WomanEchoes:
Voices in Celebration

Judith A. Cunningham

email.
Judith@gwomanechoes.com

PUBLISH
AMERICA

PublishAmerica
Baltimore

ISBN: 1-4241-5898-2
PUBLISHED BY PUBLISHAMERICA, LLLP
www.publishamerica.com
Baltimore

Printed in the United States of America

Dedicated to…
All those who deal with hard questions.

With luck and love to those who stand by while the
Person in charge of her life chooses any path that's
Right for her.

SPECIAL THANKS TO:

San Dimas Writer's Group
Wondrous Women Writers
Patricia for Poetry
Diane for Technical Assistance
Kenlynn for defining friendship
And everyone—all family and friends—
Who endured and nurtured during the creation of this book.

APRIL

Marlene sat on that hard table with her feet dangling like those of a small child, and he droned on, "Of course, there are many options open to you…" His eyes never met hers so she stared at her knees, which protruded from the paper dress with no back and which covered nothing. "There are numerous experts available to you." He paced the six feet of vacant floor space as if it were an auditorium stage behind a podium. "Now we need to make some appointments for further opinions and organize the medical team that will be working with you."

"Excuse me, Dr. Visel, this is going too fast. If you'll please excuse me, I'd like to dress. I need to think about this before I can deal with any plan of action." She dared to look up from her damned knees and at his face. His eyes didn't meet hers…*but what is his expression? Relief? God, he wants out of here as badly as I do.*

"This is news to me," she continued, "and I need to go home, maybe wash my hair. I hope you understand. Thank you, Doctor, but may I meet you in your office in a few minutes?"

He glanced a her face, but not her eyes, and said, "Of course, right down the hall to the left, third door. I understand this is difficult for you. We will get you in touch with a counselor immediately. There are so many experienced professionals who will be of great help." He put his papers together on the clipboard. "Fine, in my office. Please call the nurse if you feel uncomfortable or faint. How are you doing now? Okay?"

She nodded. *Please leave before I scream.*

He stumbled as his foot caught on the door, but he made it out into the hall. She slid off the table and went to the window that overlooked a parking lot. *But there are trees out there...trees with new growth. Winters are so desolate here in the valley. Hang on; rejoice in the few flowers and the trees putting out those glorious sprouts.* Cycles. For now that was all she needed and she turned back to dress.

Here I am, fifty-nine years old...and what have I worn to the moment when my future, or lack thereof, was laid out for me? Jeans. What happened to the power suits and blouses that told the world to rest easy? I'm in charge. Gone. Wish I'd worn the gray suit today...maybe I won't have much opportunity after this. From this moment on, vulnerability is not dependent on what I look like, but how I feel. Damn the gray suit and its false impressions. I wore that suit and it was I, not the suit, who ran my life.

She threw on the loose, bulky pullover and dumped her whole purse upside down on his precious examination table. She found her hairbrush and smoothed her ponytail. She was back on her own turf now and while she hadn't a clue what she was feeling at the moment, she was calling her own shots. She picked up the rearranged purse and went out the door.

Why wasn't she thinking of what he had said? The words were clear and fresh, right in the front of her mind, but they had nothing to do with her. It was this doctor, who perceived he was her lifeline, occupying her thoughts...well, that and how to get the hell out of here.

His office door was ajar and with a soft rap, she entered, stepping fully inside but not toward the desk where he sat with an open file.

"Excuse me, Doctor, but I think it would be better to have a detailed conversation another day. Right now, I have one question for you. What's the ballpark figure of the time I have left? Everything else can wait, depending on the answer, of course." Her attempt to lighten things up didn't work.

"Well, I can't give you a time estimate. As I explained to you earlier, there are so many courses we can take and so many opinions, tests, experts..."

"No, Doctor, you gave me a name for the illness. I'm sure you can come up with something between say four days and ten years...if it's easier, make the assumption that I do absolutely nothing to help myself. I just want to know what the realities are. Please tell me what a textbook case might be."

"Of course, there is no way of knowing…"

"God, I know that, just read the paragraph about averages."

"Mrs. Drubaker, anything I say can be dangerous. If you respond to facts that are unrelated to your case…"

"Do I have a year?"

"Maybe…maybe less."

Obviously, he was angry, but she had what she needed and would deal with him and his anger some other time.

Visibly composed, she said, "Thank you, Dr. Visel. I want some time to get hold of this information. I'll make an appointment with your receptionist to discuss all of these other pertinent facts soon. I appreciate your partnership, if we can arrange that. But right now coping and understanding are my priorities. I'll be in touch." She nodded and left the room.

He had never left his desk, or taken his eyes from her face; but he had not made her feel as vulnerable as when they were in the examination room either. That was her greatest advantage as she stopped at the desk and made an appointment. She smiled at the receptionist, told her to have a good day, and used the stairs to get back to the main floor, the front door, and the outside.

The air hit her face with a cold slap as she pushed open the heavy glass door of the medical clinic. The sensation of the fresh air was of warmth, movement, and life. It brushed her face and filled her lungs without her need to inhale deeply. There seemed to be a computer inside her head segmenting the odors…gas fumes, moist soil from under the trees, recent dog deposits, petunias, ferns and zinnias newly planted in the pots by the door, cigarette smoke, burning oil…faint but real. She sat on the cement bench near the door.

As she plopped her large leather bag next to her, she reached inside for cigarettes.

Oh, I don't do that anymore, ha, as if it matters now. She sat, unmoving, unthinking. However, she was aware, not of people, not of things, but of life.

She was simply quiet, with no sense of urgency. People walked by talking, but none of it touched her. She remained unperturbed. It was a lot like sleeping when one is ill. Something was happening inside of her, but that activity remained independent of her consciousness. She could feel and think, but she could not pin down this new awareness.

In time, she rose, picked up her bag, and walked to her car. She opened the car door, got in and turned on the motor but then turned it off, got out of the car and stood by the door. *Don't ever get in a car without knowing where you're going*, she chided herself. She didn't know where she was going…and that was the moment that she connected all that had happened to her.

"What do I do now? Where do I go?" She realized she'd said the words out loud. Tears sprang to her eyes and she got into her car, backed out of the parking space, and turned toward the street. Two blocks later, she began looking for a place to park…no easy task in this area. She turned before the next light, heading into a residential neighborhood, and under a tree in front of a house, stopped the car, leaving the motor on.

The tears rolled, no great sobs, no changes in her breathing pattern, just tears rolling down her face. There were no thoughts or pictures in her mind, just the quiet tears.

Immobility…that's my problem. I have to move, I have to act, I have to make decisions, and I don't know where to begin.

Lists had always been her lifesaver, but she made no move toward her little book. The thoughts she had were not hers, not generated from her mind, but drifting about her head like a cloud…she could reach out and claim them or just let them float. Maybe they would be there later and maybe not, but still she sat. With the tears rolling and the motor running, she put her head back against the headrest.

She became aware that she had slept. The tears had stopped and her car was still running.

*Okay, this isn't smart. I can do nothing, but I can't do something stupid. The time…*She dug in her purse for the old watch with the broken band and noted the time, two o'clock. The appointment had been at twelve-fifteen. *Okay, easy now, food. I've missed lunch and* *need to get to work by four. This is do-able.* As she opened the bag to throw the watch back in, she saw her journal and with more gentleness than anything, she had done that day, she lifted it out and held it tightly.

Then the thoughts of family came; Jessie, Kate, and Eileen…Jessie's little ones, Robert and Jane.

She clasped her paper friend tightly and said, directly to the book, "Today it's just you and I, okay? Let's keep it to ourselves for today…just you and me. What do you want for lunch? Make it good. This is our day."

The book didn't answer, but she wasn't alone now. She opted for Chinese at Chin's. Parking near the door, she entered the small, but classy restaurant. Having seated her in the nearly empty room and given her the menu, the waitress went away and Marlene acknowledged her own fear.

Dumb. Stop being dumb. She reached for her little book and placed it on the table between her and the menu. Now it spoke to her. *It's okay. Let's order and take it home. That's an all right alone place.* She patted the book and with composure, called the waitress back, gave her order with a smile and asked for it to go. As the waitress smiled back, Marlene's only thought was, *She doesn't know, nobody knows, except the book and me. That's very good.*

She opened the small, bound book with white pages and tiny pictures in the corner of each page. The cover and the interior scenes showed medieval women in all poses of work and rest. She stared at them and wondered how they would have responded to her dilemma.

Mud…bad smells…dogs and horses in the house. But Eleanor of Aquitaine, a queen of the era, clever, undefeatable, sustained in her struggle to see the throne kept in her lineage…survival. Funny, that's the big issue for all people of all times…how to stay alive forever, even when you spend all that time in a tower…but never wasting time when there was a chance that the battle for immortality could still be won.

But who else? The ones who prepared the food, produced the clothing, cared for the animals, brought in the crops, fought the wars, or, more importantly, ran to stay out of the way? Who built all those castles, churches, and home sites we visit with cameras and tour books?

Marlene thumbed the pages of the book, looking for some clue to the people who are not portrayed by Shakespeare or documented by historians.

Tiny little houses with thatched roofs. She envisioned dirt floors covered with loose thatch, no beds, a few dishes or pots and lots of those blankets everybody seemed to wear day and night...the rich embellishing them with golden threads and expensive jewels, but still blankets wrapped around themselves like ancient muumuus. She saw the woman who dominated this home.

They must have been very rough, those blankets, made from unprepared wool...but how creative to use what was readily available...and they must have smelled bad...all that wet and rain, mud, sweat, and urine...cold all the time. But people did that. They took what life gave them and they fought all the years they lived to make it work for them.

So what about This Woman? I'll call her Megan. What did she do when some pompous doctor told her she had some disease that was feeding on her vital organs? Well, in the village, she probably didn't have a doctor, pompous or otherwise and death was common. The husbands and fathers of her town died in battle or of disease, with other men or nature. The mothers and sisters died in childbirth; their children died of malnutrition, birth defects, natural disasters, and results of war or maybe were eaten by a wild animal.

But This Woman, who cooked all those meals over open fires, cared for the domestic animals and used every iota of product from those animals for clothing, food, medicines, and the teaching of her daughters. I believe Megan mourned those she had lost as she slumbered on the dirt floor of her little house, exhausted from the day's labor, wrapped in rough, smelly blankets—blankets that she had produced with no help except from the sheep that may have been sleeping in the same room. And, while she remembered, she fell asleep because her body and mind couldn't resist it.

She knew she would die sometime, this medieval woman who lived half forest, half community. Everybody did. And, while she lived, she gave everything she had to the family, to her society, to her own sense of purpose and her own sense of joy. What if she had had the luxury of foresight from some doctor? Would that have changed the way she lived her daily life? Would she have done less for her family? Or, would she have done more in preparation?

Maybe she had no one to talk to. Maybe because there was no time; maybe because no one else would sit and listen, maybe because the local counseling center was closed due to weather. Well, I think she did it herself. I think she knew, instinctively, what her purpose was and she kept doing it as long as the pain was bearable and her energy allowed her to feed the animals, the clergy, the neighbors, and her family. She still worked the wool, the loom, and the blankets and used her unassigned moments to complete the necessary items for the family's next winter.

She spent time with her daughter, sharpening the wifely skills needed in the conquest of a local man. I think she welcomed her sons returning from hunting trips and wars, giving them some sense of home before they embarked on further adventures or in search of livelihoods. I think she walked the forest in search of berries, nuts, herbs, roots, flowers, and flavors to create new and varied sights, smells, and tastes until she could walk them no more. But at the end, Megan would be cared for at home by the family she loved.

The difference was that it didn't last long. There were no machines, no experimental drugs, no 'team of professionals' to extend her pain, her vulnerability, and consume too much of the energy of her community. She just died before the family saw her unable to pee in the proper place, at the proper time; before she could no longer hold down her food or control her shit. She just died, and they buried her. They remembered her and I'll remember her and I'll learn from her. I wish, at the end she could have had one set of my smooth, colored sheets instead of those damned stinking blankets that must have scratched her body and housed a multitude of insects.

Suddenly Marlene realized the packed food was on the table in front of her and the waitress was waiting. No! Don't act preoccupied, don't give away that you have anything on your mind. Introspection is for vacations, seminars, journaling; it's not for people in control, not for women.

She paid the bill, giving the waitress a five-dollar tip, which she had never done in her life, and returned to her car. Driving home, she evaluated her behavior. *Over-tipping is a sign of insecurity—don't do that again. Be careful of appearing distracted. There will be time for exposing all your feelings, but not until you have some control over what is happening to you.*

She found a parking place on the street under a tree in front of her apartment house. She grabbed her bag and her parcel from the restaurant and ran up the porch steps. She unlocked one of the two doors in the center of the porch and climbed the interior stairs. As in many remodeled Victorians, the top of the stairs ended in her spacious entry area, which had three doors opening from it. She whipped around the railing and entered the doorway into the living room. It was a sunny, open room with windows completely across the front and one bay window on the west wall. The hardwood floors were well worn and darkened with use. The few rugs added bright color and each had been chosen, not for compatibility with room décor, but like all her purchases, because she liked the piece. Therefore, the entire apartment, according to eldest daughter Jessie, "defined eclectic."

Being alone and traveling all the time, she hadn't decorated anything. She had owned things that had a purpose. A bed—a place to sleep; a chair—a place to sit; a table—a place to eat, and if the truth were told, with her travel schedule none of them had been used too often. Now her grandchildren came for visits. Life had changed.

She had worked on a small liberal magazine from its inception twenty-five years ago. She had reported, analyzed, and written in the international section. There had never been money at the magazine to cover the really big stories, but she had gotten good at clarifying how situations evolved, mostly because she worked hard, studied much, and loved history. Her professional strengths were translating major events into issues that affected everyday people and, most particularly, understanding and relating lives of women around the world.

It had been a great life; exciting, useful, creative, and demanding. But the day had come five years ago when her granddaughter had become very ill. Marlene had been on the East Coast at the time and was torn between finishing her seminar and returning home to be with Jessie and Jane. While flying home, she realized her family, her greatest support system, took a back seat to her work, her need for adventure, and the need to have her ego fed. During that flight, she struggled over what her current and appropriate purpose might be. She determined *that there is a time for everything under heaven.* She could hold on to her memories, never forgetting them, yet moving on.

When she retired, she had brought to her new residence items of art from around the world, usually things that could be carried aboard a plane. Handcrafts done by women in rural areas had been stuffed into suitcases with collections from street fairs.

Being a grandmother, perhaps a better grandmother than she had been a mother, had been a new adventure. She had learned to balance giving and withholding, being a constant in the lives of children with very busy parents, being as supportive of her children as they had been of her when she had worked at discovering herself and was playing at her 'oh, so important' career. She had spent the following year winding down her connections and settling into her new life. The transition had been just another adventure. There had been a lot to learn and, looking back, she knew she had learned more about herself in the years since that flight than she had in the previous twenty.

She felt comfortable about who and where she was. Now Dr. Visel had given her a new concept to add to her adventure. As she picked up a plate and silverware in the kitchen and returned to the coffee table, it was with clarity and determination. She dished up the food and sat on the floor to eat the chow mien and shrimp she had brought home. Next to her plate on the table was the little book of women and days and lists.

First, she concentrated on the food and took the edge off her hunger. She pulled up an armchair to lean against. Taking a bite now and then, she opened the little book to a clean page and picked up a pencil from the other end of the table, stretching to get it; slightly aware she was risking knocking some or all of her lunch onto the floor. It was just the way she did things. With a fried shrimp between her teeth, she wrote.

He says I will die…possibly within a year.

She leaned back, ate some rice, and consciously thought, *Who's he? Some rude, insensitive, scientist who relates better to vials, disease, other doctors and data than he does to his patients. He's a man who found some things that he thinks can determine my future. Okay, I'll accept that he's found some things. Now I'll look at them again and again; in different lights and through different eyes. There's nothing that says he has all the answers or even that he's right.*

Die? So who hasn't or won't?

Picking up her fork again, she talked out loud. "That's a rather universal experience. The trees this morning outside the window, no one could have said they weren't dead this winter. They looked horrible and dark and leafless and stretched unadorned branches out in a manner that resembled arms reaching out in desperation. But they sure looked good today. When I go to work this afternoon, I'll look that good, and tomorrow and the day after.

"Death isn't a frightening thing, the pain involved is. I didn't dare ask the good doctor about that kind of stuff. It was all I could do to get him to talk at all except for his canned speeches. Let's learn about pancreatic cancer. Do this much without him."

Possibly.

After writing the word, she felt some discomfort. She put down the book and attempted to concentrate on the green bean chicken. But in her mind there was tension between what she had believed in the morning and what she had since been told.

Of course. How can I be terminally ill when I'm not even sick? A few off days, maybe my energy not as high as before, but mostly, I just keep going. How much fun we had last week when the women from work went to the symphony. Dying people don't enjoy living that much. Dinner out with people who know enough about one another to share humor, experiences and even some irreverence about themselves and their work. These are people who enjoy one another and bring laughter and substance to one's life.

Possibly is a very good word. What exactly set Dr. Visel off on his campaign to deal with a disease? (Not a woman, mind you.) It's still my life, for however long, and from this time on, he'll be the technocrat and I'll be the human rights commissioner. Sorry, Dr. Visel, that's just the way it is.

16

Within a year.

Writing those words opened the brain gate and she wrote steadily.

In the light of "possibly", that's not so bad. A year! What if that's really all I have? A year can be a long time. I used to think that to be hit by a bus and have it over in an instant would be a beautiful way to go, but how hard on those left behind. She thought of all the people she had lost in her lifetime. Daddy never got to say goodbye, never got to say, "I love you" at the end. But Charlie, my brother, yes. He died hard and long with lots of time to say things that mattered. Time to sit by his bed—sometimes all night—to remember, to forgive, to ask forgiveness, and to share funny things. For those left behind maybe that's best. But he suffered so much for so long, through intelligible times and not so lucid times. Like this morning in the exam room when I felt so powerless, that was for an hour. How must it have been for him all those years?

Somehow, there was comfort in a year. Time always goes too fast, but I'll have tomorrow, and time to learn and to plan. Maybe he was wrong anyway.

Her rumination stopped there.

She ate a little more, then scraped what was left into one cardboard container, piled everything else up on the plate and went to the kitchen. Leaving the dishes in the sink, she went to shower. It was a mindless time as the hot water ran over her and she soaped her body, a body that had served her well.

In nearly sixty years, it had suffered a couple of bouts of flu, a bunch of broken bones in an auto accident, hay fever, and a few headaches. She had kept up on walking tours of villages; sleeping on the floor in strange places and eating whatever the people ate in the places she visited. Without reference to what might be just ahead, she just said, "Thank you," to that body that had performed well.

Stepping from the shower, she looked over that body, not so pretty by magazine standards; skin hanging where she'd lost some weight.

There were some wrinkles, a few scars, nicks, bumps, and scratches. This body had conceived, nurtured, carried, delivered, and fed three wonderful children.

But this body had been loved for itself. There were men in her past who had found her body very desirable and it had given them and her great pleasure; even now, George. No, this body is not to be dumped, but to be appreciated. She would do so until the end. She pulled a long woolen dress from the closet, slipped her feet into some plain, leather, flat shoes, and brushed her hair back into the low ponytail. This time she fastened it with a clasp that was very Native America, turquoise and silver. Remembering how cold it would be when she got off work, she took a heavy shawl from the coat tree. She stopped to see that the cat had food, and then realized she had not packed a dinner for herself. She went back to the refrigerator and retrieved the carton of leftovers from lunch, slipped it into a plastic bag and started down the stairs. Then she remembered the little book and went back up to get it. Picking it up from the coffee table, she apologized to the journal by rubbing her hand across the cover and then slipped it into her pocket. It no longer had a place in the big overloaded handbag. Once again, she went downstairs and shut her door.

She was aware of how comfortable and peaceful she felt just doing what she did every day, driving across town on a familiar route to a familiar place. Things hadn't changed all that much. Like most women, she knew in troubled times you just keep on keeping on and then something else happens that often diminishes the current trouble. So she stopped at the right stop signs and changed into the proper lanes. She arrived at the church where TEEN TALK, the hotline for street kids, was housed in the basement. Pulling into the parking lot, she felt no anxiety as she stepped from her car and walked over to the short staircase.

Half of the employees with whom she worked were retired professionals, some serious about supplementing their income and some with just a need to keep working at something useful. The pay was low, but insurance was provided and a person could choose the number of hours he or she wanted to work. It was a perfect retirement job. The other half of the staff was made up of graduate students doing intern work and a couple of mothers who wanted to keep a hand in counseling while devoting time to their families. It was an amazingly cooperative group, with only one person who was still trying to define her position there. Trading hours and covering for one another was pretty standard practice, except for Linda who always found it such a big deal and never understood why people changed their minds after asking her and eventually stopped asking her at all.

Upon entering the front door, Marlene found George standing by the reception desk. He held a file and his car keys; he appeared to be stalling. His face brightened as she walked through the door.

"Marlene! Hi," he said, as he reached across the corner of the desk to take her hand. "Thought something had happened. I left several messages on your machine. Thought we might have lunch when you finished at the doctor's office. Is everything okay?"

"Oh, heavens yes, and I'm so sorry. I took myself to lunch and got home so late I forgot to check the machine. It's a really lovely day out there and I just sort of gave in to it." *Wherever in the world is there a nicer man than this? He truly accepts himself for who he is; there are no pretensions, just kindness, thoughtfulness, and open sharing.*

"I'm glad you had a good day. I apologize for jumping to the conclusion that it had been an unpleasant appointment when I didn't hear from you. I'm off to Juvenile Hall for my favorite kid, one more time. I'll come back around here when I'm finished. Maybe we can get a cup of coffee after you finish your shift?"

Her first reaction was to say no, she wanted to go home. But somehow, that didn't seem fair. The best part of their relationship was each being able to say yes or no with no repercussions or questions. But the need to keep things normal was pretty close to the surface, and a little fear began to creep in around the edges of her mind, making her want to hide, to stay by herself until it was all over. That would be the worst thing she could do. It would be the end of her, not the beginning of her illness.

She smiled at him, giving his hand a squeeze before withdrawing hers. She walked around him and put her dinner in the small refrigerator.

"Sure, that would bring my good day to a better end. However, remember I've played all day and can't stay out long. Go take care of Brad and I'll watch over all the other lonely kids for the evening."

Marlene noticed George's disappointment as she limited their time together. There were times when they stayed over at one another's houses, slept together and shared breakfast. *He's so dear and there's not a reason in the world I can't marry him, except for the fact that I simply want to live alone.* Often, she had told him he needed a real companion and suggested he see other people. Occasionally in the past, he had, but he said it wasn't any fun and that he was satisfied with what they had. From what she knew of men and what she knew of George, she didn't believe him. He needed someone there with him as much as she needed to be alone.

In passing, she recollected their meeting and connection. George, a retired high school principal and recent widower, had come to the agency looking for a place to belong. He'd been hired as a volunteer administrator. He loved working with the kids and the two of them worked well together, laughed a lot, and enjoyed many of the same things. It had taken a year of being friends before they became lovers and only then, because she believed she could do it without losing herself. Now George needed more and she couldn't give it to him.

She looked around her. The work area was not large, but very cheery and always displaying some suggestion of celebration on the wall. Each member of the staff had added some piece of themselves to the atmosphere. It was fine to share the treasures of each co-worker's personality, but when one was on the phone with a troubled kid, it was better not to be distracted. She checked the five semi-enclosed work areas to see who was here and what they were up to.

Randy was sitting in the first space with three open telephone books and one hand on the telephone in the cradle.

"Hi," he said, grinning up at her. He was young and very bright.

Marlene wondered why he wasn't interested in being a brain surgeon or world economist, but he truly loved kids.

"Marlene, I've got three kids here that I can get off the streets if I can keep them together. No foster home is available for three fourteen-year-olds. Do you have any idea where I can get money to put all three in camp for the summer?" His eyes were glistening with fun.

"Good luck, Randy. You can always take them home with you." She laughed. There was nothing else one could do except make jokes when one's heart was breaking over some kid nobody wanted.

As she entered the next cubicle, she heard a cheery, "Hi, Marlene. How's your day going?" Sue was off and running with her motherly saga of life at home. "It's been pretty quiet here, which was good. I had Becky's birthday party to plan for next month. Wish I could be sure of the weather, would really like to do it outdoors. Wanted a one-day camp out, but if there's snow…"

Sue kept up her recitation as she packed up her pictures, Bible, and notebook. Marlene pictured Sue's family as a very nice, but predictable family. She and her husband had images of raising the children to be the most wonderful of people, avoiding all the pitfalls. Out of the staff's respect for her modesty, language was always clean and there were no offensive jokes when she was around. Her scattered thinking just added to her charm.

Marlene put her things down on the desk and said, "Oh, Sue, you always do a good job with your kids. Now it's time to go home and enjoy them. Have a good night." Sue left the room, still listing options for an outdoor event to herself.

Marlene's next step was to look for Harriet. Her friend was so solid, so strong, so funny and oh, so dependable. The large, attractive, black woman made Marlene feel safe, and she looked forward to just hearing her voice. She leaned against the divider at the entry to Harriet's cubicle and watched as her friend listened intently to her caller. Marlene allowed herself a few minutes of nostalgia. She and Harriet had laughed together a lot, and they shared some tough times too. Harriet's kid, Marlene's kids, marriage, health, aging, and general moans and groans were not without disrespectful, but thorough, analysis. Harriet had grown up on the south side of Chicago, worked her way through college, and settled down with a wonderful man, who was less educated than she was. Harriet was not one to sidestep an issue. Her approach was very comforting when you discussed things with her.

Two phone lines rang at the same time, so Marlene moved away to take one of the calls. The evening was off and running and time went fast.

Marlene's flurry of paperwork began to wind down around 10 p.m. She was cleaning up her workspace and packing her things to go home when she remembered her journal. She realized she hadn't thought of it all evening. George walked in the front door and a moment of apprehension ran through her as she thought of the coffee date. But she said to herself, actually moving her lips, "You're tired and it's been a long day."

But George and Harriet met at the front desk. There was always a lot of silliness between them, making ridiculous bets about world affairs or planets colliding. While waiting for her replacement, Marlene listened to the pleasant sound of Harriet and George's banter. She waited in her workspace and prepared herself for the time with George, when she must appear completely natural. Sure, she had learned some things today, but she wanted to work them out for herself. It wasn't a case of not wanting George to know or not wanting to share, she just wanted to get a grip on it for herself right now. Not forever, just for now. She didn't want to hurt his feelings, and she was afraid he would think she didn't trust him.

As she closed her purse, she thought, *Why do men and women think they have to collaborate in order to solve things? Why is there this great need to dump everything one feels? Why does the other person think they have to fix things?*

She was ready. She wasn't hiding anymore. She could be open and honest and very much herself. She could and would enjoy herself tonight and have no regrets about how she dealt with her own personal predicament. No need to act or pretend.

Marlene picked up her things and went out to the desk just as her replacement walked in the door. Kevin was only a tad late, but she was so grateful to him for that few minutes of quiet preparation time, that she reached down into the bottom drawer of the reception desk and brought out a secret stash of chocolate cookies.

As she handed him the plastic container, she said, "Have a good night, Kevin."

"Whoa." It was Harriet who characteristically asserted herself. "What occasion requires goodies? Now we reward people for being late? Didn't I do a fine night's work here? By the way, I got here on time."

But George had to speak up. "It's the young men she's trying to impress. She thinks that tomorrow night he'll offer to taker her out for coffee and then she can get rid of the old guy."

Marlene chuckled. "I'm just grateful not to have to stay late. Instead, I'm going out to eat something that's probably not good for me. Harriet, you're welcome to join us. And, George, my gift to Kevin is appreciation. Now we're free to go play. I'm looking forward to that," and she took his hand.

Harriet scooped up her belongings and said, "Well, George, I guess that gets you off the hook. Thank you, Marlene, but no. I can't go anywhere tonight and still be at the Farmer's Market at six in the morning, well, maybe by seven-thirty. Yeah, if I agree to that, I won't feel bad when I get there at nine."

"That's why you don't get cookies," George said, relieved she wasn't joining them.

The phone rang; Kevin waved his box of cookies and headed for a workstation. Harriet, George, and Marlene went out the door and Harriet got into her ten-year-old station wagon. She waved cheerfully as she backed out.

"What I'd really like to do is drive down to the café on the delta and eat something worthy of the day I've had. What if I take my car home and you pick me up there." Marlene wasn't going to allow one of those lazy conversations that took forever to reach resolution.

"Sounds good to me, I'm right behind you." George gave her a hug, a quick kiss on the cheek and opened her car door for her.

In ten minutes, they had locked her car and were settling into his little compact for the ride. It was quiet in the car until they were out of the city, then George asked, "What brought this on? We've never been down here except in the summer. Are you sure it's even open this late in the off-season?"

"Didn't even think about it. Just felt it was time for summer. Driving, pardon me, riding, sounded like a good idea. What's so unusual? I like the heat and the summer and while I love the spring too, I'm ready for stripping down to the minimum of clothes, sipping lemonade and hearing music in the park.

"Well, I'll buy into the stripping down part, but the heat is something you can keep. What happened today to put you in such a good mood? What did the doctor have to say? You seemed a little distracted when you arrived at work, but you're plenty feisty now."

"That was just a transition from a 'heady' day back to physical realities. I drove around and looked at gardens and bulbs. Boy, we've been lazy. Many people have been working hard already. They've turned earth, cleared away winter weeds and have bulbs blooming. It's time to get outdoors and start working on your garden. After today, I'm itching to get my hands into the dirt. Maybe this year we can turn that space behind your garage into a grape patch. There's a lot of sun back there and corn can go across the yard against the fence. What d'ya think?"

"Marlene, grapes take years to produce. I thought we were going to stick to an annual garden of vegetables and whatever the fruit trees bear."

"So what's the rush? In the fall, we'll buy three-year old plants and plan this for next year. Anyway, some berries are out now and while you and Harriet were talking back in the office, I was dreaming of strawberry shortcake. That's what made me think of the Delta Café."

George seemed content. It was quiet as they continued down the road, George trying hard to follow the dark, winding road and Marlene watching the river. The moon was reflecting on the water and she, too, felt contentment.

George pulled the car into a glittery parking lot. It made Marlene smile to think that between the birth of Disneyland and the advent of the yuppie world, little Christmas lights had to be everywhere. It's not that they were unpleasant, just so predictable.

She jumped from the car. The café looked quiet. One couple was wandering along the street window-shopping. George and Marlene entered the café and found a table by the window overlooking the river. Not much to see, but a few more of the glittery lights on the shore made the trees stand out in the reflection on the water. Marlene ordered shortcake, only to find it was gone for the day.

George was determined to meet her celebratory mood, and said, "How about a plate of fried veggies and a glass of wine, instead? It's a long way from strawberries, but it's decadent enough to match your adventuresome humor."

"How clever you are." She looked at him coyly over the top of her menu. "That's entirely appropriate for whatever strange bent I'm on." She closed the menu, smiled at the waitress and looked at George seriously.

"What happened with Brad this afternoon? Do you hold out any real hope for him? How are you feeling about all this repetitive use of energy?"

George began a monologue of the conversation he'd had with Brad. Marlene was listening with slightly more than half of her consciousness, but was also aware of the quiet place where they sat, the water outside the window, the carnation on the table. She noted the way George spoke of something he cared about in a soft, pleasing voice and the connection she felt with him as he struggled with not wanting to care too much. The food came.

George continued between bites. "I know he wants a different life, but he hasn't the strength or discipline or self-esteem to prevent himself from slipping back into the only crowd he knows, which is on the street. I hate it, believing that when the going gets tough, he'll bolt. It takes so little for him to decide the going is tough." Reaching for his wineglass, George leaned toward her. "I'm sorry, I've gone on far too long about that. It's just part of what we've chosen to do in our old age, right? Let's take up stamp collecting or something less frustrating. Anyway, tell me about the doctor's visit today. I think you're avoiding that. Makes me wonder if there's more to it than you're letting on."

"No, it wasn't anything dramatic." She played with her water glass. "It's just…it's just…well, doctor or no doctor, that man is a jerk." She moved the glass away and holding her head up, looked directly at George. "I don't know if he's a good doctor or a bad one, but his social skills or bedside manner are just too…too…crass, cold, humorless.

Obviously there's nothing terribly wrong, aside from the tiredness and loss of appetite, so I said I wanted to talk to a woman doctor. I don't have to go back for awhile anyway. What he prescribed today is something my grandmother must have had on her shelf, like a tonic. In other words, the herbal teas you brought me the other day will probably do the trick. My good mood came, I think, because when I realized I was getting angry with him, I acted on it and then treated myself to a day off. Thanks for the naughty food, too."

As they finished the last of the wine, she said, "Actually, I think they're ready to close here and I'm sure it's late. Thanks again, but maybe we'd better start home. What d'ya think?"

"Well I know you wouldn't lie to me, so I won't go looking for trouble. I can't help but worry about the changes in you, but I guess we should know by now that some of our cylinders won't always perform at top speed. As long as you know you're all right, I'll take up some of the slack and we can keep on with the life we're building." Not because she needed help, but because she knew he wanted to touch her, she let him help her from the chair and he kept his arm around her as they left the restaurant.

The drive home was quiet until Marlene sat up straight and said forthrightly, "George, can we get away for a few days pretty soon? It's possible the weather will stay nice in Monterey up through May. I'd love to go over for a weekend and just hang out. Walk and not walk, talk and not talk, sit on a deck and watch the ocean and birds and do it before the summer fog comes in. Does that sound like something I could twist your arm about?"

"You're amazin', darlin'. Sure. But a while ago, you wanted to plant the backyard in labor-intensive crops. You know I'd rather go to Monterey any day over digging holes in dirt. If you've some need to play social director, just give me the itinerary. By the way, that brings up the other delicate subject. What about the month in England? When do we actually start getting that together? It's late if we're going to do it this summer."

"I thought we agreed to go in the autumn during the Shakespeare season." Marlene tried hard to sound unconcerned. "That gives us a little more time. Planning big things seems to make me tired, but little things are looking better every day. So let's assume I'm getting better and will soon be sharing your enthusiasm for a big trip. In the meantime, let's talk about going to Monterey the last weekend of the month. Will you settle for that or how do I incite enough excitement to get more from you than settling?"

His laughter was so genuine, so comforting, and so contagious, that as their hands met over the console, she thought maybe tears would come to her eyes. Instead, she replaced her left hand, which he held, with her right, putting her left hand on his shoulder. As she squeezed, she let the safety of the moment enclose her.

Too soon, they had entered town and were approaching her neighborhood. The urge to change her earlier decision and have him come upstairs was very strong. She was even prepared with some arguments for herself. *No, no. Too much new info has invaded me today. Don't risk spilling. Oh, but after the intimacy of the evening, it will appear even more abnormal if I send him away. The warmth of him feels so good, almost as if he could make the nightmare stop. That's it, the easiest thing in the world would be to lean on him, let him make my decisions, cry and fret and let him soothe and support me. No. This is mine, I'll carry it, and I wouldn't like his decisions anyway. The trap is the wonderful person he is, his warmth and comfort, the sex, the safety of him. That trap will take away all my power and I'll die one day...a sickly, dependent star of an ugly drama.* She removed her hand from his shoulder and began to collect her things. She tried light chatter about tomorrow.

"Why not come around for lunch, like one or two o'clock. I'll have plenty of time to catch up and maybe cook something fun...or open a can of soup. No promises here."

It was quiet for a minute. Then George responded, obviously disappointed. "Sure, I'll call if I get hung up somewhere. I expect to look for a place for Brad in the morning."

As he pulled up in front of the house, she leaned over to kiss him. Touching his face, she whispered, "Thanks so much. It was a very good day and a wonderful evening." She tried to get the door open before he could speak, but failed.

"It doesn't have to end here. It never has to end here."

"Yes, George, it does. It's too easy, too comfortable. It's why I say you should have someone who can share it all. Please. I don't necessarily want it to end here either. But it's best and I don't want my beautiful day to come to an unpleasant close with an argument. Thanks again, and whether you believe it or not, I love you." She touched him once again and left the car, moving quickly up the steps and waving as she entered her front door.

It was some moments before she heard the car pull away from the curb.

She climbed the stairs and saw the cat stretching on the sofa, but he got to his feet and padded right over to where she was putting her things. She reached down and picked him up. "You're really getting fat." She nuzzled the back of his neck and asked him, "Why aren't all relationships as perfect as ours? Your demands are clear and consistent. I like that. Food here, water there and litter box reasonably clean. Rub your back on the way by, if I feel like it, and then you come to tell me I'm wonderful. Yeah, I like your style."

She saw the answering machine was flashing away as if it had something very important to say. She remembered George had left messages, but he couldn't have left that many. She sat down at the desk, pulled out her pad of paper and pen then punched the button.

George: "Hi, guess I missed you. If you have time perhaps, we could have lunch after your appointment. Right now, I'm at home, so call if you have the chance. Love you. Bye."

Kate: "Mom, hi. Going to San Francisco Saturday for a shopping spree. Interested? The only bribe I'll offer is, yes, we could do a play at night if you want. Give me a call. Love."

Carolyn: singing to the tune of "Camptown Races."

"Called my friend in the middle of the day, not there, not there. Either out shopping or washing her hair, no one's there today."

"Oh, well. Mi'ja, want to do an article that has all the research, all the pictures and all the materials in one place? All that's missing is the writing of it. The guy doing it just left for a meeting in Atlanta and we really hope what he's doing will turn into a big thing. So if you want this one, it's yours. Same prices and you'll have 'til May 10th to complete it. Call and leave a message if it's a go because I have to assign it by tomorrow. When can we talk again? Seems like a long time since we covered the territory. Okay, have to run. Ha, ha, are you interested in the subject matter? South American rural development. Right up your alley. Hear from you soon. Love ya."

George: "It's twelve-thirty and I'm leaving for the office. If I don't hear from you, I'll see you at work. Hope your day is going well, but call if you need anything. Love you."

New voice: "Hello, Mrs. Drubaker. My name is Alicia Morales, Dr. Morales, and I'm on the psychological staff at the clinic. Dr. Visel gave me your name today and asked that I call to let you know that I'm available if you have any questions or would just like to talk. My number is 555-0443. Please feel free to use it any time, and I look forward to hearing from you when you're ready. I hope we'll talk soon. Goodbye."

Jessie: "Mom, don't you ever stay home? Wondering if you could watch the kids Saturday and Sunday morning week after next. Doug has a meeting in Reno and it seemed like a good time to get away for a spell. Also, Jane's basketball game is Friday night. I know you're working, but maybe you could get a trade. They're in the running for the championship. Tried that chicken and pepper recipe. It was good, but took a long…" Click.

Each one but the doctor and Jessie, who never finished her sentences, had said, "I love you." Not a bad way to end the day.

She went into the kitchen and put on water for tea and then into her bedroom to take off her clothes. She was very awake, so she changed her route and went into the bathroom and started hot water for a bath. She went back to the desk and put her hand on the telephone, but left it there while she had a discussion with herself.

I'm going to leave a message for Carolyn, I'll do the article. When do I have time to write an article? That's silly, I won't die in twenty-one days. Who's talked about dying? I just gave George two weekends and Jessie one and for sure, Kate the other. Given my schedule, my kids, my friends and a doctor's appointment or two, I'm a pretty busy lady. She got up and walked around the living room. *But all of those things are what other people want. Right now, I want to write that article. Do something familiar, something I'm good at. And it gives me a reason to be at home and not out doing what everybody else wants.*

She returned to the desk, dialed the number, and waited for the office machine to come on.

"Hi, this is for Carolyn. Love to bail you out one more time. Maybe it will give you time for singing lessons. Please send the material to my office, as I'm not always here and you'll probably want it signed for. Believe our time to talk is coming up soon. I'll be in touch when I've finished your project. Hope everything else is good. Love ya. Bye."

The tea was ready, the bathtub almost full and she dumped some bubble bath under the running water. She brought the tea into the bathroom, removed her clothes, and stepped into the hot tub. A few minutes of the relaxing warmth and the lovely smells and she began to cry, quietly. She thought about the tears. Had someone asked, she could not have said what they were for. Maybe left over from the doctor's appointment, maybe because I sent George away when I really wanted him to stay. Maybe just tired from a long day. *Maybe because I agreed to write the paper because I know I'm fighting time. Maybe because that voice of a strange doctor…intruding into my home…a nice voice…but calling my house. They think I belong to them now. Not until I call them back.*

Marlene finished her tea, washed herself, and stepped from the tub. She brushed her teeth and her hair. She took her little book and pen and climbed into bed. Sitting and holding the journal for a while, she looked above her and out the window to the sky. There were stars visible and she felt very comforted indeed. So she wrote:

Stars, planets, moon and the sun comes up every morning
Four people said, "I love you," tonight.
The trees on the river confirmed all that I saw this morning
Even with our dark and dreary winter, flowers are coming up.

After a time, she realized she could go to sleep. She set the book and pen aside and turned off the light.

If all that complex system can keep on working right, then so can I, no matter what the clashes or glitches or surprises. As she was drifting off, she felt the cat jump up on the bed and take his sweet time settling down on her feet. They were soon both asleep.

MAY

The spring sun inched towards the horizon, making the world glow, but the display was unnoticed by the sleeping duo. At one point in its journey, it entered the window of her bedroom just above her head. Marlene and her cat continued to sleep soundly. When the sun's rays were shining on the foot of her bed, they disturbed the cat just enough to make him stretch, lift his head and determine not much was going on here, not even signs of breakfast. He chose to go on sleeping with the sun on his back.

By the time Marlene woke and stretched, the sun had moved past the window awning. Her first thought was that she must have missed a glorious dawn, but the luxury of the bed and the nurturing sleep of the night before was a good trade-off. She startled herself, however, when she looked at the clock. She couldn't remember the last time she'd slept until 10:30. Now she had two perfect days in the middle of the week with no pressing tasks. Trading the weekend with Robin had been a stroke of genius.

She slid from the bed; pulled on the jeans she'd worn the day before and invited the cat into the kitchen for breakfast. She wanted to take her coffee outdoors; however, she stood by the telephone looking at it thoughtfully. She started to walk away, then, she turned and dialed a number.

"Hi, this is Marlene, is Carolyn around?"

"Mi'ja. Glad to hear from you." Carolyn's voice was soothing. "I'm so pleased with the article. Thanks again. So what's up? Are you calling because you're looking for a job?"

"Maybe. I enjoyed doing that piece, but I think I've something else on my mind. Uh…would you have any time off in the next couple of weeks if I came down for a few days?"

"Whoop-de-doo! You bet. It'd be better after next week, but yes, I can take a few days off. Anything special you want to do?"

"No. I just want to talk, hang out and, well, you know. I'd rather we just be together so don't go making plans or anything like that. A real do nothing time."

"Marlene, is something wrong?"

"Yes—no. I need to sound off and you're the best sounding board I know, like in the old days."

"Well, there's nothing I'd like better or need more. I have my calendar now. What dates?"

"Anytime. I'd like at least three or four days." Marlene was more comfortable now that when she had begun this call.

"Okay, mi'ja, two weeks from tomorrow. We'll make it a long weekend. Actually, I find your coming rather exciting."

"It's a date. I miss our vacations and stuff. Maybe we can even discuss the Scotland dream. Oh, let me ask another favor. This feels a little melodramatic, but may I say that you've asked me to come down to work on the article? I guess it sounds silly, but there are a lot of people who think they have a piece of my life right now and it's just easier not having to explain. Would you indulge me, please?"

There was the slightest pause, and then Carolyn responded, "Of course. I guess if you've something to say, you'll say it. I love ya. I'll call you on Monday. Think you'll have the details worked out by then?"

"Sure, and thanks. I love you, too. The prospect of being loose for a few days sounds great. Promise me some decent weather?"

"Hey, mi'ja. here's a thought. We don't have to decide now, but what about driving down to Rosarito for an overnight? Talk to you Monday, but I'm here if you need me."

"Thanks, friend. Go back to work and let me get some coffee. We'll talk. Love ya. Bye."

"Love you, too. Bye."

She took her coffee downstairs to the porch. She sat on the top step, relaxed in the soft sunlight, and let her mind play over the good that had happened.

Talking to Carolyn and sharing their game of 'damn the torpedoes, let's go play," certainly helped. For twenty-five years, they'd taken spur-of-the-moment vacations or short jaunts. *How do people live without sisters or best friends?* Someone who knows everything about you and still sees you as the loved one? They had laughed together, sometimes hysterically, and then they had cried. Maybe Carolyn was her other half. The best part of the arrangement was there were no deals. Each woman did what she could, and they understood there were no pressures such as you have with family, lovers, or husbands. And, there was space to screw up, which God knows, they'd both done. But it was good.

Carolyn didn't have children of her own, even after three marriages, but she was the other parent for Marlene's three daughters. Having met on the magazine where they had both started their careers, Carolyn had continued working and was now the managing editor.

Marlene thought about the article she'd just written. It hadn't been difficult, just time consuming, but very rewarding. She'd re-read the material Carolyn sent until she sorted out all the parts she wouldn't use. Then she laid the rest out on the dining room table and played at moving the pieces around until there was an order she liked. It was a lot like making a quilt and playing with pieces until it felt right. By that time, she knew the material on South America so well, it practically wrote itself.

I guess that's the way I'm running my life right now. Know everything I can about the issues and then the decisions will work themselves out. Not a bad plan at all. And, Dr. Morales thinks I'm in denial. Ha!

She got up to walk around the yard, looking at winter's damage. Thinking back on the appointment Dr. Visel had made with the psychologist made her antsy. While it had taken more than two weeks before she called the psychologist back, once they met, Marlene knew it was going to be okay. Dr. Morales was a petite young woman, forty-ish, and not at all pretentious. She had a sense of humor and displayed real respect for Marlene, simply offering to help in any way she could. The word to describe Alicia Morales was gracious. Her warmth carried across the room and she did not jump out to take Marlene's hand or grab her by the arm. Simply, "I'm so happy to meet you. Thanks for coming in, especially on such a beautiful day. Let's sit over here," showing the two soft club chairs by the window. "It's more comfortable."

"Thank you. I wouldn't have shown up at all today if I didn't have another appointment Monday with Dr. Visel."

"Well then, I'm convinced our meeting will be helpful. Tell me something about yourself and your family. Do you live alone?"

"I live with my cat, but I also have three daughters, one married with two children, and all of them living in the area. I've been divorced for thirty years and really like the freedom and independence of living alone. My job includes a lot of really wonderful people, some of whom I would call friends. So, yes, I live alone, but have a good support community. Isn't that what you're asking?"

"Yes, and you answered a lot more. May I take a guess that you want things right out on the table, no surprises, no fancy talk to cover up realities?"

"And no manipulating. I've known death in my family and in my life as a journalist. I find it demeaning to have someone else tell me what is best for me," Marlene said, as she got out of her chair and walked around behind it. "My biggest concern is that so much of my energy will be spent dealing with these people who are test tube obsessed that I won't have enough juice left to be useful to my family. I'd like to retain at least some control. If I have avoided you, I apologize, but I was afraid that you too would be committed to making me another case study."

Realizing she had talked a lot, she relaxed now and returned to her chair. "I guess they pay you for making people talk, huh?" Smiling, she added, "You're good."

The conversation strayed to more mundane things like the weather and office furnishing. It was a chance for each person to pull back emotionally for a few minutes. Suddenly, Dr. Morales returned to the subject.

"It's important that we acknowledge the reality of your health situation. Time is of the essence for treatment to begin. Dr. Visel called and asked that I begin preparing you for the process ahead. He has also contacted an oncologist, Dr. Norman Carr, who will deal primarily with the cancer. I believe you can feel confident that with a variety of people involved, no one individual will railroad you. Is that helpful?"

Dr. Morales waited quietly and patiently, but Marlene did not respond. Eventually, the doctor leaned forward and earnestly asked, as if the answer mattered to her a great deal. "Can you tell me, Ms. Drubaker, how you feel about the disease? About what is happening to your body?"

"How do I feel about it? I hate that I don't have the energy I've always had. I hate that dinner out is unpleasant because the food doesn't appeal to me at all and I need to make constant trips to the restroom. I fear the jaundice will be so visible. I hate the inconvenience of it.

"But a greater fear is the way Dr. Visel treats me as though I'm going to fall apart. My choices are being taken from me because it's assumed I'm not capable of accepting this information or intelligent enough to deal with what is happening to me. He took away my rights to react and cope as a thinking, educated and responsible woman."

The doctor sat back in her chair. "And what would your choices be?"

Marlene fidgeted because she feared she had talked too much, given too much of herself away. This Alice Morales was likeable and, hopefully, trustworthy—but she was on the team.

"I want to learn just what the possibilities of cure are. What I've read says pancreatic cancer doesn't respond well to any of the treatments. I'd like some statistics on that. I'd want to know how the disease progresses, what the deterioration will be like. I'd like to know what the treatments are and what the effects of those treatments are."

After watching Marlene's face for a moment, Dr. Morales said, "Would it be helpful to you if I were able to cancel the appointment Monday with Dr. Visel and get you in to see Dr. Carr, the oncologist? You've shown some real thought about the situation. How does my proposal sound?"

"Is the point to avoid Dr. Visel? Sure, thanks again," and Marlene pictured herself getting out of this room.

However, the doctor didn't see the same thing. "Now, may I ask you a couple of questions? They don't necessarily need to be answered now. You say you've thought about death, but I don't know if you've thought about illness, treatment and recovery. You haven't mentioned the reaction any members of any members of your support group and I would be interested to know, eventually, how all of you are coping."

Another silence.

Marlene's response had a snap to it. "I haven't discussed it with anyone yet. What was I going to tell them, 'I've got cancer and I don't know much about it and I don't know what will happen but oh well, we all die sometime?' It was all I could do to come to grips with my visit to Dr. Visel's office. I felt so trapped and he was offering me very little in the way of information. I'm ready now, though, to learn everything I can."

Dr. Morales scooted forward on the sofa and in an incredulous tone asked, "Are you telling me you haven't discussed this with anyone?"

"When I have come to an understanding, when I have something to say, I'll have no problem telling them." Marlene's tone was defensive. "People, by nature, like Dr. Visel and my family, will need to do something. But when there is nothing to do, why would I set myself up for the task of caring for them emotionally. I need to take this information in small steps and have some order in the way I approach things.

"I've appreciated your advice, Doctor, but I'm beginning to hope the hour is up." Smiling as though she knew she was about to strike a chord, she added, "Does that make you think I'm retreating again? Please trust me to make some decisions here. I'm happy, well, maybe not happy, but willing to meet with Dr. Carr."

As Dr. Morales rose from the sofa, she extended her hand. "May I call you Marlene? I would prefer to be called Alicia. I want to thank you for your openness. I hope you have a good week and I'll call you before Monday about the appointment with Dr. Carr. Here's my card with several numbers including a pager. Feel free to use it anytime."

Marlene smiled, glad to have found an ally. She returned the doctor's handshake and turned to the door. She was too near tears to risk speaking. But she felt, once more, that while Alicia Morales may or may not see things from her side, she was someone who would listen and help her gain the time and space she needed.

She became aware she had left her coffee cup on the back steps and it bothered her that she had been so distracted. She wandered out of her yard and down the street. She thought of things she might do today. She turned at the next corner and started toward home, but her reverie continued.

Family and George had used up these past few weeks, after the doctor and the article. George. The trip to Monterey hadn't worked well, but the gardening weekend had been fun. In Monterey, he had wanted to talk about 'how things were'. God, what was she to do? For all his wonderful self, he needed care and love. She didn't see herself providing that. She had her own agenda now. To hurt him was unthinkable. Yet, images of working together in the yard, when she was feeling better than she had in Monterey, brought warmth, comfort, and joy. They had given up the thought of the grapes behind the garage and he had titled the episode her 'euphoric fantasy'.

He'd said, "I have kids all the time that are planting things behind the garage, but it usually has something to do with an illegal greenery."

So on Saturday they had turned soil, pulled weeds, fed the grass, taken naps and made love. In the evening, they had built a fire, tried a new recipe, laughed, been quiet and accepted that Sunday morning would come too soon.

George had also come the weekend the grandkids had stayed with her and they had all gone to a movie and out for hamburgers. George helped Robert with a report, producing a great paper of which Robert was proud. Jane, at eight years old, was very much Gram's girl. The two of them made oatmeal raisin cookies.

When George and Robert had gone to watch a Little League game, Marlene and Jane had looked at family pictures. Jessie's collection did not go back as far as Marlene's and Jane seemed interested. Sometimes her questions seemed unending. When Marlene needed a rest, she had to think about how to ask without causing alarm. So they put on a video of Jane's choice and Marlene stretched out on the couch. She felt guilty as she dozed off but knew she had to rest up if she was going to make it through the weekend.

Upon waking she thought, *Oh, God. Will she remember me as a sick, old lady who slept in the middle of the day? Will she start to tiptoe around so as not to disturb me? In time will she learn to stay close in order to fetch and carry or to make sure I'm all right?*

To re-direct these thoughts she had said, "Jane, let's go for a walk."

***

Realizing she had arrived back at home, Marlene went into the house to fix a bowl of cereal and get another cup of coffee. Dr. Carr didn't want her drinking any coffee and she did without most days. But today was special, so she filled the cup again and went downstairs, around to the back yard. She made a serious analysis of the situation. Most of the people in the building contributed something to the yard and she could tell someone had started cleaning up. Most of the weeds were gone and a good part of the soil had been turned and fed. She determined the next step was to cut back those big bushes on the side of the house. She finished her coffee and went into the basement to get the tools.

As she chopped, she thought about Kate and the day they had spent in the city. It had been so much fun. They had shopped, dined, talked, and giggled. Of all her daughters, Kate was the easiest at this point in time. Career minded, Kate had learned about herself and her needs. Her priorities were clear and she spent her time and money in what might be called frugal but gracious living. It hadn't always been so for Kate who, like everyone else in the world, had had to work out her own place and style. It's just that she had done it well, even during those phases when the rest of the family had been climbing walls because of her. Maybe that's what Eileen's doing now. But she wasn't around often and didn't have a lot to say when she was. *Well, just trust her and she'll find her way.*

It was about here that Marlene realized she had more debris than she had dumpster space. So she chopped the larger branches down into smaller pieces and bagged most of it. When she had cleaned up the mess she'd made, she stood back and marveled at how much nicer it looked. She could visualize those plants in a few months.

She took a shower, made a sandwich and was sitting by the front window eating when she decided that she had better get on with it if she wanted to guarantee her trip to Southern California. She checked the clock, thought Harriet would be at work and went to the phone and dialed the office.

"Hello, my name is Grace, how can I help you?"

"Grace? Hi, this is Marlene."

"Hi, Marlene, how are you, dear? It's been so long since I've seen you. Would you like to talk to Harriet?"

"Sure, Grace. Thanks. Hope we have time to talk soon. Bye."

There was a pause and the cheerful voice of her friend.

"Hi, girl of leisure. Why would you call here when you could completely forget us for a couple of days?"

"It's because I like it so much, at home, that is. I talked with a friend in L.A. this morning and we decided to go play. I was wondering if you could put a sticky note on the calendar saying I want to be out May 21 through 27. Maybe I can get some trades and not use vacation time."

"Sure, sounds like fun. Maybe it's the time of the year for all of us to run away. Hey, girlfriend, is it socially acceptable to turn off the telephone at home?"

"Only if you pretend it's an accident. Turn off the ringer on the phone and turn the volume on the answering machine down. Then you apologize profusely to everyone who called and say that somehow the machine wasn't working properly. However, Harriet, I have told you this only because I trust you with my life. I use this line a lot and would rather not have anyone know how manipulative I am. I want your word here."

"Sworn to secrecy." Harriet laughed. "We could do the blood sister thing if we were younger and still had blood to spare. Oh, well, see you Friday, you go do something fun. I think there's actually a phone call or two coming in. Take care, baby. Bye."

Marlene went back to the sofa feeling as if the world were hers on a platter. Somehow, the cat knew. He came and curled up next to her and they both slept a good part of the afternoon.

When she woke, she treated herself to ice cream. She followed this with a leisurely walk to the video store where she rented a Greer Garson movie. When she arrived back home, she took a long and relaxing bubble bath. Then she climbed into bed with the video on. Just as she was settling in, the front doorbell rang. She looked at the clock—seven fifteen.

"Dammit." She got up and went to the response box in the living room.

"Hi, it's me, George."

"Oh, George, hi. Just a minute." She punched the release key and went into the hall to look over the banister.

"My God, darlin', are you in bed? Are you sick? Called a few times this evening, but got no answer. Thought I should check up on you." All this as he bounded up the steps as only a man sixty pounds overweight would bound.

"Sorry, George, but someday you'll remember my tricky phone. No, I'm not sick, I just put in an old movie and was going to watch from bed. Want a cup of tea?"

"Sure, but first…" and he took her hands, looked carefully at her and then kissed her on both cheeks. "Did you want to get back to your movie?"

She kissed him back, took her hands away, and went to put on the teakettle. "No, it's still very early." While they prepared a snack, she told him about her day and how free she had felt with no responsibilities. She laughed at the choices she'd made and added, "the only piece of the stereotype I'm missing is I didn't buy a hat. Oh, well, there's still tomorrow."

He carried the tea into the living room as she picked up the cookie plate. "You called the office today," George said after they had settled down on the sofa.

"Yeah, but it was late in the day, you wouldn't have been there."

"Yeah, I was." He paused. "But I also spent another long afternoon with the probation department. Anyway, it just seemed strange that you asked Harriet about getting days off. I can always do that for you."

She reacted in mock horror, "And what favoritism is this? George, lighten up. First of all, who expected you to be there at that hour? Secondly, it was fun to talk to Harriet for a few minutes and, thirdly, it's the appropriate way to go about things. I don't sleep with the boss just to assure days off. It's my turn to ask, What's going on here?"

"Once again, I apologize," he said and she hated how crestfallen he appeared. For some weeks, I've had this feeling of impending doom. I don't know where it comes from, but I guess it's getting a little out of control."

"Why do you assume it's me that's under a 'dark cloud?'" Marlene asked.

"You're the person I care about most."

"Well, then it appears the problem is more yours than mine. I don't know how to relieve your fears if I have nothing to refute. Have you looked at everything around you? Are you over concerned about the corn crop?"

In an effort to keep her in the lighter mood, he put his cup down and pulled her over to him so they could snuggle in the corner of the couch. She poked him in the stomach with her elbow and ventured, "You know you're getting a little boring with this caretaker posture. Seriously, George, you're not a worrier and you're not one to make up stuff, so I would trust you to think about everything that could be out there and if you can't find it, let it go. Bad stuff happens often enough. And, I'm sorry to disappoint you, but it won't be so easy to pin it on me."

"Then what's this trip to Los Angeles?"

"How do you know about that?"

"Harriet didn't seem to think it was a secret. In fact, I think she thought I knew about it."

Marlene pulled away and sat straight up. With one hand on her hip and the other flailing about, she said, "George, listen to me. Carolyn and I had a chat this morning and she needs to go over a couple of items in the article. This provides us a good opportunity to be together. It's very spur-of-the-moment, so I followed all the usual and accepted procedures for getting the time off, never thinking you would be in the office, maybe not thinking about you at all, in which case, I wouldn't have been thinking about hiding something from you. This news is less than twelve hours old, and I've done nothing suspicious, unless chopped up hydrangeas or Greer Garson threaten you. Let's get to the bottom of this so we can move on."

This time she tugged him over to her corner of the sofa and held him. Her mind was racing. *I can't believe I can lie like that. I said it like it was gospel truth, me, who would define myself as above all, honest and open everything on the table. Even Dr. Morales saw that. What am I doing to this man? Protecting him? No. Yes. No. Protecting myself. There's just no part of me that's ready to share this and no other person has the right to tear it out of me.*

He was lying on his back with his head on her shoulder and she had an arm across his chest. She began rubbing his shoulder in an unconscious, thoughtful manner.

"Look, love, there's nothing more important than feelings and we do have to pay attention to them. Well, not everybody's. If we paid attention to all of Linda's feelings, we'd be wacko. But you're a solid, take it as it comes kinda' guy. So it's necessary that you look at what's going on inside of you. But just what's inside of you. For the sake of argument, let's say these feelings do relate to someone else, like you're having some kind of psychic experience or something." She paused and rubbed her chin against the top of his head.

"Then don't those experiences belong to that other person? Maybe they feel the dark cloud too, and if they do and want to talk about it, they will. Maybe they don't have a clue and maybe that's because they don't want to know or maybe it's better they don't know. I guess I think a dark cloud is a pretty personal thing. If you're perceptive enough to grasp it, and discover it's not your dark cloud, well, I think that's pretty heavy, but you can't fix what you can't fix. How do you un-encumber yourself of that obligation? That's not a rhetorical question. I don't have the answer."

"Good lord, woman, you're good. So much for my perception. Okay, so I try to discover what's causing this anxiety. If I can't find it in myself, I acknowledge that it might be related to someone else, in which case, it's none of my business. Do I have that right?"

"How do I know? I just talk to keep you from whining," she answered lightly. "I'm sorry, I do take it seriously because I know you must have some cause or you wouldn't be into this. It's just not like you at all. But like you, I wish I could fix everybody's hurt. But that just doesn't work."

She kissed the top of his head and said, "Let's go get in bed and watch the movie. Greer Garson has the answer for everything."

He twisted around until he was holding her. She wasn't sure if he was perceptive enough to know she was squirming inside, she wanted them off this sofa, dispelling whatever mood was building. She knew she couldn't tell lies well much longer. She'd trip herself up or spill her guts and then by virtue of that information, he would own her. But she waited, and soon he whispered, "Thanks, darlin', for setting me straight. I'll work on it and I'll back off from watching every move. That's what you're asking, isn't it?"

"Yes, but for your sake mostly. Anxiety is a crazy-maker. You don't need that. It's your debonair and sprightly attitude I love so much. Heavy-handed isn't your style and it must be very draining. We all have moments when the gremlins get us, but you'll overpower these guys and everything will be well. I know you, they'll bore you to death in no time, and you'll whip them into shape. Let's go to bed and watch the movie."

As they moved off the sofa, the old banter and silliness came back into play. They snuggled down in the bed and watched an old tale of love and courage and good wins out. Marlene cried at the end. No more was said of the fear and trepidation that must surely have been lurking around the room somewhere.

In the morning after showers, she was fixing breakfast and thought, *He's going to want to do something; go somewhere.*

But as he was setting the table, he said, "I don't know what you have planned for today, but unless there's something you really want to do, I think I'll go out to the ranch and see about the expansion program for the summer. You're certainly welcome to go with me, but I guess you see this as a day off."

"Thanks for understanding. For someone who was going to buy a quirky hat, looking at housing for drug-ridden, disturbed, and abused kids doesn't sound like the best alternative. I'll probably hang around here all day unless something else distracts me. Actually, I don't have a clue what I'll do, but the fun of finding out appeals to me. That's not meant to diminish my gratitude for the spectacular offer of fun and games."

Before he left, he held her, thanked her, and promised that if he called and she didn't answer, he wouldn't panic. She left the door open by saying, "If you want to check about doing something tonight, it's okay, but I can't promise I'll be here or that I'll feel like going out. Okay? But who knows? Have a good day and don't let them beat you down, love."

As it turned out, she chose a four o'clock movie downtown and didn't get home until almost six-thirty. There were a few messages on the machine. One of them was from her youngest child, Eileen. Marlene returned that call and found Eileen was game to go for a bit to eat. As they sat in the coffee shop, Marlene was dismayed to find she was bored by her daughter's recitation of all the complexities of her life. *That's parenting.* So Marlene listened up but submitted very little advice. After an hour or so, she detected a little humor and that inspired her.

"Whatever happens, Eileen, you're smart and wise and you'll find the right direction. I love you, so I know that's true. It's just hard sometimes to find the right door when there are so many to try. You have an excellent career and the rest will fall in place. For right now, I have a book and bed calling. Ready to call it a night?"

So they had gone their separate ways, with a perfunctory hug and promises that they would see each other soon. On the way home, it dawned on Marlene; *all these people are so self-absorbed and the self-absorption is interfering with my own self-absorption and whose turn is it anyway?* The thought amused her and she was lighthearted again as she arrived home to the cat and another good night's sleep.

***

About ten-thirty on a Friday morning, Marlene left Sacramento for her trip to Carolyn's in Pasadena.

She held the cat, explained to him that food and water and litter box were all in excellent shape and that someone would be by to keep it that way. "So stay out of trouble and find something to entertain yourself, okay? Love you." She was out the door and into the car.

Three hours later, Marlene left the valley and started up the Grapevine, which took her over the mountains and into the Los Padres National Forest. A whole new set of images invaded her mind. Many years ago, she had taken the train across the U.S. and had become obsessed with the idea of people walking across this country to come to the West. Every time she drove up over these mountains, she thought about the wagons, the children, the working animals, the men, and their collective determination. Today she thought about the women.

There was great diversity among The Women. Those who wanted to be there and those who didn't; those who found it adventuresome and those who found it unbearable; those who were perpetually frightened and those who wanted to conquer their fears and the terrain. How many of these women had been given any part in the decision-making regarding this trip? How many of them wanted to leave the luxury of their homes, family, friends, doctors, churches, familiar territory, and conveniences to sit in a wagon with a bone-crushing movement or to walk alongside as the only alternative, one step at a time—for thousands of miles? They gave birth on this trip and they saw death over and over again; war, Indians, disease, stillborns, accidents, hunger, exposure, floods, wild animals and fighting among themselves.

They must have had a unique way of looking at it, not even thinking about it at night as they fell, exhausted, into dreamless sleep. I see One Woman waking in the morning saying, "Hot damn, we made it one more time." And, she began the process of survival and progress across the country again. *That's silly, they didn't talk like that. Or did they? Abigail. Maybe that was your name, Abby. A serious attitude would be a real asset on this trip.*

"So, Abby, can you tell me why we're so different today? Why we fear death and fight against it? Why we're willing to be human guinea pigs in an effort to put off the inevitable? Why are months of pain for ourselves and stress for people we love, so desirable over what you knew instinctively, death is part of living."

Conscious of speaking aloud, Marlene pulled over into the Lebec rest stop at the top of Tejon grade, a little oasis of green grass, arbors, picnic tables, and lots of vending machines. *What a relief this place would have been for them, and how convenient for me, and I use it with so little appreciation.* She walked out to the edge of the park, sat on the grass, and studied the mountain. It wasn't even hot today. She tried to imagine what it would be like climbing that mountain in the middle of summer and coming down the other side. Then she added the burden of the animals and the wagons—what about winter and snow? *I'll bet they yelled at each other a lot and often felt inadequate or foolish.*

Now, Abby, with customary attitude, has accomplished the climb, bruised, exhausted, and morally depleted. She's lost some of her provisions in the process. She needs to unload her wagon to start dinner. No microwave or call-in pizza here. Where did she get her water on this mountain? Who came in to clean up after her, put her kids to sleep or worry about the clothes destroyed by that climb?

Just looking at that mountain and trying to figure out where you put your foot for the next step overwhelmed Marlene. She got up, went over to the vending machine, and bought a coke, feeling guilty. She drank it anyway. She thought of all The Women who had made it, about their lives in the West.

The Women who had left homes of comfort and ease, who had always had things clean and orderly, who had lived by a set of rules about gentility and hospitality, made the transition in a variety of ways, some suffering with the changes. But they made it, a lot of them anyway. They got tough, they got strong; they endured...as wives, mothers, widows, prostitutes, landladies, storekeepers, farmers and community organizers. That's why we're here.

When we walk through old graveyards, it appears many of those women lived long lives. They seem to have buried children and husbands, but kept going, often into old age. Rev 'em up and you can't stop 'em. Life has never been that hard for us and we fall apart easily. We're diminished by our conveniences.

For whatever lies ahead of me, I want to be that tough and that strong. It'll be in doing what I need to do, that I'll have lived out my life.

"Thanks, girls. Lead me on. And you, Abby, with the red hair and tattered skirt, walk with me."

She got back into her car and drove on to Pasadena. She knew she had to pay attention to the changing freeways (thanks to earthquakes), and detour roads (thanks to mudslides), and closed areas (due to fire) and thank God if she just got there in the same day.

It was dark when she arrived in Carolyn's neighborhood. It had been a long day, but a good one, and when she saw Carolyn through the curtains, she knew she was expected. What a gift. She parked her car in the street and ran up to the house. Carolyn had the door opened before Marlene knocked and they were in each other's arms.

The laughter with the two of them talking at once, soon settled down to a bottle of wine, feet up with the knowledge they had several days to catch up on everything. So they talked of kids, jobs, and projects. They talked of friends they had in common, catching Marlene up on the gossip of all the people she had worked with all those years. But Marlene strongly nixed Carolyn's suggestion of lunch with some of these friends. "We promised this was our time, so no complexities. Let's just hang out."

Around midnight, they made sandwiches, ate, and prepared to go to bed. With afterthoughts constantly coming to mind, they wandered back and forth between their bedrooms and it was half-past two before they actually went to bed. Marlene was feeling safe while at the same time missing her own home and bed. She'd never mentioned why she'd come, but she knew she wasn't alone now. Eventually she drifted off into a restless sleep and woke earlier in the morning than she had intended.

Upon rising, she went into Carolyn's sunny kitchen and put on the coffeepot. Her stomach was cranky so she made some toast; should have taken better care yesterday. She took her mini-breakfast out onto the back patio and relaxed, sitting in the yard Carolyn had turned over to gardeners. It was lovely over there, but a bit chilly. She went in and took an afghan off the sofa, bringing it outside and wrapping it around herself. She decided she could sit there all day and wondered if she would doze off again. It amused her to think Carolyn might find her sleeping outside in the cool morning.

But sleep didn't come as her thoughts went over the things and people they had talked about the night before; old friends and the fun and excitement of those years. Funny, she really didn't miss all that, but it was good to remember. She thought about all the years she and Carolyn had been together, all the bad times with kids or money or work frustration. Boy, they had had some hostile moments in life before they had reached acceptance and peace. Then there were the fun times, the laughter, and the risk-taking they had shared. The bottom line was, they were always safe with each other. That's what felt so good today. No matter what was going to happen, she didn't feel alone anymore and she couldn't think of any place or anyone but Carolyn who could engender that kind of comfort. So she relaxed in the lounge chair wrapped in the purple afghan and just enjoyed the quiet and the morning.

When she heard Carolyn open the sliding glass door, Marlene said, "Don't bother me, I've returned to the womb."

"She said, motheringly. Buenos dias, mi'ja. Want some more coffee before I sit down?" Carolyn picked up the cup and went back into the kitchen. When she returned they were quiet, enjoying the knowledge they had no place to go and nothing to do.

Breaking the silence, Marlene said, "I know you know I have something on my mind, but I'm not ready yet. I will be before I go home though.

"I know." This was followed by more silence.

"However," and Carolyn began to collect the cups, "while we're waiting for that es necesario a comer. Do we cook or do we go out? Actually, after all the wine last night, I want protein. The larder is full or the coffee shop is right down the street. Either way I need to jump in the shower."

Marlene got up and began folding the afghan. "You do that. I brought stuff to make bread. I'll set that to rising then let's go eat. Let's cook for the sake of creativity and eat out for utilitarian purposes. We can head for the coffee shop when you're presentable."

Marlene went out to her car and brought in a box containing a variety of flours and utensils. She had just finished covering the starter with plastic wrap when Carolyn came into the kitchen.

"Did you think I'd starve you to death? What is all this stuff?"

"It's my newest thing and I want to share it with you. So I brought everything I needed to leave you in bread for a while. My toy, my game, but I won't let it interfere. It can sit here now until we feel like doing something with it. Ready to go?"

The two ladies walked down the street in their jeans and tee shirts, one with short salt-and-pepper hair, the other with a white ponytail. They talked, joked, and called attention to things they saw. Anyone watching them might or might not have observed their confidence. They had reached a place in their lives where what other people thought or saw was of little consequence. They'd learned over the years that nothing…well, almost nothing…was as important as it appeared. They had slain their dragons, they had met their enemies, themselves or otherwise. They had flown, fallen, and started over. They were content, sure of themselves—a match for anything. They gave themselves pleasure because they'd learned that happy, well-cared—for people are the most useful of all.

Carolyn ate a large breakfast, while Marlene explained she had eaten earlier. Sitting on the patio of the coffee shop, they dawdled and dreamed of those days they had smoked and how nice that would be now with the coffee. Then they each congratulated the other on the discipline, strength, and wisdom of quitting.

"Big deal," they both said at once and laughed. They decided to walk down the avenue and see what was in the shop windows.

"Remember the day we bought the scarves on the street in New York and discovered bird poop on them?"

Carolyn poked Marlene with her elbow. "Yeah. But I washed mine and still have it. Muy feo! But the memories are too good to give up.

Oh, God, black with tigers and gold thread. Actually, it's on the table in the corner of my patio."

I know the aqua one with orange stripes is on the chest in my entryway. Isn't it odd? I've given away jewelry. I've sent loved books to the Salvation Army and I've sold furniture. But after all these years, I still have that scarf."

Marlene brought the memory fest to an end. "Don't let anyone tell us we don't know what's important. With judgment like that—well, we could run the world. Whoa."

That set them off in peals of laughter and they headed for home and naps. Late in the day, they decided to make enchiladas. That meant another walk to the market. When the casserole was in the oven, Carolyn began making a salad and Marlene left the room to go the bathroom. Upon re-entering the kitchen, she stopped in the doorway, leaned against the jamb, and watched as Carolyn stood at the sink cleaning the vegetable debris from the counter. Her back was to Marlene.

"I have cancer. It's the bad kind." Marlene spoke with a steady voice. "I don't feel so awful now, but it's not going to get better. I have a lot of decisions to make. You're the first person I've told."

"Jesus," she said, prayerfully. Marlene responded glibly, without even thinking.

Carolyn turned around from the sink, leaned her back against the counter and her wet hands lay against her thighs as if they were in her lap. Marlene was aware of the water stains that were appearing on Carolyn's jeans.

"I waited to tell you first, because I knew you wouldn't fall apart, so please don't disappoint me. And, dear God, don't get dramatic." She had added the last part when she thought Carolyn might spring across the room and hold her. She wasn't ready for that yet.

"O…kay." Marlene saw Carolyn struggle as the color drained from her face. But she turned back to finish cleaning up the mess, dried her hands and asked, "Is wine appropriate or shall I make a cup of tea?"

"Partly because it's against doctors orders, but also because it's very appropriate, let's open the bottle of Cabernet. Also, let's set your timer.

I don't think this is worth burning up our dinner." So Marlene got glasses and Carolyn opened the bottle of wine Marlene had brought from Napa Valley. Carolyn poured a small amount in each glass and they made a silent toast. Sticking the wine bottle under her right arm, she took Marlene's hand as they walked out onto the patio.

Marlene said, "I guess I've had all this time to get used to the idea, so I'm sorry to put restrictions on your response. You know, it's really okay. It happens to all of us. I think I'm lucky. I feel good, for a dying person, and I have so much time to clean it all up; you know, say real goodbyes, and say all those things that we just don't say when we should. I want to leave things behind me in an orderly fashion, make it easier for everyone. I can say "I love you, Carolyn, but it's not enough. The truth is living is probably harder than dying, and I don't know if I'd do either as well without you. To prove my sincerity, fall apart if you want, but don't take too long about it. I'm so aware of using energy now, I conserve it as if it were limited. But," and she smiled, "it is."

"I can't help the tears, but I'll try to keep them subdued." Carolyn reached for a towel that had been thrown on the table and used it like a handkerchief, but not as delicately. "I wish you were crying. This seems so unreal. But I'm glad you made me stay quiet for a bit. It gave me a chance to avoid saying or doing something stupid. What is it you really want next…from me…from us?"

"The worst is over, I've said the words. We still have a couple of days to adjust. I find it easier to deal with it in small portions. I like your Mexico idea. Lots of diversions while having time to talk. I'll call the Rosarito Hotel now and see what's available. What d'ya think?"

"I think you're amazing, Mi'ja, and crazy and far too sensible. I feel like you're taking care of me. I'm not sure that I could drive all the way down there right now."

"We're not going right now, we're going tomorrow morning. I'm feeling good. I'll drive down and you can drive back. That's about all the time you get to straighten it out in your head and your heart. Unless you can come up with a good reason not to, I'm going to go call right now." Marlene got out of her chair just as the stove buzzer went off. She looked at Carolyn for a minute, and then knelt down next to her friend's chair. She took Carolyn's hands and held them tightly.

Her own eyes were wet as she saw the pain in her friend's eyes, but she whispered, "Everything will be fine. We've handled worse than this, because this time we have the opportunity to move deliberately. Even watching you suffer now, I know there's no one else I could have trusted with this information and my feelings and my fear. It may be a lot to ask of a friend, but our whole adult lives have been preparing us for this, the biggest challenge. We'll be good. We always have been and always will be. How do you feel if I call the hotel after I rescue our dinner?"

Carolyn was crying hard now, but she lifted her arms and embraced Marlene. "If you say so. Go save your damn enchiladas, call your damn hotel and I'll see you at the dinner table."

Marlene went into the kitchen, removed the hot pan from the oven, and looked around for foil to cover it. She saw the salad had never made it to the refrigerator, so she covered it and put it away. She looked in Carolyn's address book for the hotel telephone number. As she was sitting down in the kitchen to dial the number, she could hear her friend, who had turned her back to the door, sobbing into her towel. Marlene wished she could let it go like that. *But the minute I do, I'm dead...so to speak.* She thought of going out to offer comfort, but decided that Carolyn needed time. *When she wants me, she'll come find me.*

So she made her phone call, set the table and stayed busy puttering around until she saw Carolyn starting to stretch herself out of the curled up position she had adopted for her cry.

Marlene opened the screen door to the patio and said, "Dinner's ready when you are."

Carolyn made her way into the house and went to wash her face. When she returned, Marlene was obviously in charge and playing the host. But Carolyn let it go; that's how it should be. Marlene was dishing up food and poured another glass of wine for Carolyn. Carolyn came close to gulping it down, and then began to play with the food on her plate. In the meantime, Marlene refilled Carolyn's glass and began preparing her own plate.

Keeping her hands busy, Marlene reminisced. "Remember fifteen years ago or so when we rented a car in St. Louis and were determined to drive back to New York? No plans, no reservations—our kind of adventure. Do you recall stopping at the funny motel in Kentucky and checking our log, only to discover we had only covered sixty-seven miles that day? So we fretted about how we'd never get to New York. We felt cheated if we couldn't stop whenever we wanted.

"Then we said something like 'screw it' and went to have a drink with that lady, tasting the soda she called 'swamp water'. On the same trip, you played that nasty little trick in Virginia Beach, which ended us up in a motel in Maryland. Boy, we made up lost miles that day. And the hilarious boat trip to Tangier Island; then the finale. 'Let's stay over night in New Jersey. I'll pay.'

"We were spitting distance from home and you wanted to stay in New Jersey? 'Yes', you said, in this rational tone. 'Manhattanites can't go to K-Mart.' So the next morning we loaded up the car with ceiling fans and hardware and all the things you can't carry on the subway.

"All that, Carolyn, and we made it home on time—if I remember right, with time to spare. We're going to make it this time, too—and not miss anything along the way. We can have Kentucky, Virginia Beach, Maryland, soft-shell crab, K-Mart, and anything else we can find along the way. Which brings up the issue of Scotland. We've been promising ourselves that trip for two or three years. Now is the hour, kiddo."

So dinner was pleasant, but given the previous conversation, not much food was eaten. They finished the bottle of wine, however. They sat in the darkening room and talked quietly. Marlene started to get up to make coffee, but Carolyn said, "Think it's my turn, you turned out a lovely supper, *mi amiga*." While the coffee was brewing, Carolyn put the dishes in the sink. They decided to put on sweaters and take the coffee out on the patio.

"This is becoming a sacred place. I'd like to see more of it this summer when it's warmer."

"So that brings up the question of options." Carolyn's voice sounded stern. "How's your money? Do you need to work? What would you do with your time if you weren't working? Would that conserve energy, or make you droopy? Would that allow you to sit in my back yard if you wanted, or spend time with your kids? Would it allow you, if you had the energy, to do that traveling you said was on the agenda? I suppose money really is the issue." She put her head back and laughed, "Cuz what if you're wrong, you live forever and you've spent it all? Hmmm. *Interesante*."

Marlene looked up, curious. "What a good idea. If I cut back on the number of days I worked—say to three days a week…? I think quitting altogether isn't a good idea yet. You're right, I might take to moping. But part-time would free me up a lot without breaking off that responsible lifeline of being needed and maintaining some structure. It would also prevent a lot of questions."

She got up and walked around the garden. "Money isn't the issue. I've never touched my retirement money. It's enough to be comfortable and still do all these things. Currently I have few expenses. I was planning to subsidize my Social Security, but I guess I won't be doing that. I need to be buried and leave enough for the kids to console themselves with, but I think they'd argue that point. All we're talking about is a trip or two. I think I rather like that idea. Good work, friend." Marlene returned to her chair.

"What time do you want to leave in the morning?" Carolyn asked. It was true. Keeping it in small pieces helped.

"Any time we want."

"*Muy bien*. I need to get some sleep. We stayed up too late last night, put down more wine than we've had for years, and dealt with the most attention-getting info I've had for a while. If I took a bath and went to bed, would you feel I'd deserted you?"

They each got up at the same time and put their arms around each other.

"The secret's out, " Marlene said quietly, "We've acknowledged the facts and we're ready to do the work that goes with it. No more holding back, no more 'careful of how you say that.' No more fear. Let's both get some sleep. I love you."

***

Morning came and Marlene was up early. She cleaned up the dishes from the night before, and then began to work with her bread dough.

She wanted to let Carolyn sleep as long as needed, but still had to keep herself busy. Fortunately, when Carolyn came stumbling out, the coffee was ready.

"*Buenos dias.*"

"Don't talk yet, here's your coffee. You don't quite look like you're ready for the world."

"How long have you been up? What have you accomplished while I was sleeping my life away?"

"Not so much. I'm glad you got some extra sleep."

After breakfast, they were ready to leave. Driving down the 210 freeway, they rolled down the windows enjoying the sun and breeze then switching over to the smaller freeways in the valleys until they reached the 805 south of San Diego. After crossing the border, they stayed on the by-pass road to avoid Tijuana. They were on the toll road by mid-afternoon.

"After all the times I've driven this road, I never tire of it."

"You've never told me what the doctors are saying and what your options are. When do we do that?"

Marlene's response was to turn off the toll highway and drive down to the free road. She continued along until she came to a cluster of homes. She pulled off into the yard of a little open-fronted shack that housed a restaurant/grocery store/hangout. She parked behind a couple of cars with B.C. license plates—dusty, not new or attractive. The issue for these owners would be if those cars ran or not.

"Come on,' she said, 'let's inaugurate this trip with a Coke and savor the reality of where we are."

They stepped from the car and approached the woman in the store, who appeared uncomfortable. But by using bad Spanish with a worse accent, Marlene found people warmed up easily.

"*Buenos dias, senora. Por favor. Me gusto dos Coca-Cola diete. Gracias.*" She smiled broadly at the woman and nodded at the men sitting in the shade of the lean-to. Before long, they were all having some kind of conversation and everything seemed funny to everybody. Carolyn joined right in using Spanish that was only slightly better than Marlene's was. Soon they took their cokes and returned to the car, heading back down the road toward Rosarito.

"Okay. I have a list somewhere that gets a little more technical about what the doctors have to offer. All of their options include somebody doing something to me. I can take some medications; I'm supposed to go to Stanford where there are geniuses about this—notwithstanding the fact that their patients still die. Actually that isn't all truthful, I was supposed to go to Stanford last week and canceled. That really makes my doctors crazy. They talk about chemo and radiation, but not too enthusiastically, and in the end, I'll still be sick and getting sicker. They've used that speech about what can be learned from this experience toward the care for other people, and they throw in children, which, I'll give you, is thought provoking." She slowed the car and stopped to watch the ocean a moment before turning back onto the road.

'I know what my kids will say—do something, do anything, just don't let this get you down. But Carolyn, I don't have to prove I'm a fighter to anyone. I always have been. I was successful because I chose my fights. I have so many questions about what the quality of life will be for me, my family and to what purpose? My greatest fear is being the star of an ugly drama."

Marlene readjusted herself behind the wheel, stretching her legs in the process. "I don't want people, when I meet them on the street, to only ask about my health. I don't want my grandchildren watching me disintegrate before their eyes. I don't want my kids to spend a couple of years taking care of me or feeling guilty because they put me some place where someone else will take care of me. I can't find the rationale for that. What would I be holding onto? Bad smells, limited capacities, pain medication that wipes out my brain, and a family weakened by constant care, worry, finances, and guilt.

If I could find a reason for all that, I'd do it, but up to now I can't find the purpose. It isn't a case of 'do I want to die or not?' I'm going to die, so the only issue is how. I don't feel morbid about that. I've had a great time here. Under all the right circumstances, I'd stay forever. But not like that—not as a demanding, resource-consuming vegetable. Sad? Yeah, I'd like to see Jane and Robert grow up. I still believe Kate and Eileen might have families and I'd want to be part of that. Eileen is the only one I'm not sure of yet, but she'll find her way. I'd just like to hold her hand while she does it, as I did with the others. But we don't always get what we want and I feel so lucky that I'll probably have the time to make these decisions and say real goodbyes and hold people close. I guess it's pretty pretentious, but I believe with a little time, I can help them get used to the idea and everyone could be left with no sense of 'what if? only 'remember when'. Wouldn't that be a stunning way to move on?"

Carolyn took a deep breath. "That does make quite a picture if you can arrange all the parts, but maybe a bit presumptuous, well, actually cheeky, if you like. Sure am glad to see the road to the hotel ahead. This is getting a little deep for me."

That evening, after a nap by the pool, they walked down to the open market, had lobster in a local restaurant, returned to the hotel and had a drink where the band was playing. They avoided any intense discussions, just enjoyed the familiar surroundings. It was a good twenty-four hours, and then it was time to head home. It was Carolyn's turn to drive.

They crossed back over the border and beat the east San Diego traffic. They were getting close to home when Carolyn said, "Look, I'm not asking for facts or figures or even for possibilities. I just want to know, really how are you feeling now?"

"Physically or emotionally?"

"Both, I guess."

Marlene settled in, "Certainly feel better now than I did when I came down here because I haven't talked about this with anyone except Dr. Morales. "What will make me weepy is trying to tell you what you mean to me and what a safe and comforting friend you are. I can't think of anyone else in the world I would have been able to do this with. It's getting a little touchy right now, but you have given me complete respect and space and not pushed me for answers or decisions. Using you like this makes me feel guilty."

"Just share some of your strength with me and you'll have me convinced we can do this. I can't let you go on without me now, you know. Do I dare ask why you haven't talked to George?" Carolyn asked.

"No."

They completed the trip in the comfortable silence they each understood.

The next morning Carolyn went into the office for a couple of hours while Marlene got her stuff together and baked the bread. When Carolyn came home, they walked down to the deli for lunch and back home for naps. At dinner, Carolyn said, "I don't know how you're going to feel about this, but I made some decisions for myself, too, and I want you to hear them all the way through before you comment. Fair?"

"Sure, but it sounds ominous." Marlene grinned.

Carolyn sounded very official. "No, not at all. I want to talk seriously about semi-retirement and no, don't laugh. I'm just trying it out while saving my options. It would leave me time to be with you. There's nothing dramatic about it. What do you think?" Then she covered her head with her arm as if she were expecting blows. None came.

Marlene was deliberate in her response. "You gave me the right, or the trust to make my own decisions. How can I do less for you? It doesn't sound like you're burning any bridges." She was getting choked up and trying to hide it. "I guess I'm overcome with the reality that you'll be with me. Carolyn, I love you and if the situation were reversed, I believe I'd need to be with you, too. All I can say is thank you."

They had dinner, went to bed early again, packed Marlene's car in the morning, and stood in the yard hugging. There were no words, no warnings, and no redundant phrases about taking care. Carolyn ran back into the house and returned with two pieces of Marlene's bread, which she had torn off the loaf. "A toast," she said, and they shared this one last ritual. "Talk to you soon."

Marlene drove away toward the freeway and there were no thoughts about women, children, plans, or illness. She saw the wildflowers covering the hillsides in the National Forest. The wide stretches of purple filled her with hope and enthusiasm and peace and she just pushed toward home, aware of nothing but her knowledge that she was loved, she was trusted and she could experience her joys with no apology.

JUNE

George sat at the dining room table with paper and pencils, drawing calendars in an attempt to resolve the problem Marlene had given him.

Her excuse had been, "You want to go to London, Carolyn wants to go to Scotland, I want to go to Egypt, and I can't do any of those things and work full time."

He asked where Egypt came from and she told him, "I've no idea, and I thought I should have a preference since everyone else did."

He struggled trying to figure out a schedule that would accommodate everyone and still protect all the hours he needed to have covered.

"In order for you to have what you want, we need to think in terms of monthly hours." He was mumbling. "Three times eight hours…four point five weeks…short seventy-two hours. But you want your time contiguous, is that right?" He wasn't listening for an answer.

"So we schedule you regular shifts, use you to fill in the trades…give you the overtime someone else would be getting, and then when you're off on your own, open up the board again. I can easily fill in and the final cover is that there are always students at the University who would like to earn some extra money and we don't have to pay them benefits. So it can be done."

As if she hadn't heard a word he said, Marlene called from the kitchen, "I think this is the last bread for the year. It's hot in here. With summer coming, everyone can eat that plastic, white stuff or visit a bakery. Is it an option to go to sixteen hours a week if you can hire someone from the U?"

She came into the dining room and sat at the table with him. He began to play with her fingers as she tried to defend her position one more time. She was aware it was a trap—when one is lying, one talks too much. But she was afraid he would misunderstand, or worse, understand.

"Remember?" She said, "You said you went through it after Doris died. One can't go from the fast lane to the parking spot without burning out brakes and tires. Staying home those first few months after retirement was scary, so I found a great job that didn't create stress and had a schedule to keep me organized. But I've learned a lot about slowing down and I'm better at it now. I want to move into the next phase or down to second gear, if you like."

The phone rang and George watched as Marlene went to answer it, all his papers scattered about him.

"Hello…Hi, Jane, glad to hear from you. What's up?…Of course, I'd love it. Hold on a minute, honey."

She turned to George and, with her hand over the receiver, asked, "Would you mind if I invited Jane to spend the night? I've already told her she could come over here while her mom gets a perm this afternoon."

He looked at her a minute and said, "No, of course not."

Marlene went back on the phone. "How about bringing your jammies and staying over? I'll take you home in the morning. Seems a long time since we did that." Marlene listened while Jane and Jessie discussed the proposal. "Great. I'll see you later. Love you, sweetie."

She turned around to see George shuffling the papers back into order. "It's 10:30 and she won't be here 'til three. What do you think about dinner or a movie or something for all of us tonight? We still have most of the day before Jessie and Jane arrive."

He just sat and stared at her for a while, a strange look on his face as he tried to make the pieces fit. He put down his papers and stood up. "Let's go down by the river and just take a walk. It's warm out there, but not really hot. If we have lunch while we're out, we can come back and get some rest before the family descends."

"George, do you resent my family?"

His response was glib. "Sure, but it's a bad question, ya know. 'Do you hate babies and desire the dissolution of all family ties?' No, darlin', I'm far more dedicated to family life than that. I'm envious of the time they take and the energy you give them. But on the whole you give me all that stuff, too. There's really a lot of pleasure for me in watching a family that works well; and then, when I get included in it, I know how lucky I am. I just never liked going home alone because an eight-year-old upstaged me. Those are just the feelings of a jealous old man; so don't give them any importance at all. Jane is special and she's lucky to have you for a Grandma. "C'mon, lazy woman, let's hit the trail."

They walked along the river and up to the riverfront for a seafood lunch. They knew it would be hamburgers or tacos for dinner. After they returned to Marlene's apartment, they stretched out on the bed. They talked a little and dozed off. About an hour later, the efforts of the morning were repaired, and they got up, ready for Jessie and Jane.

True to form, Jessie was running late so she dropped Jane off and blew each a kiss. Later, Jane sat at the table with Marlene and George while the group decided what they wanted to do for the evening. They started to play a game of Parcheesi. George was fun with kids. In the middle of the game, while Jane was leaning on her arms, which were folded on the table, she said to George, "I get to sleep over with Gram in her bed."

"Wow, you're a pretty lucky kid, sleeping with Gram must be a special thing." George's face was pure innocence, but Marlene had to duck into the kitchen to get a glass of water to keep from laughing out loud.

After the game, the three went for hamburgers and saw an animated movie about baby dinosaurs. George fell asleep, which was beyond Jane's understanding. "Daddy does that and always when the movie is exciting. Doesn't make sense to me."

They had ice cream cones and then George let them off at the apartment, giving each of them a kiss on the cheek. Jane and Marlene went upstairs, where Marlene was sure Jane was ready to go to bed. But the child flitted from place to place, looking over things new and familiar. When they went into the bedroom to get ready for bed, and after all the lights in the rest of the apartment were out, Jane stood at a small table near the closet. Her curiosity and enthusiasm were wide-awake.

"Gram what are these things?"

Marlene went to look and remembered she had started a project several days before and never put the materials away. There was a book on Chinese painting with practice tools. She had made several false starts on rice paper. A book of poetry lay open.

Marlene thought she was a little tired for this, but maybe she could keep it short. "There is a poem that I really love and I wanted to put it on paper with Chinese writing. I'm not very good at it yet. Tell you what, let's go to sleep now and in the morning we'll take it into the living room and see what we can do with it. How does that sound?"

"Which poem is it you like?" Jane persisted. "Just let me read it before I go to bed."

"It's the one on page ten, called 'Life', but I think we'd do better in the morning. Poetry takes some thinking." But Jane was already reading and brought the book to get some help with a word on the second line.

Into this
Maddening world a child is thrust
Objections bursting from new found vocal chords
Two blinks, like magic; a young man stands
Objections to parental rules now bursting forth
Time has robbed us of the sweet angel child
But never fear for magical
Love soon soothes the raging beast
And sets him off in paths he'd never dreamed
When was it that this babe became a boy and now a man?
Time played a trick on those who watched and did the same.
Now age creeps quickly, slippery, takes that vibrant
Body and shakes it to a limp exhaustion.
What's left to end this weary path where love and joy have
Sustained and nurtured every step?

A place where soothing peace exists and pain
And sorrow turned boy, then man, then tired spent soul.
Willing at last to take this final step, this magical blink of time
Where time as we know it will cease to be and a new day
begins.

"Gee, that's hard, what does it mean?" Jane put down the book and
began to put on her pajamas. Marlene directed her toward he bathroom
to brush her teeth.

"Most poetry is a little hard to read, but maybe one of the most
enjoyable skills you can master. It's supposed to make you feel things
and make you say, 'Oh, yeah.' In the morning, we can go over the poem
and see if we can understand it. Then whether we like the poem or not
we can try to do some Chinese painting. How about that? Here's a glass
of water to rinse your mouth."

Marlene left the bathroom to put on her own sleepwear while Jane
did the toilet thing. As a Gram, it was pleasing to have conquered that
little problem and now they could keep the pillow talk on simple, silly
things until Jane was asleep. *Not too hard, the kid's pretty tired.*

Coming out of the bathroom, Jane went to her backpack and found
her stuffed cat, then she aimed right for the bed and was climbing up
with all the appearances of a person ready to go to sleep.

"If poetry is hard to read and hard to write, why does anybody do it?
I thought you just had to make words rhyme and tell a story. That poem
has no story and doesn't rhyme either."

Marlene sighed, "Oh, there're lots of kinds of poetry. In the
morning, I'll show you some haiku poetry Aunt Eileen wrote when she
was in school. We need to get some sleep now, Jane. Let's talk about
something else for a few minutes." And, truly believing they would
sleep, Marlene reached over and turned off the light.

Jane snuggled for a minute and wiggled around a bit while Marlene
settled in. The little girl was quiet and tired and sleep was on the way.
Marlene breathed deeply, said her 'thank you' for the grand day, and
closed her eyes.

"What do you mean by "Oh, yeah,' when the words don't make any
sense, Gram?"

Once more in her life, the test was on. What she really wanted to do was go to sleep, but her job was to get the question answered so Jane would know how important her questions were. But this could be complex, what could she understand? Mentally, she cried, *George, where did you go? And you think you got tossed out of here tonight! Wanna trade?*

"Okay, let's say I go to the beach. When I come home I call you on the phone and say, 'Hey, Jane, I went to the beach today and it was great.' I just gave you the facts about what I did. Then maybe we start talking about something else. Now, let's say I decide to write you a letter and I tell you everything about the beach. I'd probably write about the sand, the sky, the water, the tide pools, the dogs, the little boy who got lost, how we had a picnic, what we had to eat and how we fell asleep on the back seat of the car coming home. If I write that slowly and clearly, you can begin to picture the beach and maybe you'll feel the warm sun or the sand on your feet. Maybe you can imagine how the water feels so cold when you've been lying in the sun. Maybe our food was your favorite food and you begin to wish or pretend you'd been there. Okay, then I've written prose, and that helps you feel what I was feeling when I was there. Prose is description in plain sentences, but I bet it would be a very long letter.

So now I decide I'm going to write a poem and scrunch all those words from the letter down to one page. I still want you to feel exactly like you felt when you read the letter. But if I listed all those things on the page it would look like a grocery list. Right? Sun, sky, sand, baby boy, dog, water, picnic, food, and all those words. So we have to find another way to say what we want to say. Are you still awake?"

"Sure, Gram, how do you write a poem?"

"I'm not, you are. Think about lying on the beach and feeling the hot sun on your skin. What else feels just like that?" Long silence. Was she asleep?

"Sitting too close to the fireplace makes your skin get hot, but feels good."

"Great, how about the cool water after your skin is hot?"

"Huh?"

"What can you think of that feels like getting into the cold water after your skin is so hot?"

Longer silence. *This is it. She's getting bored with this game. Off we go to sleep.*

"I know. When we have to wear lots of clothes to school in the spring and then after school, on the way home, we take off our jackets and the rain gets on us and it feels good."

"Wonderful! In the morning, we'll write a poem about the beach and then we'll try to read the poem about time again. Okay? Jane, we really have to go to sleep now. Look, even the cat is trying to sleep."

"Okay, Gram, I love you. I liked the movie. Good night."

Marlene leaned over and kissed the sleepy child. She ran her hand across Jane's face and brushed her hair out of the way and thought, *if you knew how much I love you...* Then she kissed her again, and whispered, "I love you too, Jane, and I really like that we're friends. Sleep well, sweetie, see you in the morning." The house was finally quiet.

In the morning, it was neither Jane nor Marlene who woke first, but the cat. For some reason, he had determined there had been enough of this lying around and simply padded all over them until they responded. It was a good, giggly way to wake up. As Jane played with the cat on the bed, Marlene put on a robe and went into the kitchen.

While Marlene stood by the counter cracking eggs, Jane swooshed by with both books from the night before, heading for the dining room table. Marlene had forgotten the project and now realized Jane had not.

"Okay, Gram, how do I start my poem?"

"Over next to the computer is a spiral notebook. Take that and make a list of all the things you were going to tell about the beach." *Coffee, please, quickly,* she whispered to herself.

"But I forget what the list was," and Jane's voice had the slightest tinge of whine to it.

"Okay, I'm fixing breakfast right now. You think about it for a minute and I'll help you when I'm finished here. It won't be hard after you remember just one thing about the beach. Close your eyes, see the beach and start to name the things you see."

Marlene cooked while Jane thought. Hunched over her paper, Jane soon began to write. In a short time, Marlene brought breakfast to the table. As Marlene sat down, Jane handed her the list. It was quite complete. Marlene rested the page against the plant sitting in the middle of the table. Then she put the book on the other side of Jane's plate. Jessie would have a fit watching multiple activities at the table.

Do you remember last night when you were thinking about the sun on your back at the beach?"

Some pencil chewing and then, tentatively, "Sitting by the fireplace?"

Does that still feel right to you?"

"Yes."

Then you don't need to ask me about it. These are your feelings. Can you write a sentence that starts: 'The sun was like...?'" They worked while they finished eating.

And so it went until Jane had written a line for each of the words on her list. By this time, Marlene had dressed, made the bed, cleared the dishes and gone to the basement to put a load of clothes in the washer.

"Let's walk down and get the Sunday paper at the corner, Jane. It looks good out there, like summer is ready to start."

"No, Gram. I want to finish my poem. What do I do next?" Looking up, Jane saw her Gram's face.

"Okay, let's go." Jane was giving in grudgingly, but at least she wasn't arguing. So Marlene took some quarters out of the cup by the kitchen window and out the door they went. It was nice out there. The flowers were plentiful now, but still tidy in their boxes or plots. The newness of the season was present in the order of things. Trees were green, but not dropping tired wood or leaves and bushes had not outgrown their spaces. Late August would cause real conflict in these same yards as growing things grasped to hang onto life.

Jane skipped ahead and then came back to walk beside Marlene. She babbled about school and her friend Tamara. Marlene only half listened. She wanted this morning to be where and what it was. She knew how soon everything would be different, and she didn't know if she would be here to witness the next cycle. Almost everything she did anymore, she attempted to do completely. Now she tried to concentrate on what Jane was telling her and found there were not a lot of responses required. After getting the paper, they walked around her yard, while Marlene checked the condition of her own plantings. When they returned to the apartment, Jane went straight back to the table.

"Okay, Gram, now what?"

"Well, now you need to look for a rhyme or a rhythm and this will take longer. You can do it once and then rework it…maybe over and over again. Try using your word on one line and your sentence under that. Only you'll probably want to make your sentences shorter. Try that for starters, but remember to get up often so you don't get frustrated."

Marlene went to the sofa with the paper, and Jane continued to pore over her project. Marlene noticed that about every five or ten minutes, Jane got up to get a drink of water, go to the bathroom, or play with the cat. Soon Jane brought her the completed paper. Marlene was so moved by the effort and the results, she really didn't know how to say how proud she was of her grandchild.

"Jane, my love, you've done a splendid job. It's wonderful. Let's print it out on the computer and see what it looks like, okay?"

Making two copies, they each read aloud and then separately. They made a few changes. Jane had caught the need for flow and pacing and she understood she had done a marvelous thing.

"Okay, maybe we can work on the painting now," Marlene found her newspaper wasn't nearly as exciting as seeing this child so pleased with herself.

"First, I want to see if I can understand your poem." Jane got the book from the table and brought it to Marlene. Fear gripped Marlene's heart.

She didn't want to discuss this with her loved little girl. She thought, *this poem is about death, and I've taken it for my own. How can I share this with my granddaughter?* She took a deep breath and said to herself. *One line at a time and carefully.*

Jane read the first line of the poem about a child being born. She looked at Marlene with such bewilderment she didn't even try to use words.

Marlene laughed and pulled Jane into her arms.

"You listen and I'll tell you what I think it means. Then we'll look at the poem again." They sat curled together on the sofa by the window with the sunbeams resting on their heads. Quietly Marlene attempted to explain what she saw in the poem.

"It's about how time goes and yet some things stay the same. You've looked at all the pictures I have of your mom when she was little. You looked at all the pictures of when she and your dad were young, before you were born. So you understand that she was a baby and a teenager and a young woman. But I know she was. Right this minute I can feel her lying in my lap. I can smell the baby scent of her. I can hear her running through the house. I can feel how my stomach hurt when we argued during her teen years. Those things haven't gone away. They're as real to me today as when they happened. But we know that it's not the same as today. Now she's a busy, grown-up woman with a house to run, a family to take care of, and a job to do. I don't even get to see her too often anymore, but she's still here in all those other parts of her life just the same as she is now. See? It's magic. We don't lose what we are, we add to what we were.

She twisted Jane around just enough to see her face and make sure she hadn't overloaded the child. But she wanted this completed, not left half-said. She found it easier to keep Jane facing the other way while she talked, so she twisted her back again so that Jane was resting against her. She brushed Jane's hair back with her hand while she continued.

"I'm old enough to have friends who have died. Others have moved far away. Now those of us still living only send Christmas cards and these are people that I once talked to almost every day. So I don't think about them as often, but they never go away. I can pull them out of my heart, remember, and feel just like I did when they were with me. That's magic. They're not gone; the time we had together is gone. So we really don't have to be afraid of change because we can keep everything that was and still live with the new. I think Time played a trick on those who watched. She's talking about changes. The child is still a child to me even though she's grown to be your mom. Do you understand what I'm saying? Or am I saying it badly?"

Jane turned to look at her and Marlene saw with amazement that the child appeared to be taking it all in. Jane asked, "Is that why people write poetry."

"Yes, it helps us write our feelings down and that makes it easier to bring the magic remembering back. It brings the good moments back to us much more quickly. So we change and we don't change and that's the magic.

"Some day, when you go to the beach with your own children, it'll be different. You'll worry about sand in the baby's diaper, about the older children getting too near the water. You'll be afraid of the kids getting sunburned or that they will pick up some nasty object from the sand. But they'll have a good time and you'll be tired. Then when you get home, you can read the poem about what the beach was like for you when you were a child, and you'll know what a good time your children have had. You'll be in both places at the same time. See? Magic. At least that's what I think it is."

For a moment, it was quiet, and then Jane wriggled around in Marlene's arms and looked into her Gram's face.

"Are you crying, Gram?"

"No, it's just like wet around the eyes, like—well, it's good crying. Remembering is so special and today, when you wrote your first poem, will always be in my magic remembering box."

"What's a magic remembering box?"

"I think that's just what we'll call that place where we each put all those things we want to remember."

"Can we do the Chinese painting next time? I'm getting hungry."

As they went into the kitchen, Marlene knew she had given this kid too much and had turned her off with the rambling. It made her sad, but she knew she had only done the best she could. They took their sandwiches out into the back yard and sat at the picnic table.

Jane said, "It's hard for me to think about remembering so much, but I remembered about the fireplace, didn't I? And, I do know how the beach feels even though we haven't been there yet this year. So I guess it is magic. Will my poetry help me be a better rememberer?"

"It sure will, sweetie, and it'll give you a lot of pleasure." Mentally, she added, *Enough already, this is too much for me whether it is for you or not.* "How about we clean up and go to the plaza before I take you home? We can paint next time. Maybe you want to call your mom and see if she wants to meet us there."

As it turned out, Jessie did want to meet them. Then they called Auntie Kate and Aunt Eileen. The biggest surprise of all was that everyone was home and happy to join the outing. The entire afternoon was spent with all of them wandering around in and out of stores, sometimes sitting in the late spring sun and laughing a lot. Marlene mentioned she was going to spend Wednesday night with Carolyn in San Francisco and everyone accepted that as reasonable.

Jane had brought her poem and it was appropriately appreciated. Marlene was at peace. The group paired off in different couples for short periods giving Jane the opportunity to be the center of someone's attention most of the afternoon. It was a good day. When Jane and Marlene were hugging their goodbyes, Jane whispered in Marlene's ear. "See? Another day for the magic remembering box. Thanks, Gram, I love you.

Marlene thought she would stop breathing, she was so happy. She had given her gift to this most beloved child and it was accepted. She knew she was ready to cry, but Kate and Eileen had already decided it was time for the three of them to go get Mexican food. For now, her time with Jane was put away in her own magic remembering box to be coddled another time.

The next morning Carolyn called—a Monday morning habit. They talked a bit about the past week, sharing funny things, frustrations, and plans for the week ahead.

Marlene sounded as if she were giving a report. "I've traded work days for next weekend because I have to go keep that appointment at Stanford this week, I covered myself yesterday by telling the girls I was going to San Francisco with you. I go on Wednesday and will stay over until Thursday, noon to noon or something like that. So the rest of the week I have to work."

"Why don't I catch an early a.m. flight on Wednesday and go with you?"

"Because I'll be in bed for twenty-four hours and what'll you have to do? That sounds silly."

"No." Carolyn was not sounding as demanding as just down-to-earth practical. "They've got phones there so I can work or read if I choose. If I get the earliest flight in the morning and back on the latest Thursday night flight, or even Friday morning, no one here will miss me. I can get a room near the hospital for the night so I'll have a retreat if the health scene gets to me. Marlene, I would like to…no, I need to do this."

"How can I deprive you? No, I don't mean that. It's better with you there than not. I just don't want to worry about you being bored or frustrated with the sitting, of which there will be a lot…like twenty-four hours worth."

Carolyn returned to the everyday. "The drive to Palo Alto will also give me a chance to go over some of these staff issues with you. Not because you're concerned about this stuff anymore, but you have good judgment and I could sure use your input. I need a break and some of your wisdom. *De acuerdo?* Let me call you back when I've talked to the airline. Okay?"

"Sure and thanks. Talk with you soon. Had a big weekend with Jane, so I'm going to read and nap all day. Maybe I'll make an eggplant pizza. Yeah, that sounds good and would provide lunches for all week. See ya."

"Okay, bye, but I don't want eggplant pizza. We'll eat out."

"Bye, but you don't know what you're missing."

It turned out to be a quiet, catch-up couple of days. Pleasant days and interesting work nights. She turned down all coffee requests and meals out, just enjoying the time to herself. She did a little gardening and finished a book, feeling very strong and saucy when she went to the airport at six-thirty Wednesday morning to meet Carolyn's plane.

All her stuff was in the car, ready to head for the Bay Area. The trip had taken on the aura of a couple of days off instead of the horror of doctors' poking and probing. In fact, her thoughts were much more on seeing Carolyn than on the chore ahead. She was hoping, if they took off fast enough, they could have an early lunch in San Francisco before heading down to the hospital.

At the airport, Marlene parked the car and put in a bunch of quarters, no doubt, more than she needed. She just didn't want to worry about it. Then, she walked into the airport and up to the arrival area, finding a place to sit and people to watch.

She noticed the early morning travelers; most of them business people and she remembered her days of travel. All of these people appeared hassled, concerned with deadlines, clients, and customers. In addition to all their worries and anxieties, they had to consider their appearance. Did they look appropriately important? Did they remain visibly distracted? Did they appear to be completely indifferent to the flight process because they did it so often? She wanted to laugh out loud. She'd played that game. *Don't tell me that man in the black suit isn't posturing for my benefit. He knows I'm just a silly old lady in jeans, waiting for my Bingo buddy to arrive, easily dismissed.*

The door opened and people rushed off the plane. Marlene's eyes were shinning as she ran up, took Carolyn's arm, and moved her in the direction of the black suit.

"It worked...one million three and tomorrow they're filing the papers with the court."

Carolyn would have looked bewildered if Marlene hadn't pinched her arm. "I told you...six months ago I told you. We couldn't lose. Just like the last two years."

As they walked away down the corridor, Marlene got a glimpse of the black suit following them with his eyes.

At the same time Carolyn giggled and whispered, "What are we doing? Aren't you supposed to give me some warning?"

"It wasn't anything much. The black suit back there was making me crazy while I was waiting. He reminded me of myself. I thought he needed something else to think about on his flight. It's all over now. He took notice and that's all I wanted. I'm so glad to see you."

They wrapped their arms around each other and made their way through the airport and to the car. As if they were off on vacation, Marlene drove out to the freeway while they babbled and laughed all the way. Even with the traffic and the wait on the bridge, they were in The City by ten and chose the English Pub on Geary for brunch. Marlene parked the car in the very expensive parking lot nearby.

"You know, now that I've decided that money isn't the most important issue in my life, everything is so much more pleasant. Like parking your car where it's convenient instead of fighting those lots in the Tenderloin."

It was a wonderful meal and talk, and soon they were driving south to Palo Alto. The traffic was still bad, but Marlene remained stress free.

"What exactly are you going to be doing here? Or, should I say what are they going to be doing to you?" Carolyn asked.

"I don't know, but I don't think it's too important. I guess my own doctors are frustrated that I won't take this whole thing more seriously. This place is supposed to be some kind of miracle opportunity. They have procedures here that are not available anywhere else and they'll make an evaluation of my situation and offer me the world…not life, but the world. I've just chosen to play it through and see what happens; I'll hear them out. Please don't be worried about me. Read your book and walk in their garden and talk to me when they let you in and we'll be out of here in no time. Think I'll take you by the hotel first so you'll know where you're going when you take my car back from the hospital. How about that?"

They pulled into a gorgeous courtyard in front of the hotel with flowers all around the door. Inside it was very gracious indeed. As they put Carolyn's stuff in her room, she laughed and said, "See, I really understood when you talked about spending money. I also determined that now is not the time to spare oneself creature comforts. If this is truly an adventure as you say, then we need to give it our all. So don't pity me tonight when you're lying in bed being waited on hand and foot. I'm not doing too badly here. Who knows? I might even find someone to share it with."

Shortly after arriving at the hospital, Marlene checked in and went to bed. Carolyn went to carve out a space for her work, reading, and people watching. She was only admitted to Marlene's room at the end of the day when Marlene was ready to go to sleep.

"God, go to your beautiful hotel room and when you get up in the morning, take your breakfast out by the pool, drink tons of coffee, finish your book and don't come back here until near noon. This has been awful."

74

"How do you feel now?"

"I wasn't this sick when I came in here. No, that's not true, I'm not sick, just overworked, over-probed, over-tested, over-poked with not one shred of dignity left. Well, forget that. I've been divided up among a lot of people and every one of them took their share. I'm very tired and cross. Nobody's psyche needs this much invasion. I'm sorry. Please go and sleep well. I'll see you tomorrow, hopefully, in time for lunch."

Carolyn took her friend's hand, leaned down, kissed her cheek, and whispered. "Remember what we used to say about the women in the refugee camps? Well, you can do it too. You can do anything and it's only for another half day. You sleep well. I love you and I'll see you in the morning. *Recuerdas, mi'ja.*" She smoothed the hair from Marlene's face, kissed her cheek once more, and silently left the room.

Marlene rolled over on her side and allowed herself to cry, the first time since this nightmare had begun that she had cried. She cried the way Carolyn had cried that morning in the yard. It was so cleansing. When she was breathing evenly again, she rolled onto her back. She thought of the days she had spent in the camps. *I felt at home there. The people were so needy, yet so strong that they could expose their vulnerability without self-pity.*

Northern Nicaragua, early 1980's: A large metal shed with cubicles the length of a single size bunk bed and twice the width, surrounded only by blankets used as walls. One family per space and everything they owned kept in those cubicles. It wasn't the worst she'd seen, but she remembered one Christmas. Some of the families had little tiny trees or weed bouquets or pieces of wood from the ground to decorate for the season. One man had said to her, "Come into my home."

There were many young boys in that camp. Tall, apparently strong boys, but they'd held my hand as if I were their Grandma or auntie. They'd been taken off the streets of El Salvador, some of them twelve and thirteen years of age, and conscripted into the army. These boys had run off from the army and, because they were the lucky ones, had ended up in this camp. They had never talked to their mothers or fathers since the day they disappeared. To contact their parents would put whole families in jeopardy. Now there was no family, no friends, and no history; a smile was all it took to make them little boys again. And the music they had provided at night...oh my.

There was a tiny woman, Teodora. She hadn't yet obtained space inside the camp and was living with her two little boys on a blanket outside the fence in a field. There had been time that day to walk with her and hear her story. In El Salvador she had lived with her husband, five children and her in-laws. Within two weeks, all of them were dead except for her and the two youngest sons.

"I wouldn't wait for them to come and get us," she said. So she had packed what she could carry that wouldn't look conspicuous, and walked out of town. They had camped along the way and gone into Honduras, a very touchy place to be in the '80s. They had walked over into Nicaragua on the jungle side, and then made their way over the mountains into the western side of the country. And, here she was, just happy to be with people who weren't hostile, even though she was still living on her blanket. All ninety pounds of Teodora had saved those boys, these ninety pounds had kept her moving, with and without food, to make sure nobody took her sons. Why? How? Because it was what she had to do. End of discussion.

She had been a lady to giggle with, to share all our good and our bad that afternoon. There was nothing superhuman about her, just a woman doing what needed to be done. God love us all.

"Right, Carolyn, I can do eighteen more hours of this. I can do whatever I have to do," she whispered into her pillow.

Because of the exhaustion from the day, the cry, the remembering, and the pill they had given her, Marlene slept the whole night through, waking in the morning feeling considerably better.

As they were bringing her breakfast, Carolyn walked in. It was only seven-thirty.

Marlene looked up at her friend. "First of all, why are you awake? Second, why aren't you sitting drinking coffee by the pool if you insist on being awake? Third, why are you here? And by the way, good morning."

"I called when I woke up and they said I could come have breakfast with you. See, I brought my bagel and I'll find coffee somewhere around here. The nurse said you would probably do a lot of sitting around this morning while the doctors are reading your stuff. Good morning to you, too."

"What stuff? Did you bring them my old articles?"

"Sure, but they rejected them in favor of color snapshots of your guts and charts and graphs that make you look like a robot. Someone said something about an owner's manual. How did you sleep last night? Sorry, if it's rude, but I slept like the dead. So how about you? A little better than last night?" A nurse came in with a carafe of coffee and a glass of orange juice for Carolyn.

"Very good service, but I guess it's a little pricey to do it often, huh?"

Marlene, having years of experience with this kind of conversation, picked right up where Carolyn had left off previously.

"Cried like a baby after you left. That was good. It was the first time I've really let go since this started. Then thought about what you said about the refugees and I remembered Teodora. If she can do what she did, I can do this. Then, like you. I went right to sleep and they woke me up this morning. Yeah, I feel better, but not nearly as good as I'll feel when we drive away from here. What else did they tell you besides the fact that I'll be sitting around a lot this morning? I'm glad you came to act as communicator, since they don't seem to think I can do that for myself.

Carolyn was casual in her response, "I thought sitting here with you was more fun that sitting by the pool fretting about you. Now I can see you're going to be okay. Ya know, Marlene, these people are not here to hurt you. They do have some interest in your recovery or care or whatever they choose to call it."

"It sounds more like a game to me. Okay, let them do their job and I'll do mine." And, she threw her legs over the side of the bed and went into the bathroom. Upon returning, she lay back down on the bed and closed her eyes. Carolyn got her book out of her bag and gave Marlene whatever time she needed.

Twice during the morning, someone came in and took blood and once she was wheeled out for x-rays, but was back quickly. About eleven o'clock, the nurse came in and asked. "Would you like to get dressed and go down for lunch with your friend? I know the cafeteria isn't too fancy, but it beats this room. Then you can meet with the doctors in room 211 on this floor at 12:45. You can meet with them fully clothed and at equal eye level. I'm sure that'll feel better than yesterday did."

"Thank you, that'll be fine, and I do appreciate your kindness. We'll be back on time." It was a dismissal of the nurse, as Marlene had already gone and gotten her clothes out of the closet. They were down the hall while Marlene was still pulling her ponytail out from under the neck of her jacket. No time wasted here.

Marlene wasn't hungry and just wanted to take her tea out on the patio, where the sun was warm, flowers were in bloom and the big ferns cast fine shadows on the cement.

It was a silent time. Marlene watched people and imagined their stories. There were families, professionals, and a few loners who might have been Carolyn the day before. What were they waiting for? Then it was time to return so Carolyn and Marlene cleaned up their table and went upstairs.

They were in the sitting room, waiting to be called, when Dr. Ferguson came toward them. After being introduced to Carolyn, he invited Marlene to accompany him down the hall. He was in his forties or early fifties, tall, husky, blonde and he wore serious glasses. Yet for all his size, his voice was softer than average. He ushered her into a small conference room where two other men stood as she entered. She had seen all these men yesterday, been introduced to them, and then violated by them. But today everything seemed different. Probably because she was in an upright position and was approaching them as if she were an equal. They sat around a small wood table, the size of which gave the group a sense of intimacy. The absurdity of it made her want to giggle. She was proud of her ability to remain calm and confident.

Dr. Ferguson began the conversation by saying there was not much new information he could offer against what the doctors back home had diagnosed. But there were more options open to her here than in the valley.

Dr. Lynn then explained all kinds of things about surgery, medications, and life style adjustments. He was the eldest of the three and appeared to have a slightly different view of traditional western medicine. She expected him to suggest acupuncture; instead, he suggested, no cure was guaranteed. Then Dr. Bennett spoke to her of radiation and chemotherapy, again, offering no guarantees of renewed health. He was quite clear about the side effects and the recovery process from the treatments.

Dr. Ferguson ended the discussion. "Ms. Drubaker, we hope to have given you some idea of what is ahead with any of these treatments. Are there any other questions you would like to ask or any area in which we haven't been clear? It really is our intention to help you make decisions in any way we can."

"Thank you. My doctors have suggested that I'm not taking this as seriously as they would wish. I think I'm taking it very seriously. I appreciate very much your willingness to clarify it all. Let me try to be as clear for you. I have nothing to hide here. It's just not as easy to communicate. I don't have charts, graphs, and color snapshots.

"If you were to tell me I'd be blind for life, I believe I'd make the adjustment to that. If you told me I would be in a wheel chair for many years to come, I think I'd figure out how to make that work too. When it gets down to life support systems, that might be harder to determine based on my ability to communicate, but that isn't the decision I feel I have to make." In an attempt to lighten the mood, she added, "If it's a case of losing my mind, I guess there would no decisions for me to make. But what I hear is, I'm going to die. Maybe soon, maybe later. Maybe with treatment, maybe without. The discussion becomes one of time; how much of it am I willing to buy and how much will it cost me? Most of the images I've been able to conjure up tell me that the sickest people are those who are being treated. I remember time before the new technology and knowledge. People with cancer were very sick and then they died. But they were on their feet a lot, sometimes sedated, but at least minimally functional. And then they died."

Marlene paused, but she didn't want to lose their attention.

"Now we're talking about the quality of the life I can have; the quality of life I can help provide for my family. If I take it as I see it, which is what I was told in the very beginning, there really is no cure or replacement for the cancerous parts of my body. So I have to deal with the reality of death, whenever that is.

"It follows logically for me that the question is now how I choose to die. Do I go with Dr. Lynn and become obsessive about what I eat and how I exercise, reaching a time when it's the only thing I think of? Actually, I know perfectly healthy people, most of them young, who are boring beyond tears with their commitment to their bodies.

"Do I subject myself to the modern technology with Dr. Bennett and watch my flesh turn to mush, vomiting and staying sick for weeks on end? Maybe if there were to be some real results I'd think differently, but these ways appear to be tricks to buy time and that doesn't sound like time I want to buy.

"I have three wonderful daughters and two magnificent grandchildren. Oh, would I like to stay and see the children my other daughters produce? Would I like to see my youngest daughter grow into the confident, productive woman I know she will be? You bet! Do I want to plan Christmas dinners and family picnics?" She paused. "You have no idea. But there are a lot of things I don't want as well.

"I don't want to become a disease instead of a person. I don't want family members watching me out of the corners of their eyes to see how I'm doing. I don't want to see fear in their eyes. I don't want them to adjust their lives to my care. I don't want the family impoverished by the expense of buying what I now perceive as bad time. I don't want them exhausted trying to care for me and maintain their families and their jobs. I don't want them feeling guilty because they don't think they do enough. I don't want them to waste an additional couple of years after I've gone pulling their lives back together.

There are the things I do want. I want to help them understand I'm moving on. I want them to take care of their business now, while I'm here. I want to share with them some of the grief and adjustment and know they'll be okay when I'm gone. I want them to forever remember when, and never waste their energy on what if? I want them to use the energy and resources they have to make living a wonderful thing and dying just a part of that experience. I want to laugh with my granddaughter before I go, not see her cringe at the smell or touch or look of me.

"Please don't get me wrong. I'm not altogether sure how to go about all this and while my daughters are wonderful, they can be difficult on occasion. But when you list all the energy consuming things you have to offer against the possibility of making this a time of growth and acceptance for my family, well…I'm sorry, but your list just doesn't hold up. I also have no plans for the ending. I know I feel reasonably well at the moment. As that changes, I'll have to look to Dr. Lynn's natural remedies or pain control or whatever keeps me on my feet and functional. After that, I don't know what will happen. I'll have to deal with that when the time comes, won't I? I apologize for talking so long. I hope it was a logical unfolding of my thoughts, not just a lot of emotional gibberish."

It was quiet, but soon Dr. Lynn, the eldest of the group, said, "It was almost too logical and too unemotional. I guess that is what's concerning your doctors back home. I think you have thought it out very well and you certainly have my support as you make your decisions."

Dr. Bennett leaned forward in his chair, young, intense, and sincere, "The best I can give you is a little nagging about the coffee and some of the things that might slacken the nausea. Work at keeping up the appetite even when food sounds just awful. Let me suggest ice cream. It seems to stay down and cause less trouble than other things. Keep in touch and we'll work with each of the symptoms as they appear. You have my best wishes, Ms. Drubaker. I think you are a brave and strong woman."

The most quiet was Dr. Ferguson. It took him awhile to speak, then, "There's always that outside chance that something that hasn't worked before will do the trick. There's all that could be learned from your experience that will benefit children who suffer with the disease. I do hear what you're saying and I'm moved by it, but my scientist self says, 'there's always a chance.'"

With her head bowed, she spoke clearly, "Could you just let me go, Dr. Ferguson?" Lifting her head, she smiled at him. "This is good practice. I have a lot of it ahead of me. You have an agenda, Doctor, and thank God for it. But I just want to be let go, with best wishes if you can, 'to the devil with you' if you can't, as my Irish ancestors would say. Under any other set of circumstances, I would parade your talents and commitments up and down the streets, but this particular time, I want it my way. Can you do that for me?"

He moved about in his chair, tapped his papers on the table with what appeared to Marlene as finality. "Yes," he said. "Assuming you keep us posted and let us help whenever possible. I don't know whether to say thank you or, as you say, 'the devil with you.' You have my support, grudgingly, but you have it."

Marlene threw her head back and laughed heartily. "I think that's more than fair. I appreciate our honesty. You have also given me confidence as I approach my daughters. If I can convince you, there's no stopping me now."

Dr. Bennett, having joined in the laughter at the expense of his colleague, now asked, "Is there anything else we can do for you before you leave?"

Marlene reached down and picked up her purse. "I can only thank you for your consideration and support. I will stay in touch."

Dr. Ferguson began to move his chair and they all stood. He handed Marlene a manila envelope. "Here are the papers you'll need. The reports will be sent to your oncologist. Our names and numbers are in there when you need something further. I wanted to say you have a long hard road ahead of you, but now I understand.

She moved toward him with her hand extended," You've all been very kind and I thank you very much."

In the hall, Dr. Bennett nodded to her and picked up speed as he walked away. Dr. Ferguson shook her hand once again and with a smile, a courteous goodbye, he also moved down the hall. Marlene started to walk back to where she had left Carolyn, when she heard her name spoken quietly. She turned and saw Dr. Lynn still in the hall. The short, elderly man with the kindly face stepped up to her and again extended his hand.

Then he asked her, "Ms. Drubaker, are you a religious woman? I'm sorry, but this isn't a question I'd ask in a public meeting."

"If you mean do I have secret beliefs or conclusions about the next life, the answer is no. I guess I've just always been a curious traveler. Someone gave me an image once. What baby is born leaping into the world? It's a hard struggle getting here and the child seems to fight it every step of the 'labor'. I know—I had three. Maybe moving into whatever is next is like that. We'll fight it only to find that's what it was all about anyway. Or maybe not."

"Well, I admire your determination to play this out on these terms. I just wanted you to know that should you ever need anything…" It was a long pause, "Please give me a call."

She looked at the floor and asked herself, *what is he saying?* Suddenly she knew she couldn't ask him. *If I'm right, will I jeopardize his relationship with his colleagues?* So she looked into his eyes for a long moment and said, "Thank you, Dr. Lynn. I will remember and I appreciate it."

Dr. Lynn handed her his card. "Here's my office number. I pray for the best for you and your family. Perhaps we'll talk again." Then he nodded and walked away. She stayed there in the hall, taking her billfold out of her bag and carefully placing the card in the cash pocket. It somehow seemed too important an item to lose.

She went and picked up Carolyn with, "Let's get the hell out of here," and they were gone.

Carolyn pulled out of the parking lot and drove to the freeway going north. "Anything you want?"

"No, I wish I could say let's go into the city, but I really want to go home. Hope you don't mind."

"Of course not, home it is."

The trip was silent. Marlene dozed off and on. But something was happening inside her head. *What's different?* Things had changed and it took her a bit to figure out what that was. *I've made a choice. Did I make a firm determination earlier that I hadn't admitted to myself or am I such a great orator that I convinced myself? Did I just walk in, make a statement, and then decide it was the right thing for me to do? Am I acting or reacting? There's something comforting about it.* She was now on a track, going where she wanted to go.

No, it's not impulsive. I have made a commitment. It's what I've been thinking about all these months. To join The Women who do what they have to do and give it my best shot. Then Marlene slipped into a deep sleep until they were back in her town and in front of her apartment.

Once upstairs, Marlene said, "I'm really sorry, but I need to go to bed. Do you mind?"

"No, that's why I'm here. To guarantee you do what you need to do. But you've had nothing to eat since breakfast, which was minimal. Please, may I get you something? Fruit? Noodles? Cereal? Toast?"

"Thanks. A slice of toast might help and maybe something corny, like tea." She headed for her room to get out of her clothes. When Carolyn brought her the toast and tea, Marlene was in the bed.

"God, I'm tired. I feel so drained I hardly have the energy to move."

"Well, you've been through a lot. Sounds pretty confrontational to me. I don't think I mean just the doctors, but the disease. Can you tell the difference between being sick and being stressed? Go ahead and rest, we'll talk about it later." Within minutes, Marlene had eaten some of the toast, swallowed the tea, handed the cup to Carolyn and fallen asleep.

When she woke in the morning, Carolyn was still there, all signs of her bedding put away and no apparent sign of a packed suitcase. Looking at the clock, Marlene said. "Oh, you missed your plane. I'm sorry. Why didn't you wake me up?"

"I changed my reservation last night. I've been in contact with the office each day. Nobody misses me. How are you feeling this morning?"

"Actually, pretty good. Might not be up to par for a day or two, but I can take you on. How are you doing? How and where did you sleep? Wow, what a hostess I turned out to be."

"I slept fine on the sofa. Found everything I needed. The hot water is ready for tea."

As they settled down in the living room, Carolyn said, "George was here last night. I'm not yet the practiced liar you are, but I kept him from waking you up without alarming him. I think."

"Shit." She giggled at the image of Carolyn playing go-between while dealing with her own consternation. "What did you say?"

"My success came from saying nothing only that we'd had a big two days, too much wine and you came home really tired. When he got all concerned, I reminded him that he had seen you sleep a whole weekend away and then you'd be yourself again. I even aimed for a little guilt, suggesting that he was treating you like a child. I think he backed down, but you'll have to deal with any errors I made. Good luck. You know, Marlene, he really is a very nice person."

"I know. That's the problem. If he were a rat, this would be easier. But can you see how difficult it would be to deal with his concerns and caring? My choice is to go through this process with my children. I just don't have enough juice to care for extra people. He'd need care, you know. Men do.

"No wonder I went to sleep last night, maybe I can sleep through the rest of my life." She leaned forward in her chair and put her head in her hands. "The hard parts are coming up, huh? But not this morning. Let's go eat at the café in the park. How about that?"

Carolyn looked at her with wary eyes. "Tell you what. I really like that idea, but I'd like it better if it didn't mean, 'let's go watch Carolyn eat.' Promise me you'll eat something, even if light and easy. Eating is the only thing that will enable you to do all the things you have ahead of you, so let's start learning how you can do that best. Learn fast, I have a seven o'clock plane this evening. Maybe after breakfast, we can make an excursion to the market and see what can be made appealing. Okay?"

As they headed for the door, Marlene announced. "Haven't told you the latest prescription. We can buy ice cream."

With the same jaunty air, they moved into another productive, funny, and comforting day.

85

JULY

Summer was here, warm days, the trees full and leafy. Marlene found pleasure upon waking; padding around the apartment in a lightweight, cotton nightgown, wearing no slippers or shoes. She checked in the bathroom mirror to measure the jaundice that was becoming more obvious to her. She took tea to the living room where she and the cat watched the shadows of the trees on the grass. After her tea, she dressed and walked in the garden, brushing against the basil and rosemary.

The time she wasn't working was used preparing for the trip she'd organized in an effort to placate everyone.

Finally, she had just told them how this vacation was going to be. George hadn't understood the difficulty. One Sunday afternoon she had given him his choice of either going with her to England for ten days, or joining her after she had spent ten days in Scotland with Carolyn. Her last ten days were to be spent with Robert and Jane. George didn't get it. Finally, she gave up arguing and simply said, "This is how I want to do it, George. I'm sorry if you don't understand, but I've always been this way. It needs to be my choice. Which ten days do you want?"

Since he hadn't answered her, she had gone into the kitchen, but he had called her back. He began a process of sitting down, standing up, and sitting down again. His actions resembled visible thinking.

"Why don't all of us go for the whole time? We could each enjoy the kids and no one person would be responsible for them all the time. You and Carolyn could have time to go do your thing. You and I could spend some time together. I don't know Carolyn that well, but she seems flexible. How does she do with kids?"

Marlene sat for a long time just watching him. He began to play with the salt and peppershakers. It appeared he was going to wait her out.

"I'll have to talk it over with Carolyn," Marlene said. "There are no promises here, other than I'll talk to her about it" George looked at her closely, and she knew he didn't understand her resignation.

"Do you really find me such a burden?"

"Oh, no, George. You're not a burden, you're a trap, a luxurious trap, a warm, wonderful, caring trap. I think I'm the same for you. Neither one of us get all that we really need, but it feels so good when we're together that we each decide to settle. Maybe that's the way it works when people are young and need to raise families and have structure and such. But we're at the other end of the line. We don't have to settle for anything. We've done everything required of us, and actually, we've done it well. Now, before it's too late, we need to complete those dreams we had when we were young. The ones we put away for a day like today. I prevent you from having what you want and you prevent me having what I want, but second best is good, so we go on."

George paced. "How do you figure you know what I want? Who are you to decide if I'm settling or taking advantage? I thought we were pretty good at knowing we each needed some diversion. I also thought I'd been improving, learning to back off and give you space. Why isn't it enough?"

"George, you want to be married. Look, you want a family excursion here, with grandchildren, 'Aunt Carolyn', and everybody taking care of everyone else. Actually, it's a very good plan, but I never thought of it. I wanted to do the train thing with Carolyn. I wanted to spend time with you and I wanted to drive off into the country with the kids. You see, we don't think alike. Why haven't you found some wonderful woman who wants to be with someone all the time? Someone who doesn't still dream of living in La Paz in her old age? If I couldn't go, for any reason, staying here with you would be very good.

But I can go, and my questions are do I stay here because of you, or do I go see if I can make it down there? Will it be as I have always dreamed it would be? Is this really the way we want to spend our best time? Maybe it is, but I need to make that decision up front. I have to say. 'Put away those dreams and make some new ones.' I have to choose it, George, not just let it happen to me."

"You haven't talked about La Paz for a long time. I just sort of thought you'd forgotten about it."

The proximity of reality made her stomach tighten up. She was close to saying, sorry, but when you know you're going to die, you make new lists and change a few priorities. She knew she couldn't say that and since there wasn't much she could say, she needed to change the subject.

So she sat quietly for a moment and then, with her eyes a little wet, she looked up at him and said, "I'm so sorry. I've always been this restless. I just got comfortable there for a while. But this is the real me and I know and you know, George, it isn't what you want. I've taken this time from your life too. I should have known better. I apologize."

George reverted to his comfortable passiveness. He walked over and stood behind her chair. He rubbed her shoulders and smoothed her hair. "You didn't take anything away from me. You've given me a very good time. I'm not ready to say it's over, but I will acknowledge that it may be. I think we can have it all and I'll do all I can to show you how. But if you don't buy it, I'll probably fight for you, risk life and limb coming to La Paz to visit, or weep at the loss of you. But I'll never regret. Never." He leaned down to kiss the top of her head and wrap his arms around her; not to hold her, only to hug. Then he backed away.

When she was sure her voice would be steady, Marlene asked, "So what do you want me to do about this trip?"

"What do I want?" His voice was light and casual. "I want to see if it's possible for everybody to go together and yes, have a family trip. That doesn't sound so very grim to me. What will I settle for? Whatever works best for everyone."

"Aren't you afraid I'll be pissy on the trip if I don't get my way?" Marlene looked at him from the corner of her eye with her head tilted.

George laughed with his usual ease. He had moved out of the drama now and was himself again. "You're too unwilling to give up a good time. Whatever happens, you'll get on that plane ready to take on the adventure and bring all of yourself to make it wonderful. You don't have it in you to be pissy for any great length of time." He patted her shoulder and moved away toward the sofa where he had left his paper.

As he settled himself, she became disgruntled that he was letting go so easily. *Why does he think I know myself so well when I want two extremely different things and I'm unhappy if I can't have both? A lot of what I said is true, but it's exaggerated by the facts that you, George, don't know. My need for independence is not based on this relationship, it is based on my need to conserve my energy and you, my dear man, just don't fit into that equation. You'll need the care I want to give my children. Damn. Don't put me in this position.*

She went to her room and lay down on the bed, scrunching the pillow under her head. The cat jumped on the bed and curled up next to her. Soon they were asleep.

When she woke, less than an hour later, she was covered with a light quilt and the cat was back at her feet where he usually kept guard. Marlene lay there for a bit and then rose, thinking there must be something she was supposed to be doing. She found George napping on the sofa, the apartment quiet. She picked up a book and took it back to her bed. A chapter later, she heard him in the kitchen and got wondering if the previous conversation would be repeated or continued.

No, it was like always, a warm Sunday afternoon and they played out a common scene between them.

"Let's see what's in the fridge for dinner."

"Okay. I'll go get stuff from the garden to make a salad."

"There's spaghetti here from Friday or this ricotta would make a fine lasagna."

"Sounds good, but..." and they said together, "It's not Mexican. Let's go to Vallejo's." It was easy for them to be quiet together and, after eating, they decided on a movie.

When they arrived back at Marlene's apartment, the usual was only a little different. They both seemed to understand. Each wanted George to stay, but they knew it wasn't a good idea. Nothing was said, no excuses made. They simply held one another, let go and then he left. She wondered, *is it that we both know it's the end, or is he trying harder to give me space? Does it matter? Was it the word 'trap' that did it?* Aloud she said to herself, "You'd better know what you're doing and what you want. Many things are changing and you've set them in motion. There's to be no whining if it turns out to be not what you want."

She looked at the clock; quarter to eleven. Pretty late, but what the heck, and she dialed Carolyn's number. There were a couple of rings and Carolyn's voice, sounding a bit startled, came on the line. "Hello."

"Hi, were you sleeping already, or do you have company or something?"

"Oh, hi. No. Actually, I think I dozed off, but I still have the book against my legs and my glass of wine is still on the bed table. What's up? How ya doing?"

"I'm okay. It's just this trip. I think I'd rather plan a going away party for all of you and wave you off at the airport. George and I had words about it today and I promised him I'd talk to you. He really wants everybody to go together for the whole time."

"You know, Marlene, the advantage is that you'll never be alone with the kids should you have some bad days. I don't wish those on you, but let's pay attention here. It's been a while since you've gone full speed for a month. What do you mean 'you had words'? A real fight? Doesn't sound like the two of you."

"Well, hardly, we are adults, you know. You do know, don't you? But I said some hurtful things in my effort to appear honest and remain deceitful. You and I could go off, he said, even for a few days at a time. Or, he and I could go off, and we could all share in the adventures with the kids. Wait a minute, he didn't mention you and he going off; wonder if it was an oversight? Anyway, it wasn't the way I'd pictured it."

There was the sound of the sip of wine and then Carolyn asked, "So tell me how it looks to you to have everyone there the whole time."

Marlene was cautious. "You sound like it's all worked out. What are the pieces I'm missing? The part about the way you and I communicate without always including everybody?"

Carolyn giggled. "C'mon. Somewhere out there we learned a social grace or two. Dig deep, hermana, and you'll be able to remember how it goes. Yeah, I think I like this plan."

"Okay. Does it feel like I'm giving in too easily? How about Hawaii instead? The kids haven't been there and it sounds so much less complicated."

With exasperation, Carolyn replied, "I'm going to wake up in the morning and try to figure out this conversation. Just tell me where to be and when—preferably at least two hours before departure. I can see myself with tickets in my hands to Zimbabwe."

"Oh, that sounds good."

Carolyn was laughing, "Enough already, go to bed and sober up."

That was how it happened. The tickets and the reservations were ready—three weeks in Hawaii with everyone in tow. Janey wanted to talk about packing and clothes all the time. Robert was reading everything he could find on the islands. Jessie was either nervous or jealous; Marlene couldn't tell which. All in all, it was going well.

Today she was working early afternoon and had slept late, eaten well, and was feeling pretty much on top of everything. She put some cream cheese on a bagel, slipped it into a plastic bag, and determined her lunch was packed. She drove slowly through town before heading to the office.

Linda was at the reception desk sorting a large stack of papers.

"Hi, Linda, how goes it?"

"Good afternoon, Marlene. I suppose it'll go okay if I survive the mess someone made of this filing." The usual cranky, disgruntled sound was in her voice, and there was no doubt she had been put upon again.

Harriet stuck her head out of the first cubicle and made a motion for Marlene to come in. Inside the cubicle, Marlene saw Harriet was in great spirits as she pulled a gaily-wrapped package from a paper bag.

"For me? How good of you."

"No, Marlene, this is for Linda. For three days we've been listening to her complain about the filing situation. Of course, she won't let anyone help her. She seems to find it fun to be a part-time victim. So we went out this morning and bought her a journal as a 'job well done present'. I'll give it to her when she finishes and maybe shame her into smiling, even if it kills her. I'll say 'We appreciate what you've done, Linda.' How she responds is her problem. What have you been up to? You really look good. Here, sign the card."

"Yeah, it was a good day." Marlene took the pen, signed the card, and went to find a place to work. Next door to Harriet, Randy was just cleaning up his stuff, ready to leave. Marlene put her things on the floor of his space while he finished up and then she went off to see who else was around. Grace was in the next space, but she was on the phone and only smiled and waved. Sue was in the end spot and also on the phone. She didn't even look up. When Randy left it would be all women in the place. That didn't happen often. Probably some of the guys will be coming in soon. She retreated to the now empty space and set up her work area. The phone rang.

"Hello, this is Marlene. How can I help you?"

"Marlene, this is Brenda Kelly. Is Randy still around? I have some really good news."

"Hold on, Brenda, if I run I may be able to catch him. Just a sec." She laid down the phone and raced out the front door, only to nearly knock Randy down where he was standing on the top step.

"Brenda Kelly is on the phone for you and she says it's good news. Do you want to come in and take it? If you're in a hurry, I can say you've already left."

"Thanks, Marlene, I'll take good news any chance I get." She was rewarded with that big, warm smile. He went back to the space she had claimed from him. She checked on the others while he talked to Brenda. Sue was still on the phone, but Grace was filling out a closure form.

"Grace, I haven't seen you for so long. How have you been?"

"Marlene, dear. How do we keep missing each other? Actually, I just got back from my granddaughter's wedding in Alabama." The phone rang and Grace patted Marlene's hand as she said into the phone, "Hello, this is Grace, how can I help you?"

"Ya-Hoooo! We have a winner." It seemed as though Randy would burst as he tried to get everyone's attention. "Every once in a while it works, yes, sir!"

He grabbed Marlene and danced her around the small space in the center of the room. By now, Harriet and Grace were outside their workspaces and Linda was stopped dead in her tracks.

"She did it, she actually did it. Last spring I talked Brenda into taking in three teenagers and while the two boys left within the month, the girl is still there and now wants to start school in September. Wow! Of the hundred that get away, we have one that will make it." He stopped. "Sorry, Marlene, hope I didn't hurt you." They were all laughing with him, enjoying the moment.

"No, and it would have been worth it if you had," Marlene responded. "That's wonderful, Randy. Good work. Now go celebrate somewhere besides here. We couldn't be happier for you." They all offered their congratulations and shared the joy. Another kid has a chance.

"Boy, are we lucky to do this work," he said with reverence, and he was out the door with a wave.

"What a strange thing to say." Linda had not moved from her spot, and had been only a spectator to the joy.

"Well, Linda," Harriet attempted to explain. "Some people have jobs that never demand much or require much, and with that comes the fact they never get the momentous highs we have when a challenge is met and things really change. Maybe that's what he meant."

Harriet started back to her workspace and jabbed Marlene in the ribs on the way by. Marlene saw Harriet roll her eyes and they each scurried into their respective cubicles to answer ringing phones. Marlene was grateful she hadn't laughed out loud at the black woman's look of disbelief.

Marlene's next hour was spent with a boy from a different city, a scared sixteen-year-old who had been beaten by his stepfather. Marlene was able to get the kid settled with a family near his home. When that task was completed, she started to cry, and while she attempted to stay in her workspace to hide, Grace came by and poked her head in.

"Anything wrong, dear?"

"No, Grace. If I weren't post-menopausal, I'd dance around the room like Randy. We have two kids safe for the night. I'm just letting go of the stress that was created seeing it through. Thanks for asking, but let's get coffee instead." They went into the kitchen area where Grace gave Marlene the space to vent, but it seemed her crisis was passed.

Linda's voice followed them. "Well, that's over. It better not happen again soon, and by the way, friends, I'm not coming in tomorrow morning. I've done my turn as I'm already two hours over today's time." She was letting the world know she had been thoroughly abused and had survived.

Harriet called, "I don't really think you know how appreciated it is when you take on these impossible tasks and see them through to such perfection. No one could avoid paying attention when Harriet spoke and as she entered the room, her confidence and presence simply brought everyone to attention. Heads were coming out of cubicles and Linda was standing beside her completed filing job looking as if she were about to be punished.

But Harriet wasn't giving up. "We want to try to show you how much it means that you not only volunteer to take on these tasks, but you do them so well. You don't ever quit until they're complete. We want to give this to you in hopes that you can know how much we care about you and the great work you do."

Linda was nonplussed and the onlookers were amused but nonetheless, wary of how she was going to respond. Harriet had to take Linda's hand and place the package in it. On her own, Linda wasn't going to move. Sue stepped in, trying to break the stillness of the scene. "Linda, sometimes I see jobs you're doing and think how I could have or should have done that. When I think I'm going to come help you, the phone rings or a piece of correspondence catches my eye and I don't follow through. But I thank you, and maybe in the future you could holler out about needing a little help. No one means to dump these jobs on you; you just seem to take them on. Open your gift."

Grace had completed her call and come to the center of the room where everyone was. "Sure, Linda, let's see how you like it. There's nothing as much fun as surprises, with the exception of the fourth pregnancy."

Marlene became aware she was watching the scene as if she were invisible. She wanted Linda to enjoy herself, if even for a minute. Yet, watching these women try to make her happy was amazing. Maybe the kinder thing to do was to let Linda be unhappy. It seemed to be what she did best. But no, Marlene knew she had to participate, if for no other reason than to support her friends who, for one purpose or another, needed a positive response from their co-worker.

"Oh, Linda," Marlene said. "We don't party around here often enough. Let's make the best of it. You've done something that makes everybody happy. Let us share that with you." She walked over to Linda and touched the arm holding the package. She literally whispered: "C'mon, open it."

Linda opened the package carefully, not tearing paper or breaking ribbon. She looked at the journal a moment and thumbed the pages. "I'm not very good at journaling. I always end up making lists of things I need to do."

"Me, too," Marlene said. "But making lists often helps me keep control of my life."

"I use journals for doodling," Grace added, "But assume that if I'm doing nothing then my brain or my soul or whatever it is that usually does the journaling is free to flit about wherever it likes and that seems okay to me. But I agree. If you were to see my old journals, you'd find lots of lists. They must have gotten me through some tough times."

Sue entered into the conversation, but seemed a bit dreamy, as if she were already doing it. "I fantasize a lot in my journal. About things that don't make any sense in the real world. It makes me feel guilty, as if I should keep my reality in tow. I just think that I'm in reality more than anywhere else. Guess my family and church friends would be a little amazed to know that sometimes I choose the ridiculous."

Harriet brought in the final, down-to-earth stuff, in her usual strong voice that suggested; this is the way it is. "I'm not far off from any of you. I use the journal to deal with real problems, all those pro/con charts. Like should I really get a tummy tuck or pluck my eyebrows? It must work, as I haven't done either."

They all laughed at her and got deeper into it, except for Sue, who seemed to think this was pretty serious. "But what would happen if a person really thought she'd feel better with breast implants or a new nose? That stuff is important to women of my generation. We relate it to self-esteem."

Somehow, everyone got into the conversation at the same time, but it wasn't going to be helpful to Sue. All the remarks, being from older women, were facetious at best and ridiculous in truth.

"Just think what the world would look like with real Picasso women walking on the street."

"They'd have to tuck my tummy so far up, I'd have to pee lying down."

"Can you imagine after two or three facial operations, then a slip of the needle makes your mouth and ears end up on the same side of your face?"

Harriet pulled her cheeks to the hairline and exposed her teeth. They all laughed. It was very funny. Marlene was well into the humor when something clicked. It started out so logically.

"When did it all begin?" she asked. "Did someone just decide women were built wrong or that there was only one way a woman could look and be acceptable? Who enslaves us to the 'beauty secrets'? We diet obsessively and have now created a generation of beautiful young girls who think they're fat and ugly, so they're killing themselves with no food."

Somehow, Linda never saw a game when it was there. She said, "Silly children of silly adults. If Mom is so insecure that she threatens her own health and well-being to look a certain way, of course some kid is going to learn that this is the most important thing she can do." As she was speaking, Linda moved about, picking up things that she felt were out of place. It was her own way of making a space for herself.

But Marlene was on her own track now and her voice climbed to a high pitch. "I've never been considered a wimp," she said. "I've not been afraid of much in my life, but surgery is a thought-provoking opportunity. Think of being put to sleep with chemicals and having someone, who may or may not be having a good day, cut into your flesh and mess around with your very self. With fear or at least grave concern, we do this when our lives are at stake, but do we really do it because we think we're going to look better? That's insane. That carries a death wish." Marlene acted out her foolish image of a woman determined to be something other than what she was. "If I can't look like such and such, I'd rather be dead or deformed or dismissed. Who are the beautiful women?"

"Marlene." Harriet was still standing in the middle of the room, but watching very closely.

"When do we get to say how wonderful our bodies truly are?" Marlene continued.

"God, I can't believe what I've asked of mine. How I've abused it and it just keeps right on going. Every day it presents me with gifts. Like the children it conceived, nurtured, grew and delivered with great pain to both of us. I've trekked all over the world, drunk dirty water and slept with bugs. And, through all of it, my body just kept going. No body is perfect, but all bodies have redeeming features." She was speaking more rapidly now   "Look, I have great hair. Good color now that it's more white than brown. It's full and healthy. She pulled the clasp from her hair and the long white hair fell down. Should I have been dying it all these years? Should I have pretended I was other than what I am? Younger? Less experienced? I ask you, have you ever heard of a military general who wanted to hide his medals? Hell, no. Wear those suckers out there where the world can appreciate.

But my years, which to me, have been every bit as exciting and adventuresome as a generals', need to be hidden. At the same time that I have great hair, my breasts are now measured up and down instead of around. For that I should be discarded? We can only hope to even it out somewhere and remain kind to one another and to ourselves."

Sue appeared to be getting nervous. "C'mon, Marlene, let's not get into that feminist stuff here. There are real callings for women making homes and rearing children. Women who also want to make a good impression because it's helpful to a husband's career and, therefore, good for her family. We can also be peacemakers. Isn't that enough?"

Moving close, Marlene looked directly into Sue's face. "Have you ever tried to explain the clarity of tone and the simplicity of a Mozart concerto to a deaf person? Have you ever tried to describe a vista that includes ocean and mountains to a blind person? These people are missing some part of the whole, but I've never met one of either group who didn't have things to give me that I lacked. I feebly try to share those things with them and they teach me patience, courage, humor, and some of the regular stuff about which they have more knowledge than I do. Obviously, we've never met the ones who won't come out of their houses, who live ashamed and fearful of what they perceive to be their imperfection. Perhaps I've also avoided those women who feel so unworthy of their appearance that they're willing to sacrifice themselves.

"I have my eyes as long as I can find my glasses. I have my ears but at this time of life, I just turn the volume up a little. I have arms and legs with some arthritis, but by planning ahead I can do most of what I want. My stomach stays settled and my kidneys work. I have a gall bladder; don't know what it does, but it doesn't give me any trouble, so I just say thanks. My lungs are still complaining a little because of all the years I smoked, but they function. So what does it all look like? Not so hot, I guess, but it served me well nearly sixty years now and never complained. Does my body need to love? Yes, it does, sometimes just by me."

Harriet moved a bit closer to where Marlene was pacing, only trying to be in Marlene's line of vision, not really trying to interrupt. Sue had moved much farther back in the room and appeared to be inching toward her workspace.

"Sue, you think about breast implants." Marlene started to walk towards Sue. "Remember when those little buds were just beginning to bloom? It was a little scary, a lot amazing, and very exciting. Then the junior high school boys, who were equally amazed, noticed them. That was scarier yet, but so good for the young ego. False good, maybe. Did we think then that if they would grow into real beauties life would be a breeze? Maybe, but some thinking women knew better. There was the first time our breasts were handled with love by someone we cared about. Oh my, those nipples stood right up there and, those tremors, not blurry and all over, but in very specific places, were very demanding.

How were we ever to know that those breasts would be the starting place for an experience we had imagined poorly, but which was so much more?"

Now Grace grasped the edge of a table.

Marlene continued. "My women friends in war situations don't have time to worry about hair or clothes or size or appearance. They're doing the jobs they're supposed to be doing and saving, caring for and protecting children rewards them. They're feeding families and neighbors and soldiers and husbands when there's nothing to make a meal out of. They're making homes out of jungle bushes, running, or fighting in real battles when the enemy comes close, but they never lose their sense of purpose.

"When they're safe, when the children are sleeping near, when there is some rice for tomorrow and the lover is home, that body, that we hold in such contempt, for her becomes a comforting, pleasurable, reassuring place; for him, for them. From the lovemaking of bodies that may not be too healthy, maybe not too clean, maybe not too whole, comes the reassurance that life will go on and tomorrow will be another contest. And they have a very good shot at winning that one too.

"Is it important how she's dressed, if her nose is straight, if she has gained weight from lack of fruits and vegetables? No, the question is how much love can she give and how willing is she to commit herself every day to the struggle of her people, her family, her children, her husband. Does her body run down with all this strain? It gets tired, it gets sick and it knows pain, but I've never seen such a woman sit down and say, 'That's it, they can have my kids.' That only happens here, where we are so defeated trying to look better, slimmer, sexier, classier, and more successful so that we don't even manage to keep relationships together. We give up on our kids. For all our efforts, we lose in the long run.

"I love my body and want to celebrate what it's done for me. I can't find a body in this room that should be changed." Marlene began to move among the women, touching them, their faces, their hair, and their shoulders. These were loving gestures that eased some of the tension in the room. The panic left her eyes. With her hair loose and fresh tears on her face, she simply began to look sad.

"Why can't we be happy with who we are? Why can't we be proud of what we've done and could only have done with the bodies we have, flawed though we perceive them to be? Remember those days when you worked a full day, chaired five committees, baby-sat neighbors kids, picked your own up at Scouts, prepared dinner for your husband's colleagues and the washing machine backed up, threatening the new kittens that were nested behind. When the guests came to the door, you exuded great graciousness and no one ever knew you wished them dead. When they left, your loving husband said something like, 'Thanks, Hon, it went well.'"

The tears flowed more readily now and she realized she had lost it in front of these people. She muffled an apology and went to her cubicle.

Harriet picked up her own bag and went to Marlene's workspace. "C'mon, lets go get a cup of coffee. Grace will stay an extra hour and Robin will be here in a few minutes."

"Don't get dramatic, Harriet. It was just some piece of PMS that didn't get used when it was supposed to. I made a bit of a fool of myself for a few minutes, but it's over. Let's just go back to work."

Harriet just stood there a while, letting some of the dust settle, allowing both of them to have a little quiet. "I didn't say anything about you. I'm your friend and I need to talk, and I'm asking you to have coffee with me. Let's go."

Marlene looked at her friend for a minute and knew a refusal would cause another scene. She picked up her things and followed Harriet out the door. Outside, Harriet looked at the sky and said, "Let's just walk to the deli, okay?"

Upon entering the nearly empty restaurant, they each shivered with the blast of air conditioning. Harriet put her things on a table and said, "Wait here." She came back with two lemonades and almost fell into the chair.

"This was clever, it tastes good." Marlene's effort to keep the conversation normal was evident and unsuccessful.

"Okay, girlfriend, what's up with you?"

"Oh, c'mon, not much. Harriet, haven't you ever had emotional days? Or out of control days? There's been a lot of stress with this trip and trying to please everybody, and I still have the tired days. There's just a lot going on lately." Marlene went back to her drink in her effort to be nonchalant.

Harriet moved forward until her arms were resting on the table. She was ignoring her drink altogether.

"No, this is me, your friend. Lately you've been distracted and occasionally vague. I've got a feeling that something is changing. I feel this because I love you and I fear that something isn't right. Maybe it's time to talk about it."

A new wariness came into Marlene's eyes as she looked directly at Harriet and asked, "How evident do you think this is? How obvious are these changes that you perceive? Is there discussion around the office?" There was a defensiveness about her now.

"No, that's not happening. I don't think anyone in the place senses anything different. But that's the word—I sense something is wrong, and that can only be because we are attuned to one another. We've done this living thing, as women. Not together in the same place, but I believe you've dealt with things, faced things, coped with things in much the same way I have. And, so in my soul, I see you coping with something now. Don't you know that two tough broads can turn the world on its ear?"

"Make it three. Carolyn, my friend from Los Angeles knows, but she's the only person besides the professionals. The issue is one of trust. I have no problem sharing all this stuff with you, Harriet, if you trust me to make my own decisions. That's the kind of trust I'm looking for. You're beginning to look a bit tense. Guess I better get to the punch line, huh?" Marlene sat with her arms on the table, leaning forward and playing with the glass.

Harriet's chair was pushed back a bit from the table. Her body was turned half away from her friend, one arm crooked over the back of the chair. "Whenever you're ready."

"I think I'm pretty lucky. So far, lack of appetite and exhaustion are my only symptoms, but I have pancreatic cancer, Harriet, and in reality, there's not a lot they can do.

Harriet didn't move a muscle. She continued staring into Marlene's eyes as if she could see her soul. "Do you think about it a lot?"

"Actually, no. When I have to make decisions, it's part of the consideration, like taking the kids on the vacation because I really want some good time with them while I still can. But I did change the plan from Europe to Hawaii because I thought it would be less stressful and easier to cover if I needed some rest up time. I spend a lot of time looking and enjoying as if I could keep all the beauty inside of me when I go. But I don't brood."

"So where have you been letting those emotions loose?"

"Harriet, you're always the counselor. My body isn't the enemy, she's my friend. The disease is the enemy and it's attacking my friend. When the conversation in the office took on signs of another attack on her, I just needed to fight for her. It just happened."

For a moment, they were quiet. "I'm going to miss you." Harriet's voice was soft, but warm.

"Thanks. If it's possible where I'm going, I'll miss you too. You're a good friend. But for now, I have to deal with the present. Can we deal with the serious stuff when I get back from Hawaii?"

"Sure. Whatever you say. You said you were calling the shots? What about George? I don't want to say anything out of line." Harriet sounded cautious.

"Then don't say anything at all. I haven't discussed it with him nor do I intend to yet. First, this will be my problem, then my family's issue. I don't know where he fits in, if at all. I just know I need more time. That may be my trap and maybe you're a good one for watching out for that, but the time with my grandkids, before anyone knows I'm ill, is my priority. I don't mean to shock, Harriet, but this has, so far, been exceedingly easy. No doubt I'm missing some parts, but I'll commit to facing them when I return."

"I'll buy that. Just keep me posted and the rules clear, because my natural inclination is to step in and take care. I see that's not acceptable." Harriet smiled and took Marlene's hand. "Let's head back to the office. You really are okay, aren't you?"

"Yeah, I think so." They got up from the table and went out the door. "It doesn't feel any different than any other problem I've faced. One more time to figure out how to keep the family together and keep them supportive of one another." Marlene put her arm around Harriet's waist as they walked the short blocks back to the office. "If they can learn from my friends, we've got this thing whipped."

AUGUST

The days were spent in a flurry as last minute plans were completed for the trip. A schedule was made for care of the cat. Bags were packed, cars were traded, and Carolyn arrived the day before takeoff. Two days before the trip began, Marlene had a spell of such exhaustion that she was frightened of leaving at all. A call to the doctor got her a medication that would pick her up, but she was given a minimal supply and grave promises were extracted from her about coming into the office when she returned. The family had planned a bon voyage party for the night before Jane, Robert, Carolyn, George, and Marlene were to leave. She felt ready for it.

Four o'clock the next morning, Doug and Jessie were at the door with kids and baggage. They loaded Marlene, Carolyn, and George into their van for the trip to the airport. A fun breakfast at the airport cafeteria and excessive 'goodbyes and hugs' and the five travelers boarded the plane.

After getting situated, with Jane at the window, Robert next to her, George on the aisle and Marlene and Carolyn directly across the aisle, there was a moment of silence before take off.

George spoke in a conversational tone so all could hear him. "Now I hope I have this right. I have brought tweeds, sweaters, walking boots, and umbrella. Just the thing for England, right?" A startled little face came out from the end of the row.

"Oh, George, you have it all wrong, "Carolyn replied. " I have a pith helmet, mosquito netting, malaria medicine and the appropriate needs for Zimbabwe."

"Gram, aren't we going to Hawaii?"

"Yes, my dears, you listen to this. When these two grown up people say anything to you that relates to safety, like being in the water or staying where someone knows where you are, it's important that you listen and follow their instructions so we all come home well and safe. But you must also know they are just crazy old people and most of what they say is just plain silly. You have some responsibility to watch out for them too. Don't let strangers sell them any real estate and watch them when they fall asleep in the sun. That way everyone will have a good time."

Jane appeared calmed and they all settled back into their seats for takeoff. Marlene closed her eyes and in her head said something that felt like a prayer. *Thank you and please keep us safe.*

They were on their way.

***

The hustle and bustle of the Honolulu airport, combined with the heat and the confusion with the luggage plus the excitement, was almost more than Marlene could bear. But she consciously took a few deep breaths and put a smile on her face. She started giving orders.

"George, will you and Robert please go and get us a couple of luggage buggies? No one can concentrate here. Let's just make it easier."

When they were gone, she said to Carolyn. "Please watch the luggage for a minute." Marlene and Jane went to a stand to buy leis for everyone. Jane's eyes were big. She couldn't decide but looked quietly at each one, not touching anything. Finally, she made her choices, a different color for each person. They returned to the appointed spot. George and Robert had also bought leis and Carolyn had been given five of them by a hostess. They all laughed, as each person became a walking floral arrangement. *There are too many impressions to take in and remember. Thank God for the journal in my bag. I'll think on this later,* Marlene promised herself.

They made their way to the taxi stand, loaded into a cab, and headed out for the condo. Marlene was quiet, listening to everyone babble as they tried to see everything at once. It was a good moment. *Twenty-four hours and we'll be able to keep things in perspective.*

The disorder continued after reaching the condo, as the kids wanted to be everywhere at the same time. Carolyn offered to take them around the grounds to scout the place out. When they left, the noise level went from high to none at all in seconds. Marlene collapsed on the sofa and laughingly said, "I think we're a success. I truly believe they are enthralled. Wow! What a morning."

George was puttering about; delivering suitcases to appropriate rooms, checking the kitchen for utensils and generally staking out the place.

"You know, George, when a cat is moved into a new environment, it sniffs around and pees in all the corners. Is that what you're doing?"

George said, "Yeah, have to mark off my turf here, or at least know what my resources are. You really look tired." He came back into the living room and sat on the sofa near her.

She took his hand and said, "You too. Looks like you've flown the ocean and entertained the kids the whole way. It's been quite a day, but worth it. Don't forget it's three hours earlier here than back home. I vote for an early evening."

"Or we can let them run themselves out tonight and maybe they'll sleep a lot tomorrow."

"You're dreaming. Maybe three days and they'll have run down a little. Besides, the truth is I couldn't keep up with a big night. Let's just eat take-out and let them walk on the beach for awhile."

"Sounds like a plan to me." George got up from the couch and went to put Marlene's suitcase in the girls' room. He removed a light cotton robe from her suitcase. "Why not lie down for a bit? Do you feel like a shower?"

"Good idea, friend. I think I will nap a bit after taking off these clothes. They feel like they've grown attached. In an hour I'll be fine again."

However, when the kids and Carolyn came banging into the room, it had not been enough. Marlene woke from a very sound sleep and struggled to pull it all back into focus.

Jane began. "Gram, we can get to the beach in about three minutes and you can see us from the balcony and you go over these really neat rocks…" But Jane was interrupted by Robert.

"There's a restaurant right around the corner and a bunch of stores just across the street. We're set forever, and there are things Jane and I can do alone."

Jane kept going as if there were no Robert. "There's a garden that has so many different kinds of flowers it will make you crazy, Gram. Come on and I'll show you." Jane was on the bed.

Marlene laughed and said, "Wait just a minute here. I'm happy you had a good time, which is the purpose of the trip. But let me catch up with you. Did you eat anything while you were out?"

Robert offered to straighten out the confusion. "No, there's really too much to see and do. We'll eat later. We want you to see what's out there. It's really great!" Marlene looked pleadingly at George and then at Carolyn.

George risked a question, "Was there a McDonald's out there anywhere?"

"Sure, about two blocks away." Obviously, Robert liked having the answers that were required.

Moving things along, George said, "Okay, then let's go eat something before you lose your energy. We'll bring your Gram something back and that gives her time to be ready for the grand tour. How about you, Carolyn, are you with us?"

"What if you bring me something back, too? If your fear, George, is that they might lose energy, well, I say starve them from this moment on." Carolyn hugged Jane as she removed her from the bed. "This troupe is going to enjoy every minute of the trip, with food or without. But I think grownups are supposed to say, 'You have to stop to eat.' It's a great plan, but George, maybe you could eat slowly?" She grinned.

Marlene was still lying in bed, but did her share. "When you come back from lunch, I'll be showered and dressed. We'll do a short walk so you can show me the grounds. Then you may also do a walk on the beach. But after that, it's quiet time. We really need some rest. Don't forget you've lost three hours. You'll just have to trust us that we need to pace ourselves or we won't make the whole three weeks. There will be time for everything, I promise. Are we agreed?" A few hugs and the tourists left.

Carolyn began puttering about; looking through her suitcase for appropriate clothes, and said, "There's no question about the kids having a good time. The real issue is you and how you're feeling and how not to take on too much. If we're not careful we'll lose you in the process. Don't go out tonight if you're not rested. I'll cover for you."

"Thanks, but I'll be all right. I can go out with them for an hour on the hotel grounds and then we'll all take a rest. If you and George want to go out for a drink or a stroll, that's fine. The kids and I won't be gone more than an hour, so if I can get myself up out of this bed and race you to the shower, I'll be fine." The words were strong, but her actions were slow and deliberate. She stopped after each motion before beginning the next, then she went into the bathroom and turned on the hot water.

When lunch, kids, and George arrived back, Marlene was dressed in shorts, a loose T-shirt, and sandals, her hair still wet from the shower. Carolyn was in a sundress, her short hair damp but curly. "We look like a couple of tourists in Hawaii, don't we?" But the line went past the kids as they anticipated their opportunity to introduce Gram to the new territory.

"C'mon out on the balcony, Jane, while Gram eats her lunch." Marlene felt a twinge as she saw them race out onto the balcony then she corrected herself. *Children that old do not fall off balconies. This trip is about trust and helping them know they can take care of themselves. The fears and worries of old people just don't fly when little people are trying to grow into big people.* She sat at the table and ate half her hamburger, three French fries, and most of her milkshake. *Not bad.* It was a habit she'd been forming, this measuring of her food, to know she was eating enough.

"Okay, gang, show me this marvelous place. I'm ready if you are." They had her hands and were pulling her out the door almost before she had put her napkin down.

"Not to worry," George said as he headed for the table to pick up the debris. "I not only cook, I do dishes, too."

Strolling down the path out on the walkway, Marlene asked, "Is it possible for you to show me these things slowly? I really want to see what's out here and I want to take time to look over the garden you're talking about. I guess I want quality on this tour. Quantity we'll get as the days go by."

This produced a discussion between Jane and Robert about the exact activity. Robert wanted to go see the street and the people; Jane wanted to take Gram into the garden and sit awhile. Marlene listened to them and waited to hear how they would come to an agreement. It fascinated her that after a minute or two, with both of them talking at once, they actually fell into a negotiating mode.

"Okay." Robert presented the recap of their meeting. "We'll go into the garden at the other end of the complex. We can show you the waterfall, the beach, and the flowers over there. It's really neat and we can rest there for a bit. Then we'll walk a couple of blocks down the busy street. We'll come back and sit in the garden closest to the condo. It's kinda' different from the first one."

The walk was slow and deliberate, as each child pointed to things that interested him or her most. Matching the steps, the talking became softer and less frenetic. Even at eight and nine years old, they were soon having an actual conversation, each listening to what the other was saying. It was all about feelings.

Jane said, "It's funny being here without Mom and Dad. How are we going to explain to them what that tree right there is really like?"

Robert replied, "Yeah. Maybe there are some things you really can't tell someone else, like looking from this bluff over the ocean, the colors, and the smells. Maybe we have to send them here, Jane, so they can see it for themselves."

But Jane responded dreamily, "Or we can write a poem and put the whole thing in our magic remembering and it will always be with us no matter where we go. Gram, can someone else know what I'm feeling through my poem?"

Robert seemed alarmed. "What's this poem stuff? Did you do that in school this year?"

"No, Gram showed me that in a poem you can share feelings and still keep them forever and have all your good things together at the same time. It's called magic remembering. I'll teach you how to do it, Robert."

They sat for a while in the garden, and Marlene noted the greatest smells in the world, aromas possibly being more assertive than the colors and textures. They were too strong and the combination with the hamburger made her uneasy. "I want to come back here again, but let's do Robert's walk on the street now."

Just before entering the outdoor market with a thatched roof. Marlene saw a drug store. She went in and bought each child a notebook.

"This is for your magic remembering and your poems or just thoughts and anything you might want to remember from this trip. Let's agree. No one looks in anyone else's journal unless the owner wants to show you something. This is really private, because it's for your feelings about this trip and that makes it all yours."

Jane seemed awed by the availability of the clean pages and the opportunity to fill them herself. Robert was a bit confused until he found a flower that had fallen on the ground. After picking it up, he asked, "Can I put this inside my notebook?"

"What better way to remember, Robert? It's your book and you do whatever you want with it. Taking back little pieces of the trip makes the magic work."

When they got to the last garden and sat for a few minutes, it was very quiet. They were tired, whether they wanted to believe it or not. They wandered back to the condo and found a note from Carolyn and George saying they were in the lounge in the main building of the complex.

"Did you want to go with them, Gram?" Robert was doing the care taking now.

"No, darling, let's all just get ready to sleep for a bit. Leave all your windows open and you'll nap very well, I'm sure."

There was a little cuddle for Jane and an appropriate kiss on the cheek for Robert and then silence. Marlene sat on the balcony in the fading light, and tears ran down her face unchecked. Not because she was sad, but because she was so happy, because she loved them so much, because she was going to be able to share with them that joy of living before…

***

The next morning everyone was up very early and had fresh pineapple and cereal for breakfast. Each kid had a clear picture of the thousands of things he or she wanted to do first. Robert informed them you were supposed to go to the beach early in the morning or in the late afternoon because the midday sun was too strong. The consensus was that going to the beach early was a good thing to do.

"However," and Marlene spoke nonchalantly, "I have to buy a bathing suit."

She didn't want to tell them that when she had tried her old one on at home, it had all but fallen off her. She and Carolyn decided they would wear shorts during the morning and when the stores were open, around ten, they'd go shopping for a suit.

In a tenuous voice, Jane suggested, "I'd like to go shopping with you. Is that all right?"

"Sure." Marlene was pleased. "You can wear your suit to the beach and we'll carry a pair of shorts that you can slip on when we go shopping. How about that?"

Carolyn added, "It's a good plan, Jane. I'm going to have my suit on under my shorts, so when the stores open, I'll be ready."

With everyone in agreement, all the gear was packed up and the parade made its way to the beach. It was seven-thirty in the morning.

After a couple of hours of walking in the sand and along the water, the kids had found dozens of shells they wanted to keep and were getting brave enough to be in the water up to their waists. Marlene and Carolyn didn't want to disturb their progress, but didn't want to leave without Jane, so they postponed the trip to town until after lunch. Marlene was very comfortable lying in the beach chair; glad she'd brought several novels from her list of 'want to reads'. A suntan would hide the jaundice. This day was looking good.

Lunch turned out to be hot dogs at the beach snack bar and George asked, with a smirk, "How long do we have before rickets become visible?"

Both women assured him that in three weeks, both kids would still be strong enough for Jessie to repair the damage.

Afterwards, Carolyn, Marlene, and Jane went on down the avenue, with George and Robert accompanying them as far as the bookstore. When the three women entered a small shop selling swimwear, they found the skimpy, sexy suits that caused Marlene and Carolyn to make jokes. Jane, however, was so taken with the colors she didn't even notice style. She pulled out everything bright and shiny, loving them all, while Marlene was holding out for something that would cover her and still fit the purpose. Finally, in a back corner, on a rack, she found some one-piece suits in various sizes, but they were black. So she picked a couple of very bright, colorful, loose, gauze jackets before going into the fitting room.

She wasn't happy with the results, but her co-shoppers were just outside the curtain, begging her to come out and show them. Because she didn't want to disappoint Jane with the colors, she took one of the jackets and slung it around her as a dancer might and stepped out of the cubicle. She slid the jacket off, as if she'd had some stripping experience. But to her relief, the suit looked presentable and Jane liked the jacket. While Marlene was paying, Jane stood next to her and touched her arm. "I didn't know you were so skinny, Gram."

It wasn't judgment, it was concern. *I can't lie to her, but I can't alarm her either. How do I deal with this?*

"Well, then I guess we'd better go get some ice cream and try to fatten me up a bit, okay? I've been a pretty bad eater lately, but maybe I'll use this vacation as a time to try to eat better." The part about the ice cream took the edge off the rest of the statement, so Jane was satisfied. Marlene looked up to see that Carolyn had taken in the entire exchange and had to be brought back into the festivity of the excursion. She saw a rack of hats across the room; big hats, flowered hats, hats for the sun and for the celebration. "One minute," she said to the salesclerk.

"C'mon, guys, we can't pass this up." They each tried on a dozen. Finding one small enough for Jane wasn't easy, but when they found it, it was covered with sunflowers. Carolyn's choice was all purple and yellow flowers and Marlene went for red and green. They donned their hats, paid for the entire lot and went to look for the guys or ice cream, whichever came first.

It was both. Under the thatched roof of the market, Robert and George had already ordered their cones. Enjoying their snacks, the group decided a rest in the afternoon would allow them to celebrate their first full day on the island with a real dinner in a nice restaurant. They meandered down the street, looking in windows and watching people and then crossed to the condo gardens and home. Carolyn, Marlene, and George took to their beds with books, while Robert and Jane claimed the balcony, each with a book and a journal. Lying on her bed, Marlene could hear them having a conversation, but was unable to hear the words. It was a pleasant sound and she drifted off to sleep.

Once everyone was up, however, the process of each of them taking showers, looking for clothes and discussing the choice of restaurant reminded Marlene what it was like to have an entire family in action. For so many years, she'd been alone. The cat never got in the shower first or stopped her progress with dozens of questions. However, it was a fine looking group on their night out. In her effort to keep her promise to Jane, Marlene mentally determined she would eat a full meal. They had chosen the restaurant on the condo grounds, which advertised an early show of Hawaiian music and dance.

The atmosphere was everything the brochures had said, with wicker furniture and flowers and plants surrounding each table. Robert said, "We won't be able to see the show from here" A young man in a flowered shirt and lei sat them at a table and promised it would work out. The kids chose shrimp as they were unsure of almost everything else on the menu; the adults were looking at mahi-mahi, but Marlene picked a dish with scallops and rice.

There was good conversation. The twenty-four hours Marlene had predicted it would take to settle in had proven correct. She was, however, startled by the large portions of food. She completed her salad and knew it was sufficient, but she attacked the main dish with a gusto she did not feel. She would eat. She had promised Jane.

After dinner, the plants surrounding the table began to move and from the center of the room, a stage rose. It was very near their table. Drums started beating, the sound level of the guitars was heightened, and the stage was suddenly filled with beautiful, brown, young men and women, with gyrating hips moving to the island music. The lights accentuated the colors and costumes and everyone's eyes were riveted on the ritual.

The exception was Marlene whose stomach was starting to gyrate to the beat of the music and from all the rich food. A quick look to her right and left affirmed there was no escaping to the rest room without creating a disturbance. Panic began to grow and she took many deep breaths, sipping water between. When she felt Carolyn's hand on her arm, she knew her distress was evident.

The noise was such that it was hard to hear, but by speaking directly into Marlene's ear, Carolyn got her message across. "C'mon, I'll go to the rest room with you."

"No, thanks. I'd like not to make a scene if it's possible." Marlene was afraid of speaking too long for fear of losing the control she tenuously held over her stomach.

"Do you want me to move the stuff from your handbag into mine and then you'll have a container if you lose your lunch?"

"Why my handbag? Wouldn't a real friend offer her own handbag?"

"I'll carry the load and dispose of the evidence. My bag is the backup. That's all you get."

"Oh, God, don't make me laugh." But it was so comforting to have a cohort that she made it through the show.

When it was over, Carolyn suggested George and the kids walk back to the condo while she and Marlene had another glass of wine. Neither woman was sure Marlene would make it back to the room without being sick and Marlene didn't want to embarrass the children. It took the sheer force of her will, but she determined she would not subject Robert and Jane to the ugly. George and the kids left the restaurant.

As soon as the crowd thinned, the women slowly, with no harsh movements, headed for the door, then made a dash for the restroom. Marlene was very sick; throwing up several times before she dared to wash her face and begin the walk to the condo.

"Maybe I got rid of whatever it was and I'll be okay now. I'm really sorry to subject you to this after such a good day."

They ambled down the path while Carolyn reiterated her purpose. "I'm here because you need me to cover for you and to supply solutions to little problems, like where to barf. Just let me do my job and don't worry about me." Shortly after entering the condo, while her clothes were only half removed, Marlene began vomiting again.

The condo had two bedrooms divided by the living room. Marlene thought George and Robert might not hear, but Jane's bed was in the same room as the women. When Marlene and Carolyn had returned, Carolyn told Jane her gram must have eaten some bad fish and was sick to her stomach. "How about we make you a bed on the sofa, so you can get to sleep?"

Jane was concerned. "Is she all right?"

"Sure. We old people have to take it easy sometimes. We had a long trip with all that excitement and then she ate all that rich fish. She probably needs to rest a day or two, but she doesn't have the flu or anything. I'll bet you've been to birthday parties or maybe after Halloween, when you just ate too much stuff. Right? That's all it is. You settle down and get some sleep so you can tear this island up again tomorrow."

"Carolyn?" There were questions in the little girl's eyes. "Is it because I said she was skinny? Is that why she ate so much?"

Carolyn swooped Jane up in her arms and they curled up in the corner of the sofa. "No, sweetie. She ate that much because she was greedy and wanted to enjoy everything that was available. Look, my stomach's good, but my back's bad. I know that and I'm careful to watch what I lift or how I sit. Yet, every now and again, I still want to hike the hill behind my house. I know it'll make my back hurt and I do it anyway. It's trying to find the balance between being smart and being happy. I don't mean that I'm unhappy because I can't hike anymore, it's just that sometimes it's fun to do things that aren't smart. However, you make an agreement with yourself that you'll pay the price. So Jane, tell me what you really like about today."

Jane was easily diverted and talked a few minutes about the music, her new journal, and expressed pleasure that she had things to teach

Robert. "He always knows more than me, but he doesn't know how to write a poem." During the talk, she had been scooting down into the bed Carolyn had made on the sofa. She was ready for sleep. Carolyn kissed Jane's forehead, reminding her that tomorrow was another wonderful day.

Marlene continued to be sick the entire night.

A little later than the previous day, but early enough to be alarming, sounds of movement were heard from the kitchen. Carolyn looked over at Marlene's bed. Marlene's eyes were open and she was looking at her friend. Carolyn commented on the pathetic appearance of the patient and they both laughed.

"What is it in our psyches that makes everything that's horrific, seem funny?" Marlene's voice was not strong and her stringy hair, dark-circled eyes, and pale complexion added to the rueful impression, which she hoped not to show to the rest of the troupe.

What else are we going to do? Make arrangements to throw you over the balcony?" Carolyn began to plan. "The only issue is how we present this to the group. One look at you right now and party's over. I'm not sure how to fix it. It'll be hard to just tell them you have to sleep. George will be in here in a minute and the kids will get concerned."

"So let's play it our way." Marlene was depending on all her self-discipline. "Your job is to get them out of this condo as quickly as you can, but for now let's make me look worse. I'll go out there and own up to eating too much fish. We'll make a lot of jokes and behave as if any fool can overdo. I'm sure they've already heard us laugh. If we make fun of it, they'll accept it as a momentary thing. I just don't know how long I'll last, so move swiftly."

"You're nuts, but I'm with you." And Carolyn was out of her bed and into her swimsuit. "By the way, you don't have to do anything to look worse. You're at one hundred percent right now. Do you need help getting up?"

"No, just time, like three days." And, she began the tortuous effort of getting to her feet. They kept up the giggling, hoping it was heard in the next room. She was wearing the third gown of the night; it was the last clean one either of the women had. Carolyn ripped a blanket off her own bed and threw it over Marlene. Taking her hand, they entered the living room together.

"I hope none of you has eaten yet. This will scare the appetite right out of you. May I present to you the Macabre Grandmother of the Year?" There was snickering coming from under the blanket. Carolyn then removed the covering with a great flourish. There was a startling silence.

"For crying out loud, guys, I'm not dead. I just ate too much, threw up too much, and didn't sleep at all. Gimme a break here." She worked at making her voice stronger than she felt. Wrapping the blanket around her again but not over her head, she made her way to the sofa where Jane had slept and sat down on the rumpled sheets. Carolyn commented, "I'll vouch that she's a lot better this morning than she was all night. I'm up for going to the beach and sleeping in the sun and letting her mend on her own terms. Actually, I think she makes an interesting study in decaying flesh, a lot like some of the little beached sea creatures we found yesterday lying in the sand. This is what happens to a beached land creature. Has anyone started breakfast or can we just take pineapple, cookies, and juice to the beach?" She moved around George in the kitchen and started putting cereal back in the cupboard. She opened a plastic bag and began putting in things that would keep them satisfied until lunch.

Jane went to her Gram and sat beside her. "Are you really all right? You don't look very good. Would you like me to stay here and take care of you?"

"Oh, Jane, that's so thoughtful of you. If I were really sick, like with the flu or something, I think you'd take very good care of me. But I'm just tired from being up all night. All the problem food is gone now and I just need to sleep. Thanks very much, but I'm okay. Carolyn just thinks I look like Dracula and she's enjoying it a lot. That Carolyn made me laugh all night, in between trips to the bathroom. I'm sure you'd be a much more considerate caretaker and I'll remember that the next time I overdo." It all seemed to alleviate Jane's fears and she went off to put on her bathing suit.

Robert had said nothing, just watched. But when Jane went to get dressed, he appeared to have accepted her judgment and also went to change. George actually had a dark look on his face. *This wasn't flying with him.*

Carolyn spoke firmly, "C'mon, George. Don't get theatrical. She's fine or she wouldn't have been so funny all night. When young blades like us take old women on vacation, we have to accept some inconvenience. All she needs is some sleep. She's exhausted from being a comic all night. She threw up a lot, but there's no fever or weakness except in her head."

"Don't let him get to you, Carolyn," Marlene said. "George has a habit of thinking things are always worse than they are. When he sees me next, after a good day's sleep, he'll realize it's just as we say. George, it'll ruin my day if I think my silly episode can destroy your day or, worse yet, the day for the kids. I haven't had to say this for a while, but lighten up. Okay?"

"Sure." There was a tone in George's voice that was new. He sounded distrustful. "But you were a sight when Carolyn unveiled you. I also heard you all night and couldn't help but worry. Are you sure there's nothing we can do for you before we go?"

"No, but thanks. Just let me sleep it off."

The kids were back in the room ready for the beach.

"Hurry up, George. We have a breakfast picnic to attend. Let's get on with it." Very rapidly, Carolyn tied up her food bag, and started moving the kids out of the condo.

George followed. He stopped and looked at Marlene for a moment and she knew he wasn't buying any of it.

Just keep your fears to yourself, George. And, she mentally dismissed him.

She was back in her bed before they hit the walkway to the beach. She was quiet as she accepted her limitations. It wasn't going to be as easy as she'd hoped. But she would make the adjustments and see that they worked. She could be the old woman of Carolyn's imagery.

But it's not the age. A year ago, there was nothing I really wanted to do that I couldn't do. My limitations were determined by my choices. The issue is the disease and I haven't claimed that yet. I don't want to leave behind me the message that old or age is the enemy. Healthy

people of any age can be productive, capable and enjoyed by others.
But those were heavy thoughts to deal with when her head didn't even
connect with the rest of her body, probably because neither entity
wanted to be associated with the other. She got out of the bed to get a
fresh glass of water, returned to her cocoon, and went into a very deep
sleep. Around lunchtime, Carolyn slipped into the condo to check on
Marlene to see if she needed anything. Marlene rolled over and looked
up, but didn't lift her head from the pillow. "I'm okay. Are you having
fun yet?"

"Up to the point of my argument with George about who was
coming up to check on you. We'll have to talk about him, but if you're
okay for now, I'll go back to the sunshine. We're going up the avenue
for lunch. Is there anything I can bring you?"

"No, thanks, I'll just sleep. Have fun and tell George to bug off.
Good night."

Marlene buried her head in the pillow. She was still very tired, but
mostly, she didn't want to think about George and what might be
expected of her. She found it easy to drift off as Carolyn made her way
out the door.

Waking, she thought about sleep; how it repairs us, how it
straightens our thinking. It is that space in which we are most honest
and responsive to truth. Therefore, sleeping all morning, not aware of
dealing with her problems, created in Marlene new resolve. When she
woke a short time later, she was not disturbed or anxious. She was not
sure what she was going to do about the situation, mostly George, but
she felt in control again and applied herself to repairing the physical
damage of the previous night.

She showered and washed her hair. She applied some tinted cream
to her face and then over her entire body. She found a very colorful shirt
with white shorts and added some hoop earrings. *Doing my own
laundry will convince them I'm fine.* So she picked up the nightgowns,
added some of the children's clothes, went down to the basement and
put them in the washer. Upon returning to the condo, she found she
needed to sit down for a bit as the effort had caused a little weakness
and shakiness. Oops, once again she'd forgotten food. She made a cup

of tea, picked up a couple of cookies and took them to the balcony. The beach was empty and the undisturbed beauty was spiritual.

She sat. There were voices in the distance and the trees waved and nodded at her gently. She felt alone and at peace. Here, she could put back together all the pieces of the puzzle that had been falling out of place all night. Here she could focus once again on how to provide for herself, and the ones for whom she cared. Here she could envision the environment in which they would embark on this new adventure, her dying. Obviously, she was being called upon to be flexible. Plans had to be changed; George had to be dealt with. He was bound to muck up this whole trip if she didn't level with him soon. Okay. Flexible she could be. With the beauty around her and the uninterrupted space her illness had provided for her today, she faced her change in plans.

Whatever force created this beauty has also created me and that force is in me and affords me the strength and wisdom to do what must be done.

Then she remembered her nightclothes downstairs that she needed to move from the washer to the dryer. She sat a moment longer and acknowledged loneliness. She longed for the 'sisters' she had been encountering on her journey. Those women, who had coped with whatever fate had brought them, had become as necessary to her as Carolyn was in the here and now. Wherever they had gone when it was over, she'd be joining them soon. They were paving her way and giving her solace now. They were holding her hands; they were leading her along. She had concocted their names and their stories, but they were with her now and she was learning to trust them. She also knew their practical natures would have seen to the laundry, so she left her quiet and returned to the basement.

When she re-entered the condo, she picked up the books George and Robert had bought about Polynesia and took them to the balcony. First, she browsed through them looking at pictures and reading some of the captions. A few caught her eye and she thought about them a bit, but she continued flipping pages. She saw the changes in fashion and the change in the city when progress came. She followed the growth from the peaceful natural environment to the traffic and neon lights. Finally, she put the books down and sat back, returning to the near silence and total beauty of her surroundings. Her mind wandered over the sights and sounds and smells of her locale and pictures began to form in her mind about the way it might have been.

Communal. I like that. She pictured a generous space with children running about between thatched huts and airy structures of bamboo with no glass windows that could shut out the sounds and breezes. There was laughter, conversation, and the sound of tasks being completed. The children are calling many women 'mother'. *Must be extended family members. All adults stop to respond to these children. What a safe place to be. All members are moving easily, but steadily, and there is a comfortable pattern to their motions.*

Over here is a woman married to her sister's widower, a tradition that ensures the children remain with adults they already considered family. The sun, water, flowers, plants, and breezes added to the aura of a picnic rather than a stressful workday. Oops, a teen is having a hard time with his parents over there on that porch. It appears to be mutually settled when he picks up a sack, walks across to an auntie's house, and leaves his things on her porch. As he returns to his tasks, a lovely woman steps from that house, picks up his things and takes them indoors.

"Wait, I'd like to meet you." But the lady is gone. What Marlene has seen was a woman, middle-aged, plump, and easy in her movement. She had worn red, her long, black hair setting off her amazing coloring. Her face had appeared kindly and appeared to have a natural, permanent smile. But now she is gone.

How much of this easy living is dependent on the weather? It seems too hot to get angry often. Basic foodstuffs appear to be grown everywhere and there is enough nourishment in the sea to take care of all. If it's never polluted. Marlene's eyes closed as she allowed her vision to continue.

Now this woman in red is sitting inside her house with other family members; they are mourning the death of someone who is lying there in the room. Can't tell who the dead person is. Her husband? Her child?

Out of doors, all the village members are preparing a feast. But the woman sits with the deceased and holds hands with those who sit with her. Sometimes she cries quietly; sometimes she comforts. As friends come in to sit with her for periods of time, she is solicitous while tending her own need to mourn. Meanwhile, outside arrangements continue. She can hear her community making provision for the next step in the traditional process designed to bring the remaining family back into the daily life of the community.

Finally, men come into the house and remove the body to the burial grounds. All the family, friends, and neighbors proceed to the gravesite. The body is quickly put into the ground and young men of the village replace the dirt, covering the body with smooth, purposeful movements—unhurried, but intentional. With this task completed, her family takes my lady in red and, wrapping their arms around her, walk her back to the feast. She joins into the festivities at moments and other times returns to her grief. The group accepts this. Young people bring her food; sisters make sure she is not alone. Every night for several weeks after the burial, events will be planned to include her and to encourage her return to the life of the village.

That's what these months have been about for me. I'm mourning. I'm taking care of all those feelings that keep creeping up on me.

But my family—I want them to mourn, and then I want them to get on with their lives. I want them to love and nurture one another and have a big party. I want someone with them to accept their pain and then pave the way for that pain to be healed. I want them to remember me lovingly, with the soreness remedied.

She lay back in her chaise lounge and sighed deeply. This woman in red who swam naked, picked fruit off trees, made love whenever it was right, always wore flowers in her hair, found some reason to dance every day and cared about children more than anything else, had given her the plan. *I can share my mourning and begin to prepare the feast at the same time. How lucky I am.*

It was time to break the silence. She was ready. Again, it had been a sister who led the way.

The clarity gave her energy and she went to retrieve her laundry.

122

When she got back upstairs, everyone had returned. They had been a bit concerned when they had found the apartment empty.

"For heaven's sake, I just needed to wash my clothes from last night. I've slept all day and feel fine. What have you accomplished? Actually, you all look hot and tired. Let me get you some juice." Marlene went around the counter in the kitchen and set out glasses, ice, and juice. "Now, tell me what you've been doing."

Jane couldn't sit still and talk at the same time. She began to help Marlene serve the drinks. "George rented a car and we went to Diamond Head lookout and then to the Sea Life Park. There were surfers and hang gliders and all of it was fun to watch, but it looked scary to me."

Robert needed to add authority to the telling. "It's called Maapuuu Point. In the Hawaiian Reef Tank, we went to the Ocean Science Theater and saw what lives offshore Hawaii. You get to see what is above ground and under the water. It's pretty cool."

"Then we saw whales and dolphins in Whaler's Cove where there is also a big ship from the days they chased whales," Jane chimed in.

Robert interrupted. "It was a square-rigged whaler and there is also a museum just outside the park that shows you all the stuff they used to catch the whales."

To silence the competition, Marlene directed her questions to George and Carolyn. "And you two, were you part of the expedition or just chauffeur and tour director?"

Carolyn's response was easy. "It was interesting, actually captivating. The kind of stuff you'd like. It's close by so we can take you one day."

"She's right," George said. "Thought about you a lot while we were there. I know how much you would have liked it, but couldn't help worrying about you being here alone and not feeling well."

"And now you see I'm fine. Among other things, I still need time alone, even on vacation. Thanks so much for the chance to repair and regroup. I'm on again for whatever's up. What's the schedule after you all have rested?"

Jane was ready. "There's a barbecue on the beach tonight and I'd really like to eat outside in the dark. Doesn't that sound like fun?"

Marlene took charge, probably because George and Carolyn appeared to have had a longer day than the kids have had. "If it's okay with everyone else, I think it's great. How about we start the shower parade and everybody rests awhile. I think you've done a lot of running 'round in the heat and could do with some time out."

"Sounds good to me and I'm in the shower as we speak." George finished his drink and headed for the bathroom.

With easy conversation closing down, the others made their way to quiet activities, one by one. Soon Marlene was alone in the living room, very pleased with herself and the attitude that had prevailed within the group.

Following his shower, George returned to the living room and sat down in the chair across from where Marlene was reading. He sat for a while and just watched her, even though she had put down her book and was rearranging herself for a comfortable chat. She finished off her juice drink and looked interested in whatever he was going to say. But she was going to set the tone, so when he still didn't speak, she began, "Well, how are you feeling? Tired already? Seems that you've done a bang-up job so far. You have a couple of pretty engaged kids in there." Could she forestall a more serious confrontation?

"I want to know what's going on with you." George leaned forward in his chair and spoke sharply. "This trip is being diminished by the fact that I know you and Carolyn are trying to put one over on me. What's happening here?"

Marlene got up to refill her drink and pour one for George. The silence was strained, but she would have her words in order before she answered.

"Okay." She settled back into her seat and put her drink on the arm of the sofa before continuing. "There is something to tell and I don't want to discuss it here, in the condo. If I promise that tomorrow night you and I will go to dinner alone and that I'll be totally honest with you, will you accept that for now?"

George didn't answer immediately. He just watched her as if he couldn't trust her any longer. "Why shouldn't I believe you'd be totally honest? What have you had to keep from me up to now?"

"I guess that's fair. I can only hope that when you do know the whole story, you'll understand why I've kept secrets. I only meant to keep them from you through this trip and I hope you'll understand that too. Now, I'm asking you to end this conversation until we are well away from the children. I really don't want to pursue this where little ears might hear. Whether or not I owe you explanations out of friendship or loyalty is moot. I also have responsibility to follow my own counsel when I need to make decisions that will affect my family and me. I offer you tomorrow night and that's all I can give you now. I don't want this conversation to continue here."

With resignation, George leaned back in his chair. "I don't seem to have any choice. I'll have to take what I can get, satisfying or otherwise. May I just ask if you're all right?"

"Not now. Tomorrow night I'll give you all of it. But for now, please just keep things easy and make the kids happy. They're the only consideration on this trip. I'll not have their experience jeopardized, George. It's fun, fun, fun from here on. Got it? Grownups can chat on grownup time."

It was a bad spot to put George in, she knew. She could see his face as he worked out the division between his own concern and curiosity and his natural regard for the security and pleasure of her and the children. She could only hope his better side would win.

"Fine. You've got it. I hope I'm discerning enough to know if I'm getting the whole story tomorrow night. But for twenty-four hours, I'll play it your way." He got up from his chair, leaving his drink untouched. "I think I'll walk over to the bar. Do you want to go with me?"

"Thank you, but no. Think I'll read some more and make sure I'm up to the barbecue tonight. Another night like last night and I'll have put a real damper on this trip. Enjoy yourself. We all need time away, not just from the kids but from each other as well. Have a good time, George, maybe a happy conversation with a total stranger about the pleasures of this place. Just go be an adult without the constriction of family and kids."

"That's very much your way of coping. I like being with family and kids. But I'll take a walk, have a cool drink and see what other people who are alone are doing mid-afternoon. Read your book and rest, I'll be back in a little while. Anything you need me to bring back?"

"No, we're going out for dinner and there's still breakfast stuff here. We'll be fine for another day. Thanks anyway."

George left and Marlene laid her head back on the sofa, feeling tense. Now that she was committed to telling him the truth, she felt the fear gathering in her stomach. At the same time there was some hope to be found in the knowledge this sticky situation was about to be resolved. Whether it went well or badly, it would be over; he would know. Having dinner in a public place meant to her that things couldn't get too out of hand; George was too well reared to make a scene. Being in the evening, there would be no time limit, and they could see it through to the conclusion. The worst that could happen was that George would decide to go home. She could accept that if it happened, but she rather trusted she could bring him around to giving the kids all they had been promised. *Just keep appealing to his higher nature.*

She picked up her book, but couldn't relate to the words on the page. This had been a startling interruption to her quiet time. Carolyn came into the room.

"It's not the same as eavesdropping, but I just couldn't help but hear parts. I'm going to look in on the kids to see if they might have picked up any of it." While Carolyn looked in the boy's room and found both kids were sound asleep, Marlene's stomach continue wrapping itself into ever-tightening knots

"No kid hearing bad things could sleep that soundly. They're fine. They got so hot this morning and so into everything there was to do out there, they're legitimately worn out. Do you think Jessie will believe they took naps?"

"No, but I bet she'll try to bribe us to find out how we did it. How much did you hear?"

"I heard you hold to your limits and heard him agree to it, and that I'm on as entertainment for the juveniles tomorrow night. I suppose that's all I need to know except for how you're doing with this change of plans."

"Good and bad. At least it'll be over. I just can't get nervous. I have to play it straight—not let him push buttons that will make me emotional. 'Just the facts, ma'am.'"

Carolyn sat down on the sofa with Marlene and took her hand. She spoke slowly. Don't be too tough on yourself. It's an emotional subject. He's a friend and he can take it if you treat it as a genuine issue. It's not a grocery list. I love your toughness, but I love your intelligence as well. You know that soon you'll have to let yourself be more vulnerable. Those daughters of yours aren't going to accept this as a daily occurrence, and you need to practice the actuality of it. I believe George can handle it all if you give him a chance."

That's a tricky thought. It was a wall Marlene knew she had to climb and she didn't want to do it. One step at a time was her motto. Being vulnerable was not on her agenda yet.

The barbecue went well and as a group, they got up and joined a dance instruction, each doing the hula in a most individual manner. Walking home, they laughed a lot and, though they were tired, both kids wanted to sit on the balcony to put the day down in their journals. However, instead of having personal, reflective time, they were sharing thoughts and recollections as they wrote. They were enjoying each other.

The next morning, the consensus was to go to Pearl Harbor. It was a time of reflection and conversation as the children tried to grasp the reality of war and the adults tried to pace the unfolding information. When Robert and Carolyn settled on some serious picture taking, the mood lightened.

After lunch, they returned home for rest time. Jane took to the sofa, Robert and George went to their room, and Carolyn and Marlene were left alone in the girls' room. They lay on their beds until, and exactly according to their pattern, they started a chat that became silly— George and Marlene—at dinner, alone.

"Do you think it'll be like a Mafia meeting? Do you want the kids and me to hide in the bushes with machine guns?" Carolyn suggested.

Over her giggles, Marlene retorted, "What an image! No, I was thinking more of Deborah Kerr sitting with a blanket over her legs in 'An Affair to Remember.'"

"Okay, if that's the way you want to go, how about eating dinner on a catamaran and climbing up in the front to sing your story, a lot like Barbra Streisand doing 'Don't Rain On My Parade.' If you're going to do it, do it with style. The subject matter is appropriate."

Marlene needed the humor to keep the issue in perspective, but today it lacked the usual knack of causing hilarious laughter that relieved tension. The upcoming event was just too scary. It had been sitting in the back of her mind since that outrageous day in April when she'd first seen the doctor. George had been the first person she'd spent time with after that appointment. She had gone out with him that night and started the lying, the denial that anything was wrong. That's a lot of duplicity to own up to in one evening of eating out. So she just resigned herself to seeing it through and began to dress herself for the date. She'd feel good about herself even if she couldn't feel good about what she was doing to him.

In late afternoon, they gathered in the living room, preparing to leave for their different activities. Carolyn and Robert were playing with the cameras and film.

"We're going to a movie which Jane has chosen, eating some dinner and then Robert is going to try to take some nighttime pictures with my camera. The beach, cafes, and boulevard should give us some good opportunities. Y'all have a good time. We're going to." Carolyn continued to put the appropriate film into each of the cameras. Hers was a specific skill she was not giving, but sharing with Robert.

Marlene checked with each kid, heard Jane's enthusiastic explanation of the movie they were going to see, and accepted that all of them were totally immersed in their plans. They had no further need of her. She and George left the condo. It was early, warm and they hadn't spoken of definite plans. George, however, had read the tourist book on the coffee table.

"How about if we drive north? I hear that Robert Louis Stevenson's Grass House was transplanted here from Waikiki in the '20's. The Tea Room is there or we can find something else that appeals to you."

"Sounds good. A drive away from the neighborhood would be very relaxing. Thanks for being prepared." As Marlene easily entered the conversation, she thought about how much money she had with her should she need to take a cab home. *What if he leaves me sitting there alone in the restaurant?* Lighten up, she reminded herself.

As it happened, however, the strain, which they both felt, stayed just below the surface and the drive was quiet. Except for the trip to Pearl Harbor, it was Marlene's first trip away from the condo while George and the others had seen a great deal of the island. He attempted to catch her up by commenting briefly on the things they saw as they drove along. The car windows were down and the wind helped curtail much of the conversation.

They walked around the Stevenson house, but the enthusiasm they had shared in the past was overshadowed by the heavy thoughts each had. So they entered the Tea Room before the dinner crowd and got a table with a view. It could have been very pleasant. Out of character, George ordered a glass of wine, but Marlene stuck with juice. When the drinks were served, George told the waitress they would wait to order.

But George wasn't waiting. "How long do we have to spar before we get to the subject at hand?"

Marlene took a sip of her drink, a very deep breath and looked him straight in the eye. "I've been avoiding the truth with you for a very long time, George, so there's a lot to cover. Amazingly, however, the story can be told very quickly with not too many words. What will take a little time is letting you catch up to what I've known for some time now. I'm willing to give you that time and answer any questions. I hope I can help you understand that I've done what I felt I had to do." Now she looked down into her glass and was quiet.

With his arms crossed on the table in front of him, George spoke. "So out with it."

"I don't have a bug, George, I have pancreatic cancer. There's really nothing that can be done. I decided that I wanted to keep it quiet for a while, plan how I would use the time I have left and give as much of my energy as possible to family. I hope I can prepare my daughters so that it won't be so traumatic and that we'll use the months left to finish any business that might come up for them later. The secret was because I wanted this time with Jane and Robert before everything became dramatic. Carolyn consented to cover everything, like sickness the other night, hoping to allay any alarm or fear. Actually, that's all there is to it. Not so bad, eh?"

There was no response from George for a moment, and then he rubbed his face with both hands, hard, and turned to look out the window. Finally, he spoke with a slightly shaky voice, "Did you think I couldn't keep your secret?"

"I'm sorry, George, but it wasn't about you."

"Why Carolyn then?"

"She just accepted. I knew she would."

"How can you be so sure there's no hope? That seems a rather quick decision."

Marlene's breathing was more relaxed now. They'd moved into conversation about real things, not just emotions. "I have new doctors at the clinic and I've been through the Stanford course and have access to a couple of doctors there. I've pretty much covered the bases."

George had not really moved his arms from where they had been crossed on the table, but now each hand grasped the opposite elbow until his knuckles were white. "When did all this happen? I've always thought I knew where you were."

"Stanford was done when Carolyn and I made the overnight to San Francisco, 'my fun break.' The local doctors weren't hard at all. Back in April, you knew I was seeing them often."

"Are you telling me you're doing nothing to attempt a cure or at least working toward a suspension in the advance of this disease?"

Here goes the same ol' argument. She sighed. "Every possible treatment available entails severe side effects and the end, as I see it, of any quality of life. At the same time, none of the doctors, including the Stanford staff, hold out much hope of any change in the outcome. They were interested in learning about the process by invading my body and putting me through the paces. But if there's only a limited time left, I don't want to spend it violently ill with no energy left to take care of my family."

"What do you mean by 'limited time?'"

"In April, an estimate was a year or less."

It was apparent George wasn't going to be able to sit still much longer. His particular response to stress was always to pace and this wasn't a good place for that. His voice was almost too soft to hear. "Will you excuse me while I go to the men's room, please?"

"Of course, take your time."

He placed his napkin on the table and gently moved his chair back. Upon rising, he left the table quickly.

Will he come back? Sure. Choosing a public place was good for me, but terrible for him. Could I have done it elsewhere? On a deserted beach? No. It would have gone too fast, too many questions and interruptions of answers. This place precludes loss of control by either of us. It may take a little longer, but it'll be more thorough. Cold? Yea. But as Carolyn said yesterday, this isn't a grocery list. It's reality and I won't let it become an emotional crisis that buries the really important issues involved.

She looked out the window and saw George off to the side of the courtyard. He was sitting on a bench under a tree, bent over with his head in his hands. She wasn't without compassion. He was her friend and she'd sacrificed him in order to protect herself and her family. She'd rejected his friendship in favor of the legendary friends who lived only in her head. She'd depended on Carolyn to join her on the journey, when George had assumed he was her soul mate. She'd cited her daughters as the only interest in her plan while George's dependency on their friendship was discounted altogether. She wanted to defend her actions. *I'm only going to do this once, I have to be left alone to do it the way I feel best. My daughters are the primary responsibility of my lifetime...my immortality, if you will. The basic purpose of my existence. My energy level is such that I can't take care of everyone. I have to choose—my own form of triage.*

She looked out the window again and found George gone. Her mental defenses hadn't been that successful. She ached for him. He hadn't returned and she feared sitting there alone much longer. She was afraid she would, at best, start to cry, and then there was the possibility of being sick to her stomach. *Oh George, I'm so sorry. Sorry, I'm sick, sorry I couldn't share the experience with you, sorry you had to find out this way, sorry that I was never able to give you what you wanted.*

Tears welled up in her eyes and she turned to face the window in an effort to keep her feelings private. Still he hadn't returned. The waitress came and Marlene curtly asked that each drink be replenished. *This isn't her fault; there's no reason to take it out on her, but right now there's no way I can smile and chat. We'll tip well.*

The new drinks had been delivered before George returned to the table. He'd obviously washed his face recently, but it hadn't removed the redness of his eyes. He'd been crying. *God, I can't continue with this. How can I lessen his pain?* And, his pain began to take precedence over her selfish need to protect herself from the drama playing itself out.

Nothing was said for several minutes after he sat down. He did drink the new glass of wine rather quickly.

"Maybe we could go somewhere else for a while." His voice was soft, controlled, and pleading. "I don't see either of us eating right now. Is that okay with you?"

"Sure." Marlene began to organize her things and prepare for departure. "I wasn't very polite to the waitress; maybe we could compensate her for my thoughtlessness."

George put money next to his plate to cover the drinks and a generous tip. Getting out of the room was, for both of them, the most important item of the moment.

Back in the car, George did not attempt to start the engine. He sat for a while looking out the window, then reached for her hand, which he clutched tightly. He was crying again, but his head was turned to the left, away from her.

"It just hurts too much."

"I know." Her voice was quiet. This was his time now. Not like Carolyn who could be left alone on the patio to get herself acquainted with the facts. This was George, who could be so strong and so in charge, as long as he wasn't alone. She'd taken away his support system by lying, by not including him, by not declaring a need for him. *I'll sit this out for him.* They sat in the car for about twenty minutes before he was ready to turn and look at her.

She thought about suggesting a hotel. Making love would divert him; give them both a chance to hold on tight. *No, that would be a false message. Right now the warmth of another person would be very healing to the soul, but when we each let go, the reality would still be there needing to be dealt with.*

She simply sat, giving him the quiet while she held his hand and let him know she was with him, even though there was nothing she could do to make it better. *Funny, my first thoughts were of doing something...the very thing I don't want from other people. Allow him the space to take care of himself. Respect him. He can handle anything if he's given the time.*

Finally, he took a deep breath and turned back to her. "Sitting here isn't getting us anywhere. How about if we go where we can walk?"

"Sure." She made her tone soothing. "Back about a mile was a beach. Let's take off our shoes and walk along the water."

Simply because it was action, George started the car, put it into gear and backed out into the road. They remained silent while he drove back to the parking lot that had a path down to the beach.

They walked down to the water, removing their shoes when they reached the sand. Each picked up rocks or shells as they walked. Marlene dropped hers after she'd looked at them, but George threw his shells and rocks as far out to sea as he could. There was no one else around. Soon they began to walk along the water's edge and George took her hand again. "So what happens now?"

Marlene laughed a little, but it sounded more like a squeak. "I've no idea. I have never done this before. I'll take it one step at a time. After this trip, I'll need to talk to my daughters. Remember, they don't know anything yet, either."

"At the risk of sounding self-centered, where do I fit into this scenario?"

"I don't know, but I guess that's one of the things we'll figure out." Much of the tension was leaving her body as they walked. "You've done this before, when your wife died. It was another reason for not bringing it up to you. It wasn't that long ago you went through it."

At this point, there was busyness in the sand just a couple feet from where they were. Marlene rushed over to see what it was and, kneeling on the sand, discovered an unusually little creature digging furiously, spraying sand in every direction; the display was out of proportion to the size of the sand crab.

"Look, George, this tiny crab is making a fuss far greater than himself. He appears desperate; survival is his only motivation."

"I think I can relate to that now. Isn't there anything we can do to help the little guy?" George still wanted to help.

"I think not. It's his instincts driving him." Marlene sat back on the sand as she watched. "But someday he won't go fast enough, won't get buried in time and the bird will get him. Wish we could just give him a picnic on the sand before his end comes. However, I do admire his drive."

George quietly responded. "And you're really committed to creating a family picnic, aren't you? You're going to be in charge and the rest of us better follow the script, is that it?" George also sat back as the wee crab buried himself and the sand stopped flying. He looked directly at Marlene and seemed to be once again in control of himself. "Look, he lived to make it another day. Isn't that worth something?"

Marlene smiled. "Yeah, but there aren't even birds paying attention to him today. He's doing what he's supposed to do. What does he do the day there are two birds, one on each side of him, watching him dig while they know they have their dinner, right there?"

George lay back in the sand and laughed easily. "How am I supposed to have an intelligent discussion with that kind of logic? Poor crab has just had his fortune told. Okay. So how do you work out this picnic and am I invited?"

Marlene reached for his hand. "Why did I ever think I could do it without you? We just have to work out the roles. The bottom line is my need to be independent or as much as I can be as time and circumstances allow."

"It won't always be this easy, you know." George squeezed her hand. "Your spirit is contagious and buries the pain for the moment, but there will be days, for me at least, when this will be very hard. How am I supposed to handle that?"

She moved closer to him and took his other hand as well. "We won't always be alone, you know. Carolyn is here and my daughters, once I bring them around, assuming I can. You'd be amazed at the conversations Robert and Jane are having about memories, magic remembering actually. We'll be a community and that's what a community does—takes care of its own."

Playing with his fingers, hoping to prevent him from speaking, she was very quiet.

Here goes. If he decides I'm nuts, I'll have to spend the rest of my time in a straitjacket.

"I guess I need to tell you about a different community, the one I've been living with for the last four months. It's in my head. It's the women who have lived and died before me, each in her own way and often in tune with her societal traditions. Megan, a medieval woman; Teodora, from the refugee camps; Abby, a woman of the old west. This week a Polynesian woman in a red dress, Pia, who was burying a family member, joined us. I've started moving in that crowd...a form of transition, I guess. But they give me such comfort and strength and sometimes they make me laugh. Someday I'll just go away with them and you can remember that and know I'm not alone. For now, we just figure out how to help one another be the best we can be. Ready, my love?"

***

The rest of the weeks went by rapidly. The sun, the joy, the new experiences for the kids, their willingness to share in the fun, the comradeship of the adults and now the lack of duplicity with George, all came together to make a complete and self-contained opportunity for each person. There appeared to be no more glitches. Each day some group just seemed to form by itself. There was the historical excursion and a short course in the history of the islands. Lots of shopping, swimming and actually a lot of sitting about talking, resting and sharing. It was good they got a bit tired and ran too hard some days, as they learned about budgeting their energy.

There was a day Marlene chose to stay in and Jane decided to stay with her. There was discussion about how maybe Jane might change her mind later, wish she'd gone with the others, and then it would be too late.

"No," Jane said in a most adult manner, "we'll be just fine. I have lots of things to do and if Gram wants to go out, I'll be here to go with her. I'll fix our lunch and mostly, I'll be out on the balcony with my books and journal. You have a good time."

Carolyn was both amused and concerned. She gave that look to Marlene like, 'is this really okay with you?' Marlene nodded. Let Jane have the moment. So the three adventurers were on their way. Robert was leading with his information about the military cemetery and how to get there. After Carolyn had left Robert and George in the parking lot, Marlene spent the day alone, walking downtown, to the beach, and sitting where she could watch people for long periods.

So the time went by, with each person mostly getting what she or he needed each day. Moving on to Kauai for a few days brought some of the excitement back. But it was the sharing thing, the being quiet together; it was watching the kids discover and digest; it was the games at night and the funny things when everybody understood and participated; it was going off by yourself and finding it a surprise that you missed the group. It was the leisure of Victorians who rented cottages at the beach for the summer; it was the big planned excursions to new places followed by two or three days of walking on the beach, reading, eating, and assimilating all that your senses could consume.

It was one of the most peaceful times of Marlene's life. She felt pampered and strong. She felt included. She felt loved and respected. She felt needed and wanted. She felt complete and giving. She felt challenged, but by nature and love and beauty, not by the demands of people and things. She was whole. In addition, she and Carolyn had studied the flesh on both sides of her tan line. The tan was covering the jaundice rather well and she wore dark glasses a lot now to mask her eyes.

The bonus was that the family and friends arrangement worked, not only for her but also for all of them.

They returned to California rested, united, and safe in the warmth of each other. For the adults, the uncharted future was less frightening because they had learned to talk about it. The children just knew they were loved. Grown-ups, who had earned their admiration, in return had treated them with respect. Marlene thought ahead to the ordeal with her daughters and knew, in time, everything would be all right. Amazingly, she had regained control, through openness. What she had protected in silence, she had redeemed in sharing. She was ready to move on.

SEPTEMBER

Marlene and the cat got up earlier than usual and sat on the sofa in the living room. They looked out over the world through the big window. The cat sat on the back of the couch and quietly remained almost head to head with his friend. It would appear he was seeing the world through her eyes. Marlene looked at him intensely. *This is what friendship is. There's nothing he doesn't know; nothing he questions; nothing to make him anxious. If he loved me unconditionally before, then new conditions make no difference. If he demanded nothing from me before, he won't demand more now. He is; we are.* She stroked his fur and rested her forehead between his ears.

Marlene started her day with the cup of hot water, which had replaced her morning tea. That got her started. She had rested the last few days and was ready to face this one. Breaking her silence with George in Hawaii had given her another ally.

It was a group decision that she would stop working. Now she was free to enjoy her pursuits and still know she was getting plenty of rest. Her appointment today could be handled with no stress. So what's this restlessness? No reason to feel anxiety, just uneasiness that I'm forgetting something. Her appointment wasn't until two-thirty and she had all day to recall what it was she needed.

So the cat and the woman sat awhile, acknowledging the dogged heat that wasn't ready to give up, and they noted the fading, dusty gardens. They looked for the signs of autumn, which was trying to sneak in when the summer, during weak and tired moments, wasn't looking. Marlene got up to do a few tasks. She accomplished a bit of watering in the backyard, rested, made her bed, and laid out her clothes. Sitting again, to regain her strength, it hit her. Carolyn had said, "Very soon you'll have to let yourself be more vulnerable. You need to practice the actuality of it."

Being alone has been good, but maybe now I need to learn something about depending on other people. That's what she was saying about my daughters; they'll need to be involved and depended upon. I can accept that; I can even begin to practice. After dialing, she waited for only one ring before getting an answer.

"Hello." Harriet's welcoming, comforting voice exuded cheer.

"Hi. Marlene here. What are you doing today?"

"Hey, girlfriend. Good to hear from you. I was looking at the last of the berries but have decided that the birds need them more than we do. I have twenty quarts already on the shelf. What's with you today? Feeling good or what?"

"Yeah, I'm fine. Just wondering if your day was planned or if you might like to have lunch and go with me to an appointment—not to see a doctor, just business stuff. It's not critical if you're busy, just thought that if you were free it might be more fun. Everything, including lunch, would be from, maybe, one to three-thirty. Think you have time and/or inclination?"

"Sure. Where are we going?"

"I'll tell you at lunch."

"Okay, baby. How about if I'm at your house by one? There's nothing here to entice me. Can I bring you anything? How about some berries?"

"Thanks, Harriet, but I still have some of the last quart you gave me. I look forward to seeing you." After quick goodbyes, they hung up. Harriet was not one to waste minutes, words, time, or motion. Feeling easier now, Marlene stretched out on the sofa and read.

Later she dressed for her outing in a soft, pale pink cotton dress, no stockings, just sandals and her long gray hair in a knot atop her head. She looked cool and comfortable. Harriet came in with a whoosh and, pretty much taking charge, parked herself in a straight-backed chair.

The bright, red sundress with spaghetti straps would have looked absurd on any other woman her size. But it was wonderful on the dark black woman. Her large five-foot-eleven frame carried the color, her sense of confidence and joy in style. Just looking at her made Marlene feel safe. It was far too hot for physical hugging, but she felt as if she were being held in the embrace of this mother figure.

"Okay, friend, what's the plan?" Harriet dove right in.

Marlene laughed. "How about a good salad with iced tea at the patio restaurant next door to Vallejo's? Doesn't that sound good in this heat?"

"Sure, if that's what's on your mind. Somewhere I heard something about an appointment and I don't even know what for or where. Why do I feel I'm on an unannounced treasure hunt?"

"Because it's more fun that way. C'mon, let's go eat in the shade and pretend it's autumn. We have all day to take care of chores."

"Marlene, is there something weird here? Usually it's not a big secret if you want me to go with you to buy groceries."

Marlene looked at her friend for a moment and then said. "I could be asking you to do something you won't be comfortable with. But there's no need to follow through if you don't want to go and we can talk about it over lunch. It's not all that important, more like an exercise on my part. Let's go eat."

They left the apartment in the hot, dusty day believing that all was well, and ready to prove it with humor, honesty and courage.

Finding a table under a tree and next to a fence covered with bougainvillea, they could even pretend they were cool. They ordered iced teas and settled back to enjoy the respite from the overlong summer and from the duties that kept Harriet always on the go. Marlene mentally celebrated her idea of doing something with a friend. *Maybe I just conserve too much energy.*

With a genuine smile, she took Harriet's hand and said, "Thanks for coming out with me. I'm happy to be here with you, elements notwithstanding."

"Me, too. We keep promising ourselves, but we just seem to put it off. This is good. However, I'm curious about this appointment. What's up? What follows the avocado and tomato?"

"Well, let's talk about it." Marlene was amazed to find she felt no trepidation about approaching the subject. "It may be that what I want to do will conflict with your traditions or culture and religion. I don't know. But I wanted you with me today enough to risk asking. It's really okay if you'd rather not go. You still get lunch." Images flashed through Marlene's mind about the number of conversations she'd had with African-American friends about death in the past. Almost all of them had strong feelings, and nearly all of them different from her own.

"Next week, I'll be telling my daughters what's going on. I want to have some things in order, so they won't have to deal with everything all at once. I want to have a plan in place with the Neptune Society. That's where I'm going. I thought if you went with me, we could make it a bit more jovial. I don't however, know how you feel about cremation and that sort of stuff. I think I've always known that's what I wanted for myself."

"Wow, baby. Not exactly what I was expecting. But it's thought provoking." Harriet became very introspective and was more or less talking to herself, slowly, with pauses, as she worked out her thoughts. "I was prepared for some medical stuff, thinking about your illness, your discomforts, our unpredictable future. Why did the thought of your burial preparation hit me in the stomach that way? Am I preferring your suffering to your death?" Now she looked up as if Marlene had just appeared. I'm sorry. I'll catch on here in a minute."

Her eyes were shiny with threatening tears as Marlene replied. "That's it, Harriet, that's what I'm trying to get over to everyone. There can be dignity in death too. You've got it. Thanks, friend, take your time."

It was quiet while the salads were served and each woman buttered the French bread for which the deli was noted. Keeping busy seemed part of the process and gave each of them time to think about what to say next or maybe what not to say. As it happened, when they looked up at each other at the same moment, there was a connection, and they smiled easily at one another. They had joined to solve this puzzle, and there were no fears of offending.

Harriet's eyes appeared to be looking inward. "Where does this feeling of acceptance come from? It's foreign to all my conscious sentiments about death. The Christian rituals my mother passed on to me didn't allow this type of quiet approval. There was always the hushed drama, the solemn music, and the theatrical posturing of the members of the family, some of whom were unhappy being in the spotlight, while others relished the attention. But all of them sharing the grief, often quite loudly. Somewhere back in my collective memories are the spirits—the ghosts, if you will. The innate knowledge that death is not the end of the soul, yet still lacking the knowledge of what really happens after death."

Marlene's need to stick to basics launched her into speaking her own theory. "Harriet, why not? We're women who've done all the things expected of women. We fixed the washing machine by sticking socks in the drainpipe so the water could be diverted to the flowerbed, thereby avoiding the stopped up drain. Some cat having kittens behind that same washing machine on the same day it ran over never daunted us. It was our job to divert the water, save the kittens, and still have the wash on the line before the fog came in. We never had the luxury of creating nuclear waste knowing someone else would figure out what to do with the residue. What we invented, we took responsibility for, all the way down the line. We learned the hard way that reality is the only way to go. We made choices when we couldn't change the reality."

Marlene heard herself preaching and softened her voice. "Whose bloody idea was it that death is the ultimate awful? If we can't change the reality, let's make the best of it."

Harriet sat back in her chair with her glass of iced tea resting on her ample stomach and laughed heartily. "Why do I feel like one of the bigger rocks in the sack on my back has been removed? Chile, let's get on with what we must do. I consider it an honor that you asked me to join you. If I get prickly in the process, it's only because it's a whole new way of doing things, but I like the challenge and I'll catch on. Just give me the chance."

Lunch was fun after that, and the conversation moved back and forth between gossip and thoughts or suggestions about the plan they would soon be putting on paper. After lunch, they left the restaurant with a sense of adventure, not one of facing an unpleasant chore.

They found the Neptune society in an old Victorian house, which had been made over into offices. However, the visions of families coming and going in times of stress explained it to her; funeral home images after all. Marlene and Harriet entered the building not knowing what to expect. It was plain, very clean and, Marlene liked the "Shaker" feel of it.

Rhonda, who had spoken to Marlene on the phone, greeted them and showed them into her office. Harriet was introduced and everyone shook hands and took seats, Rhonda behind her desk.

The desk was not as tidy as Marlene would have expected. She remembered the offices of funeral directors she had visited as being clean, to the point of suggesting that everything that had passed here before was—GONE. Rhonda obviously wasn't all that together. *It's comforting to know that at least there will be a piece of paper to validate my prior existence.* Rhonda's physical appearance followed the pattern. Wisps of hair escaped from a coif that indicated a period of time with dryer and curling iron, followed by 'what the heck' and fingers run rampantly over the scalp whenever she was thinking. These characteristics endeared her to Marlene, who was more comfortable with real people than with designer creatures. She wanted to say something to Harriet; she had an insight she wanted to share, she wanted to laugh, but knew it was completely inappropriate. *Other people in this business would lead one to believe that no mishap could occur to one's remains. Rhonda makes one think 'accidents happen' but that she wouldn't give up until the situation was corrected and the remains were back where everyone believed them to be.*

Marlene had lost a bit of what Rhonda was saying during her own reverie but she worked at getting back to the conversation. What she was being offered were as many or as few services as she chose, and the nice, helpful lady behind the desk kept interjecting the prices to prevent surprises. The body would be retrieved from the place of death, and cremation would occur within twenty-four hours. Offshore distribution of ashes was available, and the family or Marlene could arrange any type of service. Urns were available, as were simple metal boxes, but should the family, or Marlene, have an art object or container with particular memories, it could be brought in and the remains would be put into that container and sealed.

Marlene couldn't quell the humor in her head as she thought about one of her youngest daughter's earliest gifts. *I wonder if that pottery piece Eileen brought back from Mexico when she was nine would work or if it's possible to get all the ashes into the very skinny neck of that vase.* She had to be practical. "What are the procedures for donating any organs that might be useful?"

"It's necessary that the patient be on life-support systems at the time of death in order to harvest any organs, with the exception of corneas. For life support, you'll need a power of attorney and hospitalization. Please remember, I'm not a legal advisor." Rhonda was covering herself. Marlene mentally responded, *Harvesting?*

The next few minutes were taken with Rhonda giving Marlene forms and brochures covering all the laws.

"The ideal is that your physician has seen you within twenty days of your death, but he or she can sign the death certificate up to 120 days after his last visit. If you haven't seen a physician in that period of time, the law requires the signatures of both the coroner and a physician, and that entails an autopsy. It's best to stay in touch with your doctor. "She handed Marlene another set of pamphlets. "Here are the laws of other states, should you be away at the time of death. They're complex, but your family can give us a call and we'll walk them through it."

Marlene looked at Harriet for a second or two. Looking back at Rhonda, she moved forward in her chair, taking her checkbook from her purse. She was ready to do business. "I'd like to have the basic services. I believe you said the price is $811. Then I'd like to add a couple of hundred dollars for an urn, should they, my family I mean, choose to do that. They'll probably be taking the ashes to Mexico. I believe I could be happy in the water there." She smiled at both women. "What I really wanted was assurance that one phone call will take care of all the immediate concerns; the body picked up and cremation accomplished as quickly as possible, and that all legal papers will be filed. After that, the family will be free to do anything they feel the need to do. I don't particularly want services and such, but I won't be there, and if it helps them bring closure, I want them to know it's their decision."

Rhonda leaned across her desk, and the professionalism she had attempted was dropped. A woman, a friend, a cohort replaced the frazzled businessperson. There was no sympathy or teary eye, just the ability to deal with truth and reality. "You speak as if this is near at hand. Is there anything else you would want to share with me that might ease the situation?"

Marlene met the mood with all the poise she had sensed in Rhonda. "Reasonably soon. I have a cancer that isn't treatable and I'm attempting to put all my ducks in a row, if you will. When I discuss this with my children, I want all the business end of things taken care of so we can spend our time in a more fruitful manner. I also wanted to know that the person they will call when the time comes would be human, competent and kind. You've relieved any fear I might have had about unnecessary bureaucracies."

"Please know, Marlene, that we will make any changes or adjustments you may want during this time. I will be available for anything they want or non-existent if that's easier. I'll be sending you the cards which clearly state the instructions for use at the time of death. Once your family has made the phone call, they have nothing to do but pick up the urn and copies of legal papers. If you want these plans so they can change them after your death, sign on this line. If you want things left exactly as you say, sign on this line. Just let me know if there's anything you need from me. I simply suggest that you stay in touch with your physician and follow the time limit requirements."

There was a comfortable comradeship among the three women, one of them a stranger. Yet, their common responses to the situation, their acceptance of each other and the mutual acknowledgement of things as they really are, gave them a temporary bond easily recognized by each.

The three heads moved towards one another over the desk as Harriet talked about her African-American traditions and perceptions and how very different they were from the experiences of both Marlene and Rhonda. They were moved as Rhonda spoke of families where this process was the only acceptable one in unusual circumstances. She talked of personality types and how impossible it appeared for some people to deal with death at all.

They finished their small talk, Marlene wrote her check and Rhonda completed the paper work. "The cards and certificates will come in the mail to you in about seven days."

Rhonda was cleaning up the files and talking at the same time. Then she stopped, stood up, and walked around her desk. She put out one hand to Marlene and extended the other to Harriet. "It's not every consultation that I find this affirming. I wish for you the very best and remember I'm here any time.

Marlene and Harriet squeezed the hands that had been presented to them and, among a few non-sensible syllables, thanked Rhonda for what she had done.

Harriet added, "And for yourself."

The two women left and walked to the car in what was now extreme heat. Little was said until the air conditioner had cooled things down.

Harriet spoke first, "May we please have something cold to drink, and may I say, as a blind date, you're hard to beat."

Marlene glanced at her friend to make sure Harriet was joking, then laughed easily. "You've just walked over a bridge into territory you haven't trod before. Was it disturbing to you? I found myself using humor to keep it from getting maudlin."

Harriet was wiping her brow but answered quietly, "No, baby, just learning something new and different about you. Sometimes that takes a minute or two of adjustment, but I do appreciate that you took me on this foray. I guess you trusted that I wouldn't make a scene."

"What if you had?" Marlene turned into the parking lot of an ice cream store. "Let's get something fizzy and cold where the A/C works well." They left the car and entered the shop that was a bit noisy and rather crowded. Harriet claimed a table and Marlene ordered old-fashioned sodas.

When they were seated at the table with their drinks, Harriet ventured. "What's next?"

After a moment, Marlene responded in a soft voice. "Now I have to tell my daughters." She stared off into a far corner of the ceiling. Past the fans and the ads and the people and the noise. Harriet let her friend take the time she needed; not speaking or touching.

Soon Marlene came back and smiled at Harriet. "They're coming to my house for dinner next week—just my kids and me. I've thought a lot about the fun part of it. We have this traditional dance when we're together. After a little pulling by one, a stepping back by another and, if no one exerts too much pressure, we always end up in a reasonably good place. They are each so different and that's good, but now I have a chill telling me it won't be all fun. That's what next."

"Anything you need?" Harriet asked.

"You know something." Marlene became somewhat animated as she leaned onto the table toward her ally. "I thought I asked you to go with me to make final arrangements because I wasn't sure how easy it would be. It was a piece of cake, maybe because you were there, but I think it was straightforward. However, my inner comforter knew that today I would face that reality about my girls and that's why you're here. Thanks, *Madrona*. Now that I've said what I need to do next, I'll figure out how to move."

Marlene sat back in her chair, but Harriet hadn't moved. Marlene looked at her and said, "I'd venture to say that the look on your face says 'incredulous'. What? You thought this would be a picnic?" They were very quiet. "I know, me too."

After finishing their drinks, they drove back to Marlene's house. It was too hot to stay outside and talk and too late for Harriet to come in, so they held each other a moment. Harriet said, "I'll call you tomorrow. Love you." And, she was gone. Marlene made her way up the stairs and entered her apartment. The cat looked up at her and put his head back down. It was too hot to even deal with your best friend.

Marlene went into her room and removed all her clothes. She threw on a shift and went into the kitchen to pour some water. She sat in the living room by the window. It was only minutes before she thought, *"What I want to do is take a nap. What I have to do is plan this dinner and conversation.* Her eyes strayed out the window and beyond to something that was drawing her; her friends, her women—but now they were the mothers who had inflicted pain on their daughters, each for her own reason.

Not the woman out of control for whom abuse is a release, but the women who are required by the society to perform certain acts, who have to make decisions which will cause pain but will enable their daughters to remain an integral part of their society. It's just more of the reality of living and the challenges that require courage.

There's the woman of old China who spent her entire life crippled and in pain. Now she is required to break the bones and bind the feet of her own daughter. Even today, female circumcision is performed as a regular religious rite in some countries. In both instances do all the aunties and wise women of the community perform these acts? Is this because each mother, singularly, could not do this to her own daughter?

In the seventies and eighties, we rebelled against the customs of our society that limited the career possibilities of women. Being good bra burners, we reared our daughters with images of great and glorious futures. How often did we break the hearts of these young girls who had other dreams, not our dreams? What was the greatest pain I inflicted on my children? Probably the divorce. She became very quiet inside herself as she relived the horrors of that time. Energies seemed to come from all her corners to wrap themselves around those memories…allowing her to remember, but not to touch…allowing her to glean, but not to wallow…allowing her to visit, but not to stay.

Those three little faces, "Daddy's going to Venice, in Italy, to live. You'll be able to visit him there." *Sam and I had agreed that we would present this together, that we'd look united and give them some sense of security. So there he was putting on a big show to make them think it was a circus, but they weren't fooled a bit, especially Kate. Quiet Kate, taking it all in but knowing she was being left behind. Watching her face, I think I could tell the moment she decided to play along. But it was an issue all their lives. They had visited him and his new wife once, but then had never asked to go back. They received the Christmas box every year, but birthdays were neglected.*

We became a good team, the four of us women, but I think I said to myself the day Sam and I talked to those girls that I would never again do anything to hurt them that much. Now I feel like this is one more broken promise. And for one of those few times, she put her head on the back of the couch and let herself cry, just hard enough to get the knots out of her stomach.

"Hold me, You Women who say in the morning, I have to do this thing and I'll do it now—bind the precious feet, perform the clitorectomy, remove the stable underpinnings of this child's world, and prepare them to say goodbye."

The morning of the dinner party, fall was trying again to make an entry. The out-of-doors was cool and breezy and there was that autumn smell in the air. It was a good day for walking and cleaning up in the yard. Marlene wanted to stay busy all day. She was ready. Carolyn had flown up last weekend and they had cried it all out together. They'd talked about the things that would be hardest to say, analyzed which words would be easiest understood without being brutal, and practiced the lines that might choke her up until those words lost their power over her. She could do this alone now.

Yesterday, she and George had driven to Reno for lunch. Rolling through the mountains and watching fall make it's moves on the forest had made Marlene feel hopeful. They strolled the streets for a bit and ate at a buffet in one of the casinos.

This trip was one of George's good ideas. It was distracting and amusing. It had required no effort to be a part of the action. More than anywhere else in the world, Reno is a place where you can be alone in a crowd. They had laughed together and giggled as they watched people so intent on their 'dream chasing'. Sometimes, holding hands, they had walked and observed the glitzy casinos; the outrageous effort management had made to capture the minds of the players, and the players themselves. Now she realized each person had come for a specific reason. Hers was amusement, diversion, and distraction. The gamblers? So many possibilities; she wanted to make up stories for each one. Instead, she wished them luck with their gambling and their lives.

The weekend of reality with Carolyn and the day of diversion with George had done their jobs well. She was very composed as she planned her day—a little exercise, a trip to the market, a rest in the afternoon. She was ready.

Early evening came and Kate arrived first, exceeding all the attitudes of celebration Marlene hoped would set the tone. This middle child, the peacemaker, had brought flowers and after a big hug, went into the kitchen to put them in a vase for her mother. As she placed the flowers on the table, she appeared to be looking around, maybe for some sign of dinner. Then she sat on the opposite end of the sofa chatting about current activities and made the small talk that enabled each of them to catch up on what was new, or so Marlene wanted Kate to believe.

It was twenty minutes before Eileen arrived, complaining about parking. She sat down in a chair, forgetting to kiss her mother. "Don't tell me I beat Jessie here, I've never beaten her anywhere, ever. What's your word, Mom? Sloth? Aha, it's the first time I've ever been able to use it on my big sister." The youngest of the three began a litany of the things wrong at work; at her apartment complex and how even her friends were behaving badly.

The eldest daughter, Jessie, wasn't far behind. Her entry suggested relief. "Finally, a whole evening without people to take care of. Until school starts next week, there's no routine." She kissed her mother and looked around the room and at the table. However, Eileen beat her to the question.

"Ummmmmm, dinner. I thought we were invited to dinner."

Marlene looked at each of them and grinned. "Well, it's like this. Jane and I have had so many conversations lately about when all of you were little that I wanted to relive some of it. Come with me." She got up from her chair and they followed her into the kitchen"

"Now," she said as she opened the refrigerator, "there's enough food in here to make a variety of menus. First, we get to decide what we want and then we divide the chores so that it all gets done—exactly as we did it when you were little. I think it sounds like fun. How about it?"

Jessie, being oldest and currently responsible for a family, analyzed the situation quickly. "I believe that when we were little we used up much less hip space. How are all of us going to fit into this kitchen and work?"

"Resourcefully, that's how." The negative energy of her sisters drove Kate mad. "Okay, gang, what's it going to be? I like tacos and enchiladas myself. Mom, how were all those decisions made? Did we fight about menus too?"

"No." Marlene wanted them to remember their younger days. "I think you took turns and then the others had to help with your menu. Remember, Eileen always had frozen fish sticks and French fries. You were very little then, but you always prepared a proper salad and set the table well."

As Marlene ran her hand over Eileen's hair, there was a moment of hesitation in her youngest daughter's eyes, maybe even nervousness as she responded. "Give me a break! I was also the first one to conquer roast beef, so you won't have to eat frozen fish sticks now. I second Kate for the tacos and enchiladas. I'll even chop onions. I can do that at the end of the counter and not have to bump butts with the rest of you."

Jessie, obviously disappointed she was once again in a kitchen, covered her dismay well. "Gotcha. I'll grate cheese and Kate, you can work on the meat. Mom, that leaves you with vegetables, at least for now."

"Wait a minute here," Eileen stopped taking onions from the bin. "The way I remember it there weren't as many pairs of hands as we have now. Mom, you were either at work, working at your desk in your room, or calling to say you'd be late." The tone was accusatory. "Did we really do this together back then?"

Jessie tried to smooth things over. "I think that's unfair, and the timing is a bit off."

"No." Marlene's voice was strong. "This is the perfect time for all those issues to come up. If we don't deal with them when we're together, I don't know when we'd deal with them. Right, Eileen, I was always working. I thought it was an issue of keeping a roof over our heads and food on the table, but I think the part that may have hurt was that I enjoyed my job so much. I can say that I'm sorry, but I can't change what I did. I can only tell you that any thought of life without you three would be mighty bleak."

Jessie kept grating the cheese but looked up and said tentatively, "We never talked about what life was like for you after Dad left. I think we were too young and then we just grew up doing all of it ourselves. Did you ever hate him for leaving us like that? What was it like for you? I can't believe I've never questioned that before."

Marlene left the lettuce and tomatoes she'd been slicing and went to sit at the kitchen table. She and Carolyn hadn't thought to discuss this, "This is really important. I think we should have discussed it years ago, but maybe we weren't ready till now. He told me he was leaving and it was less than a week before we told you and he was gone. Thank heavens Gram and Grandpa were around then because they really took care of you." She reached nervously for a saltshaker, but not wanting to appear ill at ease, she pulled back her hand.

I didn't want you to see me cry. I didn't think you needed to know that caring for you by myself scared me to death. I certainly didn't want you to see me wringing my hands trying to figure out what I was going to do. So I brought you home every night from Gram's and pretended that it was terrific and we'd be fine. Then I took you back in the morning to Gram's so I could wallow in my fear and anger some more. One day Grandpa sat me down and said, 'Okay, enough grief. Make a plan and start working it. Those kids need you, not us. You be the mother now and we'll always do what we can to help'.

"So I did and as the years went by I perceived us as, pretty much, a complete family. We did what we needed to do, we leaned on one another and I thought we did okay. Each of you became so strong, sure of yourselves and what you want. You are all committed to overcoming the tough times, to accomplishing what you've dreamed. What else is a family except a place to grow in those directions while being loved and kept safe? We did that, and I can't ask for more." She paused, looking down at her hands. "Except maybe acknowledgement of the things I didn't do as well and then we can move to forgiveness."

Amid some monosyllabic sounds, Marlene interrupted them and said, "Come on, it's easier if you let it go. Look what happened when Eileen mentioned how often I was away from home. It helps each of us understand where we are in this family. I think it's a worthy effort."

Marlene got up from the table and resumed slicing the tomatoes. All the work had slowed down, but it wasn't forgotten. The room was quiet as each woman committed herself to her task.

When Jessie finished the cheese, she looked for a skillet in which to heat the enchilada sauce. Then she tore open the large package of tortillas. "Mostly it was okay. Mom, I know I missed you when you were gone and I guess I got pretty bossy with you two girls, but actually, we were always safe and warm, and we knew that you, Mom, loved us. I think I remember hating the responsibilities I had, but when I did well in school or in sports, it felt good to know I'd earned that. I guess I remember more about being proud of myself and my accomplishments than I do about housework and child care."

Eileen took her large bowl of uniformly chopped onions and placed them near the stove for the enchiladas. Then she spoke directly to her eldest sister. "But look, Jess, what a tyrant you are now about your own kids, everything has to be perfect for them, they can't be left alone, everything has to be done for them. That must come from somewhere."

Marlene was trying to give Jessie some time to build a response. "I found those kids to be very responsible, creative and curious while we were in Hawaii."

Kate stepped in. "When I think of not having a dad, I think of social events like Father/Daughter dinners, when I just didn't want to be different. Then some friend of Mom's, of ours, would take me along and it would be okay. We really had a lot of nice people in our lives. I guess I think that we had a very big family made up of people who came and went but always cared about all of us."

The work went on and the meal continued taking shape. As Marlene opened a bottle of wine and put a glass near each woman, the three daughters began to talk about their younger days, laughing over the fights and vowing that they'd still get even.

Jessie finished the pan of enchiladas, bumping into Eileen when she backed up and bent down to put the pan into the oven. Eileen slapped Jessie's backside and said, "See? You still take up all the room. Give a guy some space."

Jessie stood up and attempted to put her arm around her younger sister's shoulders, but she wasn't fast enough. Eileen slid around to put the tortillas near the stove for Kate who was ready to fry the tacos. As if to stay out of the reach of tender embraces, Eileen began setting the

153

table and carrying the bowls of chopped vegetables to the dining room table.

When everything was ready, each woman took her glass of wine to the table, with Jessie bringing the enchiladas, Kate the tray of tacos and Eileen the bottle of wine.

As each plate was filled and bowls were being passed, Jessie took up the subject from where she perceived it had left off. "There's a lot of complicated feelings about the way we grew up. I felt such pride in you when I could say, 'My mom's in Uruguay, and can't come to the school playoffs'. When I took things to school that you'd brought back or the articles in the magazine that had your byline on the front page, I knew that the kids knew you were special. But at the same time, I wanted you at those playoffs and I really envied the kids whose mothers were there giving rides, selling hotdogs, and in on all the school gossip. Some of those mothers knew the story of every kid and could say things that would make that kid, a stranger really, feel special. I don't think I thought about changing the way things were, I guess I was just asking to have it all."

Sometime during her talking, Jessie had folded her paper napkin into the tiniest bundle.

Eileen reached across and took the totally crumpled napkin away from her sister. She held it up for Jessie to see and nearly sneered. "See where letting feelings go gets you? Here's one destroyed napkin and Mom looking like she's been hit in the stomach."

"Mom, do you feel like you've been hit in the stomach?" Kate asked this as she reached back to the cabinet near the table and got another napkin for Jessie.

Marlene moved back in her chair with a sigh. "No. If we can talk about the things that bother us, we can begin to fix them. Most of what you've said leads me to believe I was a better parent than I thought I was." Now she leaned into the group and said, "Never, never, never did I ever think I wasn't making mistakes. I spent time fretting about how to do things better and how to give you all the time and energy you deserved while still providing a living and enjoying my work at an interesting job.

Kate, the middle child, the thinker, the take-charge-quietly kid, offered her conclusion while sitting back, completely relaxed in her chair. "I don't know one single kid, or adult for that matter, who's had a perfect life. You gave me something I didn't recognize until college. We, the girls in the dorm, would sit around and talk about our mothers a lot in the night and maybe that was because we were blaming you for everything, but I listened to those whose mothers had been at home. Sure, they were at all the school functions and always available when kids came home from school. And, that was very good for many of them.

"But somehow those students also had a smaller vision of the world. You taught us, through your lifestyle, that life was for living, risks were for taking and never say 'no' out of fear. You were always stretching and for myself, well, I learned to stretch too. As a role model, your style was best for me. I guess I never said thank you for that."

Marlene knew her eyes were tearing up and that it wouldn't help the ensuing conversation. But Kate had to be acknowledged and thanked. Marlene got up from her chair, hugged Kate where she sat and said, "What a gift of support. I can't thank you enough, any of you, for crediting me with what I knew was never enough." She moved around the table touching her other two daughters and then went into the kitchen to start a pot of coffee, the purpose being to get herself back together. From the kitchen, she called out another memory.

"Remember the first time Carolyn and I took you all to Ensenada and the motel room that had more than its share of roaches? You talk big now about risk-taking and facing fear. Where was this bravery while we wrapped you in blankets and left the lights on all night so you could trace the journeys of your new, multi-legged friends?" She returned to the table and sat down.

Eileen took up the challenge. "Yeah, and you and Carolyn slept through the night, actually snoring. As if we alone, the little kids, would protect all of us from the varmints. See, Kate, we didn't learn lack of fear from modeling, we learned that after three nights without sleep, watching them sleep, until we finally had to turn out the lights and give up the fight." She softened a bit when she added to her sisters. "I think I remember that you two took pretty good care of me that time."

Marlene, seeing her chance, jumped on the statement as she reached over and took Eileen's hand. "That's what it's about. We're all afraid sometimes, but we take turns being strong and that way someone is always in the nurturing position, even though it's someone different each time. Actually, that's not only what it's about, that's all it's about. C'mon, Eileen help me get the coffees and cups."

Jessie stood up and said, "No, Mom. You sit there and I'll help Eileen."

From the corner of her eye, Marlene looked at Kate. *I expect you now to be the strong one.*

When they all had their coffee, they made jokes about the division of labor they had utilized as children—mostly who was loudest or biggest or crankiest made the rules for the moment.

"Jessie was always bossy, but there were times we each had to give in because one of us would be wounded or blue or PMS-y." Eileen seemed to be thinking about something that didn't include everyone else. Then she straightened up and looked at her family around the table. "Okay, Mom, so we learned that too. I'm glad you didn't tell us we were learning. That would have taken the fun out of it."

Once again, Marlene reached for the hands of her children who were sitting on either side of her, Kate to the right, Eileen to her left. At the same time, she looked across the table, directly into the eyes of Jessie, her first born. She was conscious of her voice, not wanting to sound too serious.

"Well, I'm certainly glad you did learn it, because I have something I want each of you to do for me. I don't want arguments or excuses about why you can't. It's my turn to be appeased, just as you took care of one another." Now she looked at each one and smiled. They were looking a little startled and she didn't want them afraid. "I want each of you to make an appointment to have a complete physical exam. I want you to do it quickly. They've found some cancer in me and I'm really bugged about the genetic thing. Do I have your promises?"

"What cancer?"

"When?"

"Why haven't you told me?"

"What are they doing for you?" The questions all came at the same time, and all three voices were mixed up in the inquiring.

"No, First I need your promises about the exams. That's the most important and I won't go on until you have each given me your word. Can I count on you for this?"

"What I want to know is what's happening and why you haven't told us anything." Eileen was once again the assertive intruder.

Jessie had already started to tear up. "How could you not have told us?"

"That's what I'm trying to do now. Please let me have your pledges that you'll take care of business, then I can feel free to discuss what's going on with me. "

Kate would pull this conversation into a constructive form. "I, for one, promise to make an appointment within the next week. I'll tell you when that appointment time is and I'll report everything I learn. Okay? Now come on, you guys, we can eliminate some of her stress by doing as she asks and protecting ourselves."

Jessie was wiping tears from her eyes. "Sure, I understand. It's just really scary to think of you being sick. You never have been. I'll match Kate and make the appointment right away."

Marlene looked at Eileen and waited. Eileen was looking at her coffee cup, her face closing up as she stared. "Then she realized that everyone was waiting for her. "Yes, I'll do it."

Kate refilled everyone's coffee cup, giving a little space for each to calm herself. "Okay, Mom. You have our promises, grudgingly or otherwise, but we'll take care of it. Now can you tell us what's happening? I wasn't even aware you were ill. Has it to do with the tiredness you complain about?"

"Wait." Jessie nearly jumped out of her chair as she suddenly leaned forward onto the table. "Jane mentioned that you got sick in Hawaii. Is that what this is about? Did you know before you took the kids on vacation?"

Marlene allowed herself an easy laugh. "If I just sit here long enough you'll have figured it out and won't need me to explain anything. Yes, I've known for a little while, but really needed to work it out for myself.

"Why did I take Jane and Robert to Hawaii when I knew I was ill? Because I really wanted to have a time for them to remember before everyone started treating me as sick. I need to tell you that's my greatest fear. The first person to whisper behind my back or help me to a chair when I'm perfectly capable, will find out quickly how much strength I have. There'll be times coming when I won't be doing so well, but we'll all handle that when the time comes."

Eileen interrupted, "Is that related to the chemotherapy everyone talks about? Is that the part that'll be hardest?"

"No." And Marlene tried to look at them full face. "There won't be any chemotherapy."

Kate found her voice. "Please, Mom, start at the beginning. What kind of cancer is it? How long have you known you've had it"? How advanced is it? What are they doing for you? Have they told you what to expect?"

They're talking about an illness, not my death, Marlene thought, but Jessie had her questions, too.

"How are you now? You appear to be okay. I'm feeling guilty that I didn't notice any changes."

That's easier, I can deal with these questions before I tackle Kate's. "Actually, I'm doing well. It's pancreatic cancer and it affects my eating, digestion, my energy and the yellowish color of my skin more than anything else. The sickness in Hawaii was because I forced myself to eat a big, rich meal so I wouldn't look puny. It was a bad plan and I heaved all night, but the rest of the trip was fine. Tell me, in reporting the trip, did the kids talk about me being sick a lot?"

Jessie was on safer ground, too. "No, they made it sound funny. Otherwise, they said nothing about you being different."

"That was the plan."

Kate was not to be dismissed. "Please share some of the facts with us. What's really happening—in your body, I mean. What are we to expect?"

"Not a lot. Things will go on as they are now. Eating will be my major effort, but actually I do almost everything now that I did before— just less of it."

Eileen went straight to the heart of things. "Just a minute. What are you doing for yourself? What are they doing for you? What treatments do you take? I want to know what you'll need during that treatment period. I've heard that can be pretty tough."

Marlene swallowed the lump that suddenly rose in her throat and reached for Eileen's hand. "There won't be any treatments at all. It was pretty advanced by the time it was discovered, which is why I'm so inflexible about the precautions I want you to take. I also made some decis…"

Eileen tore her hand from her mother's and stood up so quickly she tipped her chair over. Her voice was cold and hard. "Are you telling me you're not doing anything? There's no end to the things medicine can do now. Sorry, Kate, but if this is the kind of risk-taking that impresses you, it does nothing for me."

"Eileen, sit. Mom has a right to be heard. What decisions were you going to tell us about?" Kate spoke calmly and evenly, but Eileen didn't sit down. She began to pace the floor, refusing to look at anyone. She also didn't pick her chair up off the floor. Jessie had started to cry, quietly, as if she were alone.

Marlene spoke with quiet authority. "Every scenario they painted was pretty bleak. There were no guarantees of any recovery, and being sick from chemical treatments until the end didn't appeal to me. I want to be with you and yours. I want to be involved in your lives as long as I can be. I want us to prepare ourselves so that we have no thoughts of 'what if?' only 'remember when."

Jessie spoke through her tears. "It's so unfair. My children have no grandfather and now they'll have no grandmother. I don't even know how I can raise them without you. Oh, my God, when Jane gets married you won't be there. I can't even imagine that."

Eileen returned to the table, gripping the edge with her hands. She leaned on her arms and looked at Jessie with contempt. "You have children old enough to remember her, you have a husband and a home. I have no children yet. My children will not have memories, they'll never get a trip to Hawaii, and they'll have nothing of my history. It will have ended before they arrive. I don't want to hear how bad it will be for you. She won't even be at my wedding for God's sake. I want to know why Mom has chosen to just end it as if it were another adventure she had to take." She walked away from the table again.

Marlene's thoughts were to take Eileen in her arms and make the pain go away, but she knew she would be rejected. She remembered how she had let Carolyn face the facts without hindrance. She remembered how she had had to sit by while George coped. It was a sign of respect to let people deal with pain on their own terms, but one doesn't ever want to watch a child ache so intensely. Another thought came to her, these three will need to learn to take care of one another now. She was glad they were together and that she had subjected each of them to the soreness of the others at this difficult time.

Kate rose and began taking dishes into the kitchen. Eileen headed for the bathroom. Jessie let herself cry and moved into the chair Kate had vacated, reaching for her mother's hands. "I don't want to sound selfish, really, but it's so scary."

"Of course it is, darlin', that's why it took me a while to tell you. I had to get over the scary part too. You'll get beyond this, I promise. It just hurts so much at the telling. We have time to mend, Jess. We can say all the things that other people wish they'd said. We can be together in ways we never thought to be before. It's all a part of living and we know we're strong enough for that."

After a moment of quiet, Marlene softly suggested. "If you're okay to drive, why don't you go on home to Doug and the kids and give yourself a little space. I love you so much and I love that your home is where your comfort is. We'll talk tomorrow or whenever you're ready." Marlene loosened one of her hands from Jessie's grasp and ran it down her eldest child's cheek.

Holding Jessie's chin gently, she kissed her on the forehead. "If you've believed anything I've ever told you, Jess, believe this. It will be okay in time, because we'll work it out together."

Jessie put her hand behind her mother's neck and pulled her face close. Pressing her forehead to her mother's she was silent for a minute. When she released Marlene, Jessie's face was calmer, if sad. "I'll call you in the morning, if it's really okay that I go home now. I guess I do need my family and Doug particularly. But I love you so much."

"Knowing that is what makes it bearable, dear. You go on home, and we'll still have lots of morning calls. Kiss the kids and Doug for me."

Kate was standing in the kitchen doorway for the last bit of this conversation. For the first time in many years, Marlene watched Jessie get up from her chair and go over to kiss her sister's cheek. They exchanged a hug, and Jessie picked up her things. She hugged her mother one more time and left the house.

Kate returned to the table, picking up Eileen's chair. Just as she was sitting down in it, Eileen came back into the room and said, "I'm sorry I can't be as passive about all this as the rest of you. I will find out about what treatments are available and tolerable. I will find out what can be done to stop this ridiculous, heroic drama. I know there are doctors out there you haven't even heard of yet, and I will find them. I'll not let you sit and allow this to happen." She started to pick up her things.

"That's good, Eileen. There may be things I've missed. I'll wait to hear what you learn." Marlene rose and touched Eileen, not wanting to risk the rejection of a hug. She was rewarded with a peck on the cheek

"Sure, Mom. I have a few places I can call tomorrow to get me on the right track. I'm a researcher for God's sake, I ought to be able to handle this. Goodnight, Kate. Bye, Mom." Eileen left.

Marlene listened to the footsteps on the stairs and heard the front door open and shut. Then she turned and said, "Let's heat up the coffee for you. We can sit a few minutes while the whirlwind passes by."

Kate took the rest of the dishes from the table leaving only her own coffee cup. She had nothing to say, but when she had her coffee and Marlene a glass of water, they returned to the table and Kate took Marlene's hand. Maybe it'll be easier for them because they can blow off steam, indulge in self-pity and anger."

"But you, how are you doing?" Marlene was so comfortable talking with Kate about feelings.

"I don't know. We're too much alike, I guess." Kate had an expression that was both coy and imploring. "I can't bring it up to the surface until I've had some time to let it stew. Where did you learn that, and how did you pass it on to me; segmenting things until you can deal with them in private places on your own terms? There are other things

I need to talk to you about, but they'll have to wait. Even those of us who can repress have limits." She smiled at her mother. "Are you really feeling that good and is it going to be a long time before you become visibly ill?"

Marlene asked herself one more time. *How honest can I be?* "Most of the time I feel pretty good as long as I take care. Drinking the wine and coffee tonight is going to give me something to think about tomorrow. But it's fine for the time being. Nobody really knows what's next."

They chatted quietly for a while about other things; about the classes Kate was teaching this year, what Marlene would do now that she'd stopped working. Marlene thought maybe it was joint denial, but at least it was acceptable and it kept the two of them steady. She knew Kate would deal with things in time, on her terms, much as she herself had done.

As they were getting her things together, Kate suddenly stopped and dropped her handbag and jacket. "I was going to go away and leave you with all those dishes. I can't believe it."

Marlene reached down and picked up the bag and jacket from the floor. She laughed as she forced them onto Kate. "There's all the time in the world to do dishes. If I do them tomorrow, fine. If not, I'll get to them next week. By then, you'll have stopped by again and if they're still here, then they're waiting for you. That's not what's important anymore. Right now, we need to say goodnight and get some rest. Let's face it, this wasn't the usual 'let's get together and have dinner' kind of an evening and I can't thank you enough for being so tough. But don't forget to take care of your needs too." She helped her daughter on with her coat, then kissed her and hugged her lightly. With a firm hand, she led Kate to the head of the stairs and said, "Goodnight, I love you."

When the downstairs door had closed and Marlene had heard the car drive away, she turned back into the living room. She stopped a minute, seeing the phone. Carolyn was probably on pins and needles knowing what this evening had been about. It was only kind to put her mind at rest.

Marlene dialed the number. On the second ring, Carolyn said, "Hello."

"Everything went okay. We're all fine and you and I can talk about it later. Right now I want to go to bed."

"Thanks for calling. I love you. Goodnight." Carolyn hung up the phone.

Next Marlene thought of George, *but he's coming for breakfast in the morning, that's soon enough.*

Marlene looked around the room; it was a bit disheveled, but not bad. She reached into the bookcase and withdrew a picture book Carolyn had edited many years ago. She took it to the bedroom with her. As she climbed into her bed, the cat, who had been mysteriously missing all evening, came and climbed up to lie on her feet. She opened the edition and looked at the photos she'd taken for a series of articles. Next to the illustrations were short texts telling stories of the women in the portraits. She knew those stories by heart.

She looked only at the faces, sometimes running her hand over a photo. It gave her a feeling of compassion for others and a feeling of gratitude for what she had. Still she felt some connection to these women who were dealing with life the only way they knew. Frances had sat every day on the corner in San Francisco when Marlene's office had been on Market Street. Marlene yearned for her, wanting to comfort her, but Frances was removed from her now. All these women had nothing and no one. She had everything and everyone.

They were the homeless women of the world who lived on the streets for whatever reason. No one knew it when they died. No one cared.

OCTOBER

Marlene and Carolyn were sitting on the beach in La Paz under an umbrella, in beach chairs, each wearing a ridiculous hat. Both had more wrinkles and sags than the average person would expose, which struck Carolyn as funny. "In our heads, we're sweet young things exciting the staring males and working on our tans when, in reality, we're two ole' women taking in the last bit of sun we'll see for awhile. Those people over there are wondering how we got away from the old folks home in Florida." She laughed, lifting her hat to run her fingers through her hair. "You're the only person that would let me acknowledge this and not be embarrassed for myself. Move over, ole' lady, your hat brim is knocking my sunglasses off."

Marlene looked at her friend from the corner of her eye. "Speak for yourself. If I choose to see myself as a sweet, young thing then that's what I am. However, I don't usually stay awake long enough for it to matter much. The daydreams are shorter these days and the naps are longer. Please don't allow me to sleep in public with my mouth open, okay?"

"I'll try, but I don't know if it matters." Carolyn reached for the sun block, then lay back and picked up her book.

Marlene continued to sit with her chin on her arms, watching the water as her thoughts wandered. So much had happened in the last two weeks. She'd called Carolyn in the middle of the day and announced. "I've got to get out of here. This may be our last chance. Let's go to Mexico for a week and just be dormant." So true to their style, they'd picked up and gone.

But a few things were different. This time, Carolyn had flown north so she could be with Marlene during the entire trip. There had been some lessons from George about the schedule of medications Marlene would need. George and Carolyn agreed there would be no more pressure on their friend to eat or rest, just let her call the shots. Marlene had put her foot down, and there was no more talking. If the experience was teaching them anything, it was the importance and the freedom of honesty.

She stood and walked the short distance to the water. *But my God, my kids. Jessie's solicitousness is going to drive me nuts. Oh, that's so unkind. But she's taking more than her share of my time. Maybe she'll calm down soon; it's early yet. I'll have a chat with her when I get home. And Eileen. She hasn't been around that much, but when she does come, it's always with armloads of reports and doctors' recommendations that I really don't want to deal with. Took some of the wind out of her sails when I told her I'd been to Stanford. I hope it reassured her that I can still call on the doctors there, if need be.*

Looking up, Marlene was startled to see she'd walked a good distance down the beach. It took longer than she expected to return to the spot where Carolyn sat. "The water feels good on the feet, lazy one. Must take a nap now, it was a long trip."

Carolyn didn't even look up from her book as she responded, "Rant on."

Marlene focused on the local children playing; children with no fear, children for whom it was natural to look out for younger ones. It made her happy and made her think of Kate.

There's work to be done with Jessie and Eileen, but Kate is my rock. There's the same strength in Kate as in those other women who live in my head now. She shows up or calls more often than before, but it's never overwhelming. I love the way she takes up some small chore, sometimes, without asking, and just sees that it's finished. But there's something else there and I can't put my finger on it. Actually, not a thing but a feeling in my gut that she has something to say. Thanks, Kate, that whatever is on your mind, you're not going for the drama.

With these thoughts, she fell asleep under the protection of the umbrella, the hat, the sun block, and the ultimate knowledge that she was loved.

***

"Hey, where are we going to eat tonight?" Carolyn was picking up all their belongings, folding towels, and stuffing them in the bags around books and water bottles.

Marlene folded the chairs and tied her wrap about herself. "I've never understood why we haven't formulated a plan about this dinner thing." She smiled at her friend and then waved to a hotel staff member to come get the umbrella and chairs. "Almost all of our vacations have revolved around where or what we ate. One would think there would be a more formal design for these decisions. Funny, even now, when food holds no interest for me, dinner is what I look forward to all day."

"Marlene, we don't need a plan. Mexico means seafood. I hate to admit that there's a certain freedom in being the one to choose now that you've taken eating on as a spectator sport. "

"Watching you eat seafood, Carolyn, is a national spectator sport. I see people from other tables enjoy watching you indulge." They were making their way back up to the hotel, mere yards from where they'd been sitting. Yet, with every sentence, Marlene had to stop and put her energy into either walking or talking. "I love watching you eat a crab or a lobster. You always begin by almost stroking it as you remove the shell. Then comes the actual act of eating it; intensely, but gently; determined, yet so patient; uncompromising, but with such visible pleasure, rigorous, yet so tender. And then, there's nothing left but a few smears of butter, a many times broken shell, and a look on your face of absolute satisfaction. My God, I've just described the ultimate sexual experience."

Carolyn didn't laugh, but stopped in her tracks, looked directly into Marlene's eyes, adjusted her head to see under the big hat and said, "At your age it makes you jealous, huh? Furthermore, on such an occasion, and at my discretion, I'll get up and go home when I choose."

With these comfortable digs and jabs, the last day of their week in the sun began to wind down. The old days that had been spent wandering about enjoying sights were left behind in place of reading quietly in the room. The walks in the marketplace were replaced by naps. Carolyn very often ate breakfast and lunch alone, bringing ice cream back to the room for Marlene.

On the last morning, they sat on the beach wall. It was too early to doze. Carolyn held a book and Marlene stared out across the water. They sat this way for a very long time until Marlene spoke in hushed tones. "Further out is so peaceful." She nodded toward the calm water beyond the breakers. "When the sun gets so damn hot, well, it would feel good to just slip into the water and swim—out there. I can imagine sometimes floating to rest and then just keep going—on and on. What a respite from the real things, the people I still have to take care of, the pain that is becoming more persistent, the tasks to be completed before I can move on. Anything as blue as that water can only be kind…" Her voice trailed off.

Carolyn's response was slow in coming, and she matched the same soft-spoken tone that Marlene had used. "I know. A decision like that opens so many other opportunities and choices. I hope you look at them seriously. Like," she paused. "Marlene you get a few feet away from the shore and that water starts to get really cold and continues to get colder the further out you get. Then there are the new friends you'll meet out there; very big fish, with very big teeth. I'm sure they'll mean to be companionable, but in truth you'll be invading their turf, sorry, surf, and they are into eating." Carolyn paused to glance at her friend. "Finally, as you consider me your friend, please don't go off doing something silly without leaving me the words I can use when I return home without you. I fear someone will notice your absence and, somehow, 'oh, she's still swimming' won't close the subject for your family."

Marlene had her knees bent and her arms folded across them. For a moment, she put her head down and just looked at Carolyn. Then she began to giggle. She reached out and took Carolyn's hand. "No one else in this world could get away with such morbidity and sarcasm, and no one else would deliver it with such respect for my weak moments. Thanks for putting things back into perspective. When I do die, my final wish will be for you to encounter that hungry fish on a plate for the ultimate seafood dinner." They sat holding hands for a few moments, re-enforcing the bond; the commitment, the assurance and the joy of what they'd had over so many years.

"Going home won't be so bad." Marlene began getting down off the rock wall. "Let's get our stuff ready so I can rest before we head for the airport. I suppose you need one more lobster lunch."

"Going home is what we came here for. Are you ready? Did the sun infuse you with all the courage and gallantry we came here to garner? Are we now dauntless?" Carolyn stood her ground, waiting for an answer.

Respectfully, Marlene addressed the issue. "I feel I'm hearing your version of Henry the Fifth's St. Crispin's Day speech. Sounds a little militaristic for an avowed pacifist." Playfully, she saluted Carolyn. "Yes, Sarge, I'm ready to do battle with life and all that goes with it. Let's get our bags packed." As they headed for the hotel room, Marlene was humming, "Onward, Christian Soldiers."

***

George met them at the airport. After claiming their luggage and storing it in the car, he concentrated on moving out into the traffic. Then as he brought them up to date on the home front, she sensed his normal manner of accommodating without interfering.

"I had to get a little heavy-handed with those headstrong daughters of yours. They had every intention of descending on you in a swoop and delivering you home with as much commotion as they could muster. Well, it wasn't their intention, but commotion would have been the result. So Kate helped me sell them a plan that was less wearing for you." He looked over his shoulder at Marlene. "No one will be there or call you tonight. I'll call them after you've been safely delivered and let them know that you're alright, and hopefully tell them you had a good time. They'll call you tomorrow, but only once. Then you're on your own. I couldn't get further than that. But for now, you don't have to walk into the chaos, caused, I may add, because they care."

"George, you're truly brave and efficient." It was disconcerting to think of so much caring at one time. She so appreciated his efforts. "We

168

had a fine time. I'm tired from the flight. Well, very tired, but none the worse for all that." Marlene was in the back seat, but still noticed the glance that George and Carolyn shared. Putting her head back, she closed her eyes. "Thanks, guys."

When they arrived at her apartment. Marlene went directly to the bedroom and lay down to rest, but not to sleep. Not yet. She listened to the exchange in the other room. Carolyn was matter-of-fact. "I need to get our tired friend bathed and into bed. She really did quite well and you certainly made the return easier. Thanks."

"I hope we agree that we're in this together." As she heard him say it, Marlene gauged that George was making his own position secure. "I'm ready to do anything you need to make it easier for her and for you. We just need to be open and clear about what's needed. We both want to do something. So maybe we can help each other in the doing. There's also that 'overbearing' tendency I've heard enough about. That requires some supervision." Hearing that made Marlene smile.

George appeared at Marlene's door. "Goodnight, world traveler, I'll talk to you tomorrow. Sleep well." Turning to Carolyn, he said, "Thanks, and have a good night." With no further words, he left and Marlene heard his steps slowly descend the stairway. Then the front door opened and closed.

Carolyn helped her friend wash and get into bed. The night was long as Marlene wasn't able to sleep. "Too tired to relax," she said. Several times in the night, she had needed medication for pain.

The next morning, Marlene heard snatches of conversation on the phone. Carolyn called George and asked if he could help change her plane reservations. "Our friend needs some time to get into the swing of things here. She's had a bad night and is still restless. I want to stay a little longer."

Evidently one of the kids called early in the morning because Marlene heard Carolyn suggest that "You could call back in a couple of hours. She's really not awake yet."

Marlene turned her face to the wall and wanted to sleep But sleep wouldn't come.

Sitting by her bed, on the wall side, was Teodora, the woman from the refugee camp. She was crocheting something very bright green in color, but the object in her hand had no form.

The woman just kept putting the hook in and out, wrapping the pretty string around the tool. Marlene lay very still, watching the woman and wanting to meet her eyes, but it was not to be. The brown and weathered skin of the very small person and her dark hair streaked with gray spoke of hardship and long periods of anguish. Yet, there Teodora sat, unwilling to share her fears and worries, making herself useful as long as there were things to be done.

Tears came into Marlene's eyes, and she turned her head away to avoid the challenge of the woman's action. It was only a few minutes later that Marlene sat up in the bed, responding to the determination of her imaginary friend; determined to dress and at least move to the sofa. *When there's nothing left you can do but crochet, then at least crochet.*

It took a little time for Carolyn and Marlene working together to get Marlene comfortable on the sofa. They had found a loose dress that was easy to get on and off, and threw an afghan from the back of the sofa over her legs.

Carolyn being authoritative was amusing. "We agreed on dauntless before we left Mexico. Here's the test! I'm going to soft boil an egg for you and toast a slice of bread. Think of it only as what is needed to get you through the day. You had nothing at all yesterday, except one bowl of ice cream, and it's nearly noon. Can you give it a try?"

Marlene's stomach was the first to reply with a vehement 'no'. But the unseen lady with the crochet hook prodded her along and she agreed to Carolyn's challenge. When the food was served, Marlene could only keep it down by sheer force, using the toast as weight to hold the egg down. Using that method took a while, but the task was completed and she did admit to feeling stronger.

"Okay, I'm going to get some fruit and yogurt and put it in the blender for your dinner. Carolyn was preparing herself for a serious bout of nursing.

"I'm cooperating, so you don't have to describe it to me. Just bring it on when the time is right. Carolyn did the laundry from the trip and changed Marlene's bed linens. Between tasks, they sat together. But as the minutes went by, Marlene became more like herself and Carolyn appeared willing to play the games that came so naturally to them, serious discussions interrupted by nonsense and quiet time. There was a magazine nearby, but it was left untouched.

It was noon when the phone rang. Carolyn answered it and said, "Sure, she's right here. Just a second, Jess." She passed the phone to Marlene.

"Hi, sweetie, how is everyone?" Marlene's voice was strong, clear, and happy. *No one could know that Teodora from Nicaragua had that crochet hook pressed up against Marlene's spine.* "I'm fine. I'm pretty tired and Carolyn's making me eat things I don't want, but actually, I'm fine. George is right, dear; I need to get caught up before we can do much running around. But I don't want you to worry. I'm just going to take lots of naps for a couple of days, eat Carolyn's dreadful cooking, and then I'll be great. So tell me what's been happening with you and yours."

Marlene fell quiet. Jessie, having taken the lead, was going to talk non-stop for a while. Marlene rolled her eyes at Carolyn and kept the phone near her ear, but not on it. The good mother remembered to put in an 'uh huh' every now and again, and that was all that was expected.

"I think you really made the right choice, Jess. I'm proud of you for being so firm." There was more silence on Marlene's end and Jessica, beginning to run down, finished her story.

Marlene led toward the goodbye. "I'm sure Jane is pleased with that outcome and I'd guess her teacher is too. Sounds like a good plan to me. I'm so glad you called and I'll see you in a day or so. We're doing laundry from the trip, so I probably should go help. Thanks again for calling and give everyone a kiss for me, okay? I love all of you." Another moment and then, "Yes, I'm glad to be home. Bye, bye. Love you." And the phone went in its cradle.

Carolyn got out of her chair. "You're sure going to look silly going up and down those back stairs doing the laundry I hear you're helping with. Guess I'll go get some out of the dryer and you can start to fold." Carolyn got up and headed for the back of the apartment. Marlene put her head back on her pillow and felt very pleased with herself. It's going to be all right.

When the phone rang around two o'clock, they were sitting at the table in the kitchen. Carolyn answered the phone and said, "Sure and good afternoon to you, too. Your mom is right here, just a sec…Pardon me?" Short silence. "Oh, we had a very good time. Can't say we burned up the town, but we spent a lot of time on the beach and struggled with age issues. I think we're ready to admit to getting old…Ha…Let me get your mom."

Marlene took the phone gladly. She knew it had to be Kate if the caller was including Carolyn in the conversation. "Hello, m'dear. How goes it?" She laughed, and continued, "No, she's wrong or partly wrong. She's the one getting old, couldn't keep up with me. We had a very good time even though I slept a lot. Read a good book while I was gone, about adventuresome women in history. You can have it now if you want. What did you do while we were on the prowl?"

She listened a moment. "How wonderful. It's the perfect time of year up there. Did it get hot at all? Who went?" She was intent on the answers she was hearing.

"What do you mean 'some guy you don't know'? I'm your mother. Isn't it my job to clear all your friends before you leave the house?" More laughter. "Oh, thirty-one! Are you really? When did that happen?"

The conversation continued along those lines of sharing and laughter and often included Carolyn. After a time, Marlene said, "I'm glad to be home and I look forward to seeing you. Maybe you can come for dinner before Carolyn leaves. However, you'll need to talk it over with her. I've never asked her how long she's staying. It's really nice having her here." After some additional chatting and goodbyes, Marlene handed the phone to Carolyn and listened while they made plans. When the phone was back in its cradle, they were quiet until, "How did I manage to get such a together person for a daughter?"

George came by late in the afternoon. For dinner, the patient got her concoction of yogurt and fruit and the other two ate what they found in the fridge.

Over dinner, which was eaten in the living room near the sofa where Marlene sat, George asked Carolyn when she was planning to return to L.A.

"No, no, George." Marlene tried to protect the status quo. "If we don't ask, maybe she'll forget she doesn't live here."

"Let's try a little up front talk here." Carolyn appeared to be at ease and comfortable with herself as she sat back in the big chair. "You're already stronger. Another few days and you'll be on top of everything. So how about I fly home Monday and Tuesday to square things away. I'll come back on Wednesday. Are you up for taking charge that long, George?"

Marlene started to protest, but was quieted when George looked directly at her. "Marlene, she's right. We need to talk about this. There are questions you need to answer, like where do the girls fit in? When do we call them to help? How can we be clear about what you need and when you need it? When are you really comfortable taking care of yourself? No one wants to take away from you the right to make all your own decisions, we just need to be clear about what they are so we can be useful."

George moved over to sit on the coffee table, facing Marlene and took her hand. "Boy, do I remember the talks we had about what is 'my business' and what isn't. It was a hard lesson, but I learned it. Now you can help me be good at it by sticking to our agreement about being open, honest, and clear. I really want both of us to do this right."

There were tears in Marlene's eyes. "This is the part I didn't want. I don't want to talk about who needs to do what. Okay, I know, it's necessary, but I don't like being so helpless."

Carolyn joined them, squatting at the side of the sofa and put her hand on Marlene's forehead. "This is the way it is, Love. You told me that you could do this your way because you had George and me; that you trusted us and had no reservations. We want you to call the shots and keep us informed. We only want to take care of the parts you can't and no more than that. Now is the time to start leaning on that trust. Or-r-r-r-r and her voice went into the upper range, "we could let your kids come take over, and then we'll see..."

Marlene was laughing through her tears, a welcome release from her inner tension. "Now that's a picture. Talk about losing control of one's life. Okay, no more meandering into long, thoughtful discussions." She patted Carolyn's hand and said, "Go back to your chair. You weigh too much to squat Asian style for any length of time. Now, while I don't want to put too much on George, flying home and back inside of two days is too soon and seems very stressful. And I'm probably going to be okay by myself most of the time."

"No, I'll fly from here in Sacramento instead of going to San Francisco. That cuts the time way down."

"Carolyn, use your head. That's very expensive."

Carolyn got up and started to pick up dinner plates to take to the kitchen. "Don't worry about it, I'm charging it to you. So, George, do we have a plan for the next week?"

As George was ready to answer her, the phone rang. Carolyn simply put the dishes in his hands and went to answer the phone. "Hello...Well, you can ask your mother, she's right here. Eileen, those are questions for your mom, not for me. Let me put her on the line. No, no. Of course, you can speak to her. She's all right, just tired...No one was suggesting you were banned...It's okay that you called. She just needed to rest a bit...I'm going to put her on the phone now, so goodbye."

Covering the mouthpiece of the phone, Carolyn looked at Marlene. "She's still angry and thinks she's been banned. Do you want to talk to her or can George or I put her off awhile?"

Marlene reached for the phone. "No, I can talk to her now. Why put off the inevitable?"

"Hello, darlin'. How are you and what have you been doing while we were off enjoying the sun?" She ran the sentences together in an attempt at humor. George and Carolyn left for the kitchen so as not to cause additional trouble. But once there, they were able to laugh quietly, peeking around the doorjamb back at the speaker occasionally. Only these two friends could understand the look on her face and know that it was fine to tease.

Marlene was saying, "Yes, Eileen, I know it's been hard for you this week, but I'd like to share with you the very good time we had. You could have come over any time, but I did need to rest after the long plane ride." This was followed by a long silence.

"Eileen, I believe you're reading far more into this than is involved. Whom would I want near me if I really were ill? You, my precious daughter. Now that that's been said, I'd really like to hear about what's going on with you. You still haven't answered my original question. How was last week and what new happened while we were gone?"

Marlene played with the edges of the afghan while she listened to the tirade on the other end of the line. It seemed to go on forever.

"I think that's very interesting. You must have learned a lot having talked to so many medical people in so short a time. I appreciate what you're doing and how concerned you are. I would like you to come over and talk about all this, where we can listen, carefully, thoughtfully and with some patience on both our parts."

Following another quiet time Marlene's voice became a bit firmer. "The illness is a reality and there's not a whole lot we can do about it. It's like…well, when it rained on your prom night. All the hysterics in the world didn't change the fact that water and green satin don't mix. What we needed then was the creativity to cover the dress with old cleaner bags. Remember? We made that balloon skirt from yards of plastic, and when you got home the dress was ruined. But you'd arrived at the prom in fine shape, to the envy of your friends whose dresses were soaked before they got there. What I need now is more creativity, not hand wringing. Let's deal with symptoms when they appear. Now, tell me about your week, ask me about mine or let's wait until later to continue this heavy conversation. Your choice."

The conversation came to a slow halt after that. Marlene reported later that while Eileen had tried to make small talk, she wasn't very good at it. "She's coming Sunday afternoon. Maybe I'll have adoption papers ready just in case." As she got up to go to the bathroom, she stopped and looked at Carolyn now standing at the kitchen doorway. "God, how unfair I am. I have to remember her pain is real, and she's as scared as she can be. But I need to protect myself from her fear. I've got 'til Sunday to figure that one out." She left the room as George brought tea. He and Carolyn resettled themselves in the living room.

**

Friday afternoon, George came and they all went to a movie. Afterwards, Marlene's response was lukewarm at best. "While I liked it in the beginning either the chair was too uncomfortable or the story line was too weak to hold my interest. Maybe from now on I'll stick to books."

Sunday morning the women rose early, preparing for Eileen's arrival and Carolyn's fast approaching departure.

"Are you sure you want to go through with the confrontation with Eileen? I hate to see you use yourself up with a problem that's really hers." Carolyn wandered into the kitchen where Marlene was laying out the food from the fridge.

"Wow, that's all I've been thinking about this week. But ya know, she's my kid. I owe her some time and energy to help her deal with this. I promise, I'll keep it to lengths of time and frequency of sessions that I can handle. But Carolyn, what else have we done in this life that's more important than these kids and helping them be strong and capable and fearless." She sat down at the table and twirled the small vase that held the flowers from the yard.

"The last flowers." Her voice was far away.

Carolyn's hands were flat on the table before her when she said, "I'll give you this, it's the most important part, but I hope we take the time to remember and celebrate the good times we've had. We've brought some laughter and joy to other people. We did work that was useful. We learned to play nice, share, be courteous and watch out for each other; and sometimes, other folks where we could." She got up and went to the sink where tomatoes were waiting to be sliced. She reached for the cutting board and penetrated the ripe fruit with her knife.

While she worked, she continued, "No, we didn't build a university or discover the cure for this damn disease. But we did take responsibility for the things that came our way; we gave a laugh to some people, who, on their own, couldn't see the joke; and we raised these women you call daughters. Okay, so Eileen is having a tough time with control and Jessie is a little self-absorbed, but they'll work it out for themselves. You've enabled them to find strength. Then there's Kate. I think I'll take credit for that one. Not only will she be fine, she'll be the rock for the other two. You can rest knowing Kate will pick up where you leave off."

Marlene smiled. "Yeah, I'm asking a lot in a short time. Since we're using the 'we' word, let's give what we can to them and hopefully they'll soon be able to join us as we celebrate the good parts." She got up, took the knife away from Carolyn and continued making the salad. "I hope I last long enough for us to see that happen. Remember? We laughed harder and more often when times were tough."

When Eileen arrived, lunch was on the table and Marlene encouraged all of them to sit down. "I wouldn't rush you except Carolyn needs to meet someone at one o'clock and I'd like her to enjoy her meal. Eileen's face softened when she heard Carolyn was leaving and she'd have her mother to herself. She didn't seem to notice how small the portions were her mother took; nor, at the end of the meal that the same food was still on the plate. Mostly, the two travelers discussed the Mexico trip even though Eileen's responses needed to be elicited vigorously.

After the meal, Eileen moved to the living room with her mom, letting Carolyn clear the table.

Carolyn glanced at the clock, "I'm going to put these in the kitchen, but I won't actually clean them up until I get back. Just leave them, please." On her way out, Carolyn said, "Take care, you two. I love you both." She brushed a kiss on the cheek of each, giving Marlene the slightest unseen pinch and went down the stairs.

Eileen took no time at all getting out a mountain of materials, preparing to do battle. "I will not watch you go without making some effort to help yourself. This is the twentieth century and…"

Marlene interrupted. "Please come and sit on the sofa with me." Her daughter disregarded the request. Marlene repeated herself. "I need you to come over and sit with me here." After an attempt to argue, which was cut off by her mother, Eileen begrudgingly came to sit at the far end of the sofa.

"Now I want you to lie down and put your head in my lap, please." This suggestion by Marlene was met with an indignant guffaw from

Eileen. "You've told me all about your research. You've told me how you feel about the process and your determination as to how I'll respond. Now it's my turn to tell you how I feel and I want to do it where I can touch you. Will you please do as I ask?"

The body that stretched out toward Marlene was stiff and unyielding. But Marlene ignored that and began to stroke her daughter's hair. "If there was a way I could let you know how much I love you and how badly I want to stay with you, I'd do whatever it took. But those are things you'll understand when you have children of your own. You've made me very proud of you with all the things you've accomplished, what a good student you were, how energetically you entered into activities from sports to drama and music. You were willing to go for the long stretch in business, successfully rising in a good company. Mostly, I'm happy that you have work to do that you love. Use the passion for that work to make your life as full and satisfying as it can be. You're a beautiful, strong, capable woman and I find great comfort in that fact. I also know that right now you're very frightened of what may be coming." She paused as she looked down at her beloved child. "Me, too, darlin'."

Marlene, aware of her own physical weakness, thought for a moment that the young, lithe, healthy body was relaxing in her lap, but she felt it stiffen again. She didn't change the pressure or the pattern of her strokes, nor slacken the tempo of her speech.

"What you've done these weeks is important to you. You needed to know all you could about what was happening to me—to all of us. I had to do that too, which is what took me so long to tell you. And now we have to compare what we've learned and share our feelings about all of it, the good and the bad." She felt the slightest jerk, as if Eileen were fighting a tear, but still Marlene didn't change her movements.

"There are so many things I want to do with you, tell you, hear from you. Time is always too short and now it's finite. I don't want to spend it hashing over things that have nothing to do with us. I want this time to be the most special time we've ever had, giving to each other all the things I fear we may have missed. It's special to have that kind of time, not what one gets when the person we love is killed in an accident and never even gets to say goodbye. It's a choice…" The front doorbell rang.

Damn, Marlene's worst fears surfaced. *What if I don't get another chance with her?* She attempted to hug her daughter, who had sprung up from her lap at the sound of the bell.

Eileen appeared liberated. She pushed the door button and leaned over the banister as someone entered. Marlene heard a murmured conversation coming up the stairs, and Harriet appeared, arms laden with a large casserole dish and a cloth bag. With her normal, commanding voice, she said, "I feel like I've interrupted something, so I'll leave these in the kitchen and go. It's just some custardy stuff that I thought might appeal to you, cool and smooth. The other is for anyone else around, just a vegetable ragout which can be heated whenever it's wanted."

The sturdy, tall, confident, black woman took herself into the kitchen and put the containers in the refrigerator. When she returned to the room, she sat on the edge of a hardback chair and the two women began the patter of friends. Eileen sat hunched back in the chair nearest the door, arms tightly crossed, head down so that she watched Harriet by raising her eyes.

"…gals at the office send their best. We could have lunch with them some day, but there's no pressure. This is the last month for the Farmer's Market, so I'll have more time now. Oh, by the way, we saw the exhibit in San Francisco last weekend. You would've loved it, girlfriend. I admit to being a little sad wishing you were there."

She rummaged in her very large handbag and pulled out a packet of brochures. "Here, brought these for you. I know how much you love the impressionists." She put the packet on the coffee table. "How's Carolyn doing?"

Marlene had to laugh as her friend took over the room, the atmosphere, and the mood with her down to earth hominess and attention to business. "She's still here, but out for the afternoon. It's Eileen's turn to keep tabs on me. They seem to think I'll go out partying if they don't keep an eye on me. Tell me about David's senior year. Is it going well?"

The two women chatted on for about twenty minutes while Eileen never moved from her chair of observation and judgment.

In time, Harriet got up from her chair and went over to rub her friend's arm. She bent down and kissed Marlene on the forehead. "I'll talk to you in a few days, baby." She headed for the door. Eileen was right behind her. As they reached the landing, Marlene heard the hard edge to Eileen's voice.

"I really thought you were her friend. All that time you were in there, you just kept babbling about nonsense. Are you aware you never even asked her how she was?"

Marlene visualized Harriet slowly turning around, perhaps putting her handbag on the floor as she leaned her back against the banister.

"Darlin', I know how she is. She's sick—she's damn sick. When she's feeling some better, she tells me so. If it's really bad, she tells me. But we're not going to spend the time we have left together discussing the inevitable when there's so much around us that is living and sweet and worth holding to ourselves. This is the time to celebrate all the things we mean to one another, not to discuss medical procedures. Let me ask you something. Do you know how to make that famous crab salad of your mother's?"

Marlene tried to imagine the discomfort of her daughter. Instead, she knew there was no more than a shaking of the head.

She heard Harriet continue, her voice still firm and strong, with no patience for foolishness. "That, baby, is the only thing you can do for her and for yourself right now. Spend a wonderful afternoon with her learning what you can always remember. Then know that it will make you famous someday, too. Every time you prepare it and serve it, you'll be with her again. Eileen, it's your choice how you spend these last months with your mama. Don't build up things you'll regret. Love her with everything you've got and she'll be with you the rest of your life. Take care, young'un. I'll see you both soon." Marlene heard Harriet descend the stairs.

She waited. Eileen re-entered the room, tears streaming down her face. She avoided Marlene's eyes as she slipped to the floor next to the sofa. She put her head on her mother's knees and let the tears flow, unrestricted. At last she was letting go of all the safety factors she had used to protect herself from this pain. Marlene held her lightly, crying along with her. This was different from the experiences she'd had with either Carolyn or George. This was her child.

NOVEMBER

Even knowing that Carolyn would be back soon, it was hard to let her go. Marlene thought of how she had come to depend on her, even now, when she could still do a great deal for herself. George was anxious to take Carolyn's place. As much as Marlene had changed her thinking about men in general and George in particular, she was still apprehensive about depending totally upon him. Aware she was losing control of her bowels; she wasn't ready for that to happen when only George was here.

So the morning after Carolyn left, she was up when George came. Up for her now meant out of bed, into a dressing gown and settled on the sofa. He immediately got her a cup of hot water. He also gave her the morning paper. She hoped he would sit down and not fuss.

"Sit down, George. If you want to fix yourself some breakfast, help yourself, but don't putter about me. If I want something I'll ask for it."

"Somehow, I know you will." George brought a cup of coffee for himself and sat in the easy chair across from the sofa where Marlene was lying down. "Do you have a plan for today? Anything I can get you?"

"No, not right now. Maybe, if it warms up enough, we could take a ride. I'd like to be out of the house as much as possible while the weather's good."

In the afternoon, he helped her down the stairs and into a chair in the backyard. *Maybe I shouldn't let him see how weak I'm becoming,* she mused. *This probably wasn't a good idea.* They sat quietly and occasionally spoke of the fall plants coming along and remembered the summer flowers that had faded. Withholding any bitterness from her voice, Marlene said, "I guess all the gardening is up to you now. I'm not even going to be able to put the garden to bed this year. But you know, I'd like to come and watch you if you're willing to do that for me."

He smiled at her, looking into her eyes. "I'd like you in the audience while I work. But we've taken turns at that before. The best part will be the memories of the gardening and the projects we did together. I want to put this yard into good shape for you." He paused and looked at his hands before he looked back at her. "I want you to see spring. Is that too much to ask of the gods?"

She smiled back at him. "We'll try. We made a couple of good gardens, even the year we started one in your yard that we never finished." They both laughed and George rose, wandering over to one of the flowerbeds. *Does he need to be alone for a minute? I can understand that,* and watching him, she thought back to the night last April when she had first lied to him.

It had been dark that night with a misty rain. It was the day she had learned she was ill—and terminal. Her original thoughts that cold, wet night had been that what was ahead of her was the work of women. She had determined she wouldn't be able to take care of any extra people now. Her priority had to be her children. All her energy had to go to her daughters. She had to leave them strong and independent while they learned to care for each other.

Her second line of defense would be her closest, living women friends because they would be able to support her and they were the people who would be there when the going got tough. They were the ones who would understand about her daughters. They would have the power to bring those young women full acceptance of real life, which included death. They would be there after the fact to fortify these children. Look at Harriet and Eileen. She had loved George and enjoyed their time together. Yet, she had known real work was ahead of her and she had chosen women.

Yet, here he was. He'd accepted that he'd been relegated to a lesser position. He followed the requests she had made in Hawaii. He hadn't run and that confused her. He was willing to take care of her and keep his good disposition intact at the same time. He was here for her and she had tried to make him go away. It was disconcerting, but she was grateful he had refused to go.

When they returned upstairs and settled into the living room, George brought some ice cream to Marlene as she half-lay, half-sat on the sofa. "Get a hose and pump it into me so I don't have to sit up," Marlene said, while at the same time, she was attempting to pull herself to a sitting position.

When she was comfortable, George said, "I've wanted to ask you a question and maybe it's one you don't want to answer." He sat back visibly relaxed in the armchair opposite her. "If so, okay, but I'm curious. In Hawaii you mentioned some friends," and one eyebrow went up in disbelief. "I believe at the time you said, 'in your head.' It sounded important, but you never did explain. Can you tell me what it means?"

Marlene chuckled. There would be no putting George off now; she had never lied to him again after Hawaii. All their shared good times had earned him honesty.

"Now that, my friend, is a challenge. Maybe it's like asking the mental patient to explain his or her psychosis. It started innocently enough, just daydreaming about women I've studied or worked with. They came from different eras or cultures or circumstances." She was quiet a minute while she took another bite of her ice cream.

"I would see them doing things that were scary and unpleasant, making choices no one really wants to make. We're still here, so they must have pulled it off. Then the daydreams became more personal. I would see a very specific woman and somehow get into her skin. It made me feel less lonely and oh, so much stronger. And, these women knew how to laugh.

"No matter how you slice it, George, we've never had to face anything too terribly difficult. These friends have. It made me proud to be a part of who they were and to learn how to cope from them. That's all it is, but it's still important to me."

After that speech, she lay back down on the sofa, hoping he'd babble for about an hour so she could pretend she was listening. Instead, he said, "Thanks, it makes sense to me." Then he reached over and took a magazine from the table. "Just rest a while and let my fine cooking do its job."

So they were quiet. Marlene dozed and George refrained from watching her. Finally, he slipped into a shallow nap, too.

When she woke, George was still sleeping in the chair. She thought of the Sunday afternoon naps they had taken together; of the fun and intimacy they'd shared, of the time each had filled the other's life. She knew it could not have been different for her, but she wished...*Oh hell, I wish this whole sickness thing could have been different and all my tricks hadn't been necessary.* It was the first piece of bitterness to find its way into her soul and it scared her.

"George wake up. I finished your damned ice cream and now what I really want is for you to go to the video store and bring home something with Joseph Cotton in it. We haven't done a really old-fashioned movie for a long time." She began to get up, wanting to carry her own dish to the kitchen. "While you're gone, I'm getting ready for bed, just in case I don't stay awake until the weepy part."

George pulled himself together and then out of the chair. "Any particular Cotton movie?"

"No, anything with Greer Garson, Claudette Colbert or Jennifer Jones. Just some simple old movie where everything turns out well and everyone retains his or her dignity.

The challenge had been, back in April, to conquer the disease, the reality, the living 'til you die. This was good time. Time to be treasured, time to be enjoyed. Time to love and be loved. By itself, love would take care of those around her. No need to work so hard now.

***

Within a week, Marlene was feeling really rough. Finally, when the diarrhea had continued throughout the night into the next day, Carolyn called George to ask for a little help. For two days, they took turns sleeping on the sofa so that one of them could always be with their friend. Then they came together to Marlene's room and asked her if it was all right to have a little talk. She was so weak she simply nodded and looked at them.

Carolyn looked at George and then began as gently as she could, "We're going to need a little help here from someone who can give you something for the pain, the vomiting and the diarrhea. Is it the local doctor from the clinic that you want us to call? You won't be able to take much more of this and it isn't likely to stop on its own."

"Look in my billfold. There's a card."

George got the purse and looked in the billfold for a card. There were several, covering a variety of things. He looked questioningly at Carolyn.

She asked Marlene, "What kind of card are we looking for, mi'ja?"

Marlene sighed deeply and turned her head toward them. "The doctor from Stanford...the one who came into the hall? He said, 'If there's anything you need...' and he gave me that card. If I'm wrong, I can jeopardize my own care. If I'm right, I could jeopardize his situation."

"Marlene, would it be alright if I called him?" George moved to the side of the bed. "I think I can be discreet enough to see how he sounds or what he offers."

She looked at him, but was too ill to discuss it further. "Sure."

Later that same day, the two caretakers returned to the room, ready for another talk.

Having slept a bit, Marlene was stronger and asked Carolyn to help her sit up a little with a pillow. "What did he have to say?"

George tried to be clear and brief. "He remembered you, but thought by now you would have been gone. He also said that as long as we have all these papers completed, he has no problem and will see you as soon as we can get you there. It's necessary that he see you again to be listed as your Physician of Record. Don't forget the 120-day rule.

"Now we need to get the girls here." Even as weak as she was, she could see he was watching her for signs of stress or discomfort. "You need their signatures, making sure they understand what it is you want. They will have to be your advocates now." His voice softened and he stroked her hand. "How're you doing? I've already gotten the forms. What do you say?"

"In the top drawer of my desk is a gray travel folder. It has in it my will and all the papers from Rhonda, the woman who will take care of everything after I die, including the cremation. Also, the instructions for care are in there. Meant to give it to the kids, just never did." She closed her eyes and saw the Hawaiian woman in the red dress; the lady surrounded by that community that would care for her. She was unquestionably an independent woman, yet she accepted the help of her family and friends with such grace. *Let me be as grateful and gracious.* "Thank you, George."

He left to get Marlene a glass of water. To Carolyn, Marlene said, "Why didn't I let them know it was getting more difficult. This is no way for them to see me."

Carolyn took the chair George had vacated. "Remember Hawaii? We're pretty good at glossing over reality. It's expected that you'll have a bad time occasionally. No one has said this is the end and I think the pain just got to you. Let's tell them you're going to a really good doctor, and just need these papers signed saying what you want medically. What do you think about offering to let them go with you if they want? It's not that George and I don't want to do the care-taking, but it's going to be important to them to be involved. 'Besides, both Eileen and Kate have called and we've told them you were really feeling rocky. We promised to let them know if you needed them, but right now, you just need rest. You really do seem better to me. How about a hair brush?" Carolyn retrieved the brush from the bathroom and gently stroked back the hair that had stuck to Marlene's face.

"Maybe I feel better because I know that something is going to be done. Thanks."

"You gave us a choice and this is what we committed ourselves to. There's nothing to thank us for. We love you. This is necessary for us if we're ever going to live easily without you."

Marlene touched Carolyn's arm, but went on to something else. "I think I can call them myself, or at least Kate. When she tells the others I called her myself, some to the fears will be lessened. Is that like Hawaii?"

"See? You're great. Everyone will be fine."

"What time is it? Is she still at school?"

"Quarter to three. Do you know the number?"

"Yeah."

"Hello. I'd like to leave a message for Kathleen Drubaker, please. This is her mother and I'd like her to call me at her first opportunity. Would you please tell her I called? Thank you. Goodbye."

As she replaced the phone in the cradle, she asked, "Should I call the others myself?"

"How about their pagers and voice mails? That won't sound so urgent and it will be your voice."

"Good plan." When that job was completed, Marlene scooted down into the bed and closed her eyes. She heard Carolyn sit back in her chair and pick up the magazine she had tried reading earlier. It wasn't too long before the phone rang.

Marlene looked up at Carolyn with questioning eyes. "Tell her I'm in the bathroom, okay?"

Why didn't I give some warning? *Red dress lady, are we given clemency for lapses of thoughtfulness? How can I let my daughters see me like this?*

"Hi, Eileen. Yes, your mother called you, but she's in the bathroom right now. She's not feeling so hot and needs to go over to Stanford. Dr. Lynn, her favorite Doctor, can't change her medications for the pain unless he sees her. Before she's admitted to the hospital, some papers need to be signed and some understanding between you, your sisters and your mom as to what the medical directives are. Is it possible for you to come by sometime this afternoon or evening so we can get all this in order?" After a pause. "Yeah, Eileen, she's not feeling well at all, but we can expect that. Right now, she's taking care of business. She wants all of you involved in the decisions to be made. Can you make it soon?" Longer pause. "Thanks, kid. We'll see you then."

Within a couple of hours, all three were there. Marlene stayed in her bed. They came into her room and said 'hello' to her, but none stayed long. They had adjusted to the fact of her slackening strength. Marlene heard Jessie go into the living room and assume a voice of authority. Jessie asked George to explain what was needed, what the options were and what preferences her mother had expressed. Marlene listened and smiled at her eldest daughter's acceptance of her newly claimed position of family coordinator.

George was reading from the papers Marlene had shown him earlier. "She only wants what will make her comfortable, pain control and supportive care. Nothing more. She'll accept antibiotics, intravenous fluids and oxygen. Here, see where she checked the options, 'Patient to remain pain-free, receiving supportive care only, no CPR.'"

Kate entered her mother's room and squatted down next to the bed. She reached for her mother's hand as she laid her head down on the bed. Only then, did she look directly into her mother's eyes. Is it very bad? The pain?"

Marlene, holding the hand her daughter had offered, rubbed it between her fingers gently. "Better since Carolyn got into the drug supply, but I need to see the doctor before we can do that too often.

"Kate, there's something I want from you when we get the medications straightened out. All these months I've lived with women in my head who have become my best friends. I want to tell you about them and I want you to write down what I know about them. They're such a comfort to me and I believe they'll be a comfort to all three of you too. Okay?"

"Sure. But Mom, where are we now? What comes next? Is this what the end is like?"

"We won't know that until the end comes, will we? In the meantime, let's just be thankful for the time we have, like now. I haven't tried to share my friends with you until today. This is important time, but when the end comes, we'll be ready."

It seemed to her that Kate had passed over that barrier between intellectual acceptance and emotional acceptance. *And, I have to trust her. I feel too rotten to check it out. My acceptance has to be that she'll be fine. Oh, well, I'll have another day.*

Kate returned to the living room after planting the lightest of kisses on her mother's forehead. Marlene heard them discussing her choice of options and their plans for care giving. They told one another where to initial and sign.

Jessie remained in charge. "Now that we've done all that, Carolyn, I think it's time to give Mom the medicine for traveling, and George to see about the bed in the van. I suppose we'd best discuss exactly who's going with her."

Soon Carolyn entered Marlene's room with the glass of water and the pill. "I guess within the hour we'll be ready to hit the road. Now's the time to get yourself prepared to sleep the trip away."

Marlene took the pill without urging.

Carolyn returned to the living room and there was more discussion of a less orderly fashion. Marlene chose to turn her head and close her eyes. The time was fast approaching when the family would need to take care of everything. *Maybe it's not an issue of accepting help from someone else when I've always done it myself—maybe it's just someone else's turn. Have I taken away from them some of that initiative by selfishly insisting on doing for myself, wanting to be strong or at least perceived as such?*

Carolyn returned to sit in the wicker chair and asked, "What else can I do to help you get ready? Do you mind awfully that the crowed is out there planning your excursion?"

With difficulty, Marlene pulled herself up to a sitting position against the pillows. "No, I think it's up to them now and they seem ready to handle it."

"Okay. They've been discussing the ride over. At first, they all wanted to ride with you and then, with their own judgment, decided that it would be best if they waited here. They believe you, George, and I should go and we'll keep them posted. The final decision is that they'll come over to Palo Alto if you don't come home tomorrow."

"Sounds fine."

Jessie came into the room. "I think we have it all under control. I'm not sure about the bed in the back of the van, but it's on the floor so you can't fall off, and is a real mattress. With Carolyn hanging onto you, the trip will be a breeze—if you stay asleep, that is. But I'm assigned the task of explaining why none of the three of us is going with you now. No matter how sick you may be, you're still the 'mama'. That means that you remain aware of what we say, do or feel. Do we need something? Is there something else you should be doing? With Carolyn you appear more relaxed and less responsible—oh, I said that badly."

Marlene smiled at her eldest daughter. "You may have something there. I have been worried about the three of you, but you know, every day I see reason to worry less. I appreciate your thoughtfulness and even the 'evil Carolyn' has acquired the nursing knack, which surprises me immensely. I guess we're just used to each other. Thanks, Jessie, for your thoughtfulness and to your sisters, too."

George helped Marlene down the stairs and into the van. As she settled into the bed on the floor, each young woman leaned in, kissed her, and said, "I love you and I'll see you tomorrow, either here or there." No more heroics, no more drama, no more self-pity, or unacknowledged fear. No more sniping, denial, hidden agendas, or pretense. *It isn't fun, but we're doing okay."*

While Marlene thought that perhaps the shocks on the car were not as modern as the vehicle, she was dozing off about the time they got to the freeway. She had no idea where they were when she became aware of the covered wagon and the woman walking next to it. In her half-consciousness, Marlene recognized Abby, the heat, the dust, the direct sun of summer, and the unending steps this woman took. *But she doesn't know I care about those rocks under her feet.* In her mind, she saw herself step out of the van and walk next to the woman, matching the pattern their feet were making in the sand. There was no conversation. The woman just kept staring at the horizon and moving forward. *None of them will look me in the eye. They've become so important to me, so precious to me and yet they never acknowledge I'm here.* But walking along with the woman, Marlene at least felt they were together. It came as a jolt when she heard the woman say, "If ya try to figure how far ya have to go, it'll make ya crazy. At night, I only think of how far we've come." The idea of the woman speaking, yet not taking her eyes off the trail she still had to cover, startled Marlene and brought her back to the van.

She saw Carolyn sitting in the dark, on the floor next to her, but didn't attempt to explain what she had just witnessed. In a short while, Carolyn realized that her friend was awake and "How ya doing?"

"Pretty well. Where we're going doesn't matter, it's only how far we've come." She closed her eyes and slipped back into her fog, unaware that Carolyn couldn't possibly have known what she was talking about.

The medicine allowed her to remain somewhat oblivious to the process of arriving at the hospital, the necessary paperwork of admittance, for which George took responsibility, or the nurse who put her to bed. She slept through the night, but woke in the daylight feeling quite strong and clear-headed. She had expected Carolyn or George, but it was Dr. Lynn who came into the room. He was deliberate in his movements and appeared confident, assured and comfortable. It made Marlene relax even more. His smile was as warm as she had remembered. The sound of his very quiet, inquiring voice reminded her of the short, elderly man in the hall, those many months ago, hesitantly offering his assistance.

"So it was a very nice surprise to hear from your friend yesterday. It looks like you've done quite well for yourself. Can you tell me about the last five months? What was it like for you.,"

Marlene was slow to answer. She wanted her words to be as to the point as his were—no rambling. "I appreciate your willingness to see me on such short notice. As to the way I feel, some days are better than others. There's been a gradual decline in things I can do and the pain increases. But it happened slowly enough to make adjustments easily. It's only been this week that I began to feel this terrible. It hit hard and I guess I wasn't expecting that."

"Well, I'm very glad you called when you did and I'm very pleased that you've done so well. Remember it's up to you to control your comfort level. You'll have to ask for pain relief when needed. Don't be afraid to do so."

The doctor rearranged the clipboard on his lap and leaned forward with his elbows on his knees. "As for the other symptoms, the nausea, vomiting and diarrhea. That's little harder to handle. But don't you find them much easier now that you've almost completely lost interest in eating?"

He smiled and she only nodded. He continued. "Let's put our efforts into pain control. From now on, I believe you'll sleep more and more.

What you're feeling right now is the weakness that will continue as you, well, actually starve yourself. It's a natural process and if you accept it, everything will be much easier for you. Does it frighten you when I speak of starving and constant sleep?"

"No." Just having a conversation with someone who knew what she herself had come to acknowledge was giving her strength. "I left here five months ago with an agenda; a list of things I wanted to do. I've pretty much accomplished all of them. I'm happy with the months I've had, but now it's getting difficult. I'd rather sleep than complain."

"You amaze me as much now as you did when we first met. Let's get this morphine patch started and let you learn how to control it. Today we'll give you a thorough exam…and I know, I'm sorry." He waved his hand at her as if to say, 'don't argue'. "It won't be fun, but it will probably be the last time. It will give me the information I need for the state and county. Do you still want to die at home? In Sacramento?"

"Yes." Her voice was strong and confident. "We're doing quite well as I seem to have an inexhaustible number of caregivers. Just so, I don't become personally difficult and give them all a bad time. I need to stay appreciative." She smiled at him with some of her old mischief showing.

"Mrs. Drubaker, you aren't able to give anybody too much trouble. I'll come out to see you before the holidays just to check on your social skills. For today, let's do the exam. The nurse will apply the morphine patch for you today and teach you how to do it yourself. Okay." He had been gathering up his things. Now he came to stand by her bed and he took her hand. "I think that if you rest well tonight you can probably go home tomorrow. All this okay with you?"

There were tears in her eyes as she said to him. "You'll never know how much I thank you." To avoid crying, she said no more, but relaxed into the pillows behind her head.

During a break in the activity, George and Carolyn came into the room. They'd been told about the extra day and took it well.

George said, "Carolyn's been here before, you know and she knows the hot spots. At any rate, she got us rooms in the classy hotel with all the gardens. Obviously, we're going to be just fine. What about the kids?"

"Do you think I could call them myself? How do you make long distance calls on this phone?"

George called the operator and arranged for Marlene to call home. She called each one to find they had been talking to each other all day.

"Shouldn't we come over for the evening?" each one asked.

"No. I'm fine and I'll take some of their lovely dope and sleep away the whole night. I look forward to seeing you tomorrow." Each conversation was more to the point and more concise than she could ever remember. There was nothing draining about any of it.

Next morning, Dr. Lynn came in again and looked her over, punching a little here and poking a little there. "Does this hurt?" he would ask. She'd simply reply, "It doesn't feel good. I'd rather you not do it again." When he was finished and had made notes on his ever-present clipboard, he sat down in the chair.

"So, generally, how are you feeling today?"

"I'm okay. I haven't been up or tried to do anything. They aren't forcing me to eat, which makes it easier. My energy has been used meeting your needs and that wasn't too demanding. Actually, I'm pretty comfortable right here with your happy pills."

He smiled, that warm smile which convinced her he was her friend. "Mrs. Drubaker, you've done an amazing job of taking care of yourself. You've extended your active life beyond what we would have imagined. But I want to be honest, as I believe we agreed last June. The hard part is here and we need to be clear about the length of time and discomfort ahead."

She was able to look him in the eye. "If it's the hard part, then I wouldn't want it to take too long. Actually, Doctor, I've had precious time with my family and friends. I spent a wonderful month in Hawaii with my grandchildren. The priority was seeing my daughters accept my choices. They've pretty much accomplished that and watching them become a unit was worth the entire life's journey. They have each other now and don't need me as much." She was quiet for a moment, but then looked back up at him. "What about the holidays?"

He appeared to think for a minute, then smiled and said, "For anyone else I'd venture a guess. Not for you. We'll prescribe everything you need to keep you comfortable. Yesterday you got the morphine patch. It works on the pain steadily and prevents those dips in and out of pain. You may be disoriented some days, but it won't be the medication as much as it is just your body beginning to pull away from the reality of this life." Appearing slightly uncomfortable, he took a sip of the coffee he had brought in and left on her bedside table. He said, "I have a suggestion. A hospital bed in the living room will make things easier for your caregivers and will keep you in touch as people come and go. You can sleep to turn them off if you want, or pretend to sleep, but I don't see you hiding away in a bedroom. Mostly, it's up to you now. If, as you say, you helped your family adjust, then it's time for you to concentrate on what and how you're feeling. Do whatever it takes to keep you comfortable. I'm not counting you out until it's over. I'll be back in a few minutes." He prepared himself to leave. He watched her for a few seconds. She felt cared for and appreciated. *Doctor Lynn, if I had more energy and time, I'd fall madly in love with you.* Instead, she smiled, thanked him, and closed her eyes.

A nurse helped Marlene wash up and put on her clothes. Then she lay back down on the bed conscious of how tired just that little bit had made her.

Carolyn came in and said, "They tell me I can't stay long as the doctors are coming soon. How was your night?"

"How would I know? I wasn't aware of anything and it wasn't dark yet when I floated away. Oddly enough, I didn't have my women dreams last night." At that, the door opened and both Dr. Ferguson and Dr. Lynn entered. Carolyn started to get up.

Marlene reached for her friend's arm. "I'd like both of you to meet Carolyn Green, who is my primary caregiver. I'm sure anything you have to tell me would be put to better use by telling her. So I'd like her to stay." She looked up at Carolyn and said, "I think you should take notes since it's me you're taking care of. Wouldn't want to hear you puttering around saying 'now what did they say to do?'"

She looked back at the doctors and grinned. "I'm afraid we've always been like this and it's too late to change us now. She's kept me going by giving me space to do what I wanted to do and filling in when

I wasn't able. She also keeps me laughing, sometimes very inappropriately."

The choices Marlene and Carolyn had made were affirmed. There was no reason to force the patient to do anything that wasn't what she wanted to do. Not eating was acceptable, as food had such undesirable effects. However, the ice cream was firmly endorsed as the primary food source. They assured her that by reducing the pain, things would be much easier for her, even if she wasn't pain free. When necessary they would change to other methods of pain control. They didn't discuss what that might be.

She was most impressed with the respect they showed her. Despite what she perceived to be her unpleasant appearance, her odors, her crankiness, they treated her as if she were a whole pampered, attractive woman. *Amazing.*

So, armed with the information and the medications, they reversed the process; getting her back into the car and driving Highway 80…home.

***

A few days later Kate came by to talk about her new boyfriend and she and her mom planned a meeting for the following week.

"I want you to know something so it doesn't come as a shock I'm asking you to visit the first of the week because we're putting a hospital bed in the living room on Thursday. It'll be much easier for Carolyn. Let's meet this Jason before it gets all that dramatic. How about Tuesday?"

"Mom, are you sure this move is just for Carolyn's benefit?"

"Kate, darlin', we promised ourselves honesty. I won't be getting out of bed much more. I'm just getting too weak. So, while I have no trouble lying in my own bed, it's really tough on the caregiver with so much bending and twisting. I appreciate the fact that the only difference between us is that I'm sick and she's not; but Carolyn isn't getting younger, either. Maybe you'd be willing to prepare your sisters so they don't panic."

"Sure. But that means before the holidays, huh? Okay, we can handle that, and I'll get the word out. Thanks. I remember the promise—no more secrets. Anything coming down the line is easier now when we know what's up. I guess I'd better go and let you get some rest. I'll talk to you tomorrow." She leaned over and kissed her mother goodnight.

A complete reversal—or the world goes 'round and 'round, Marlene thought.

The next day she received a call from Dr. Lynn to find out how she was doing. He asked her about the holidays and how she thought she'd like to spend them. "Remember, the best for everyone is that you do exactly what makes you feel most comfortable. It's also fine if you change your mind about your activities at the last minute. Do you think you can be clear about that with all of them?"

"Oh, my, yes. Dr. Lynn, these months have been very productive. I really believe all of us can cope with just about anything now. Are we sad sometimes? Sure, but we're all in agreement that the time left is to be enjoyed. So, Doctor, do you think I could make it out to my daughter's house for the Thanksgiving activities?"

He laughed at her. "There's almost no other time in your life that you're as free from convention as you are now. Come, go,—sleep or not. You won't want turkey, so take your own ice cream, then change your mind any time you want. You make the rules."

"Wow, with images like that I can't wait. But seriously, is there anything I haven't encountered yet that may come up? I just don't want the melodramatics on a holiday with everyone present. Will I have reasonable warning if something new is going to erupt?"

More quietly now, the doctor answered. "What happens from here to the end is you'll sleep. The patch will reduce the pain and you'll just sleep more and more. Part of that is the weakness. Remember, at this point, you're starving yourself to death. But there is a phenomenon about the patients who choose to die at home. They appear so much more quiet and peaceful near the end; they sleep a great deal, often using less and less medication, sometimes down to none at all. We doctors talk about it a lot but haven't come up with a scientific explanation.

"My theory is that when a person is in familiar surroundings and being cared for by people they know well, a level of trust is attained that allows them to completely relax. Hospital patients are receiving very good care, but a lot of it. Strangers coming at you with needles and food, a change of shift and a new caregiver you never saw before can be disconcerting.

"Of course, I can't guarantee anything, but unless you break a leg or something, I don't foresee any really big events. Just listen to your body and yourself and set your own limits. We'll do our best to take care of the pain.

The following week there was a short visit with Kate and her obviously very good new friend. Marlene liked Jason a lot. The young people were kind to one another and thoughtful. *Is that new love? No, Kate would be that way with anyone she respected. Being that way, she wouldn't be hanging around with anyone who couldn't play the game her way.*

After a very pleasant and relaxing time of talking, laughing, and sharing, the lovebirds got up to leave. After the usual, 'so happy to meet you,' etc., Kate and Marlene's good night kisses, the couple started for the door. Jason stepped back to where Marlene was sitting on the sofa.

"For whatever it was you did to make Kate the way she is, thanks. She's a special woman. She's funny and bright. She has a constancy about her that feels safe."

Marlene asked, "Does her strength bother you a little bit?"

He paused. "No. I don't see myself as much of a wimp either, so perhaps I see each of us secure enough to be strong in many ways, like being able to trust someone else sometimes."

Marlene smiled. "I think, Jason, you just passed the test. I couldn't ask any more of anyone than to accept who she is and continue to expect the best from her. If each of you can appreciate yourselves, you'll be able to appreciate one another. So I can only say, in return, 'thank you'. We'll see you at Thanksgiving." She reached out and shook his hand as they smiled at one another. Then they were gone. She lay quietly until Carolyn and George returned. "Well, how did it go? George was the first to ask, but Carolyn was looking over his shoulder as if she were also very curious.

Marlene only smiled and said, "How could I have doubted her? He's fine, very fine. She's too self-assured to make it with someone who's weak." *There's a lot I have to learn from that. Sorry, George, I never gave you a chance. I assumed you'd be weak and needy. You've proved yourself strong and constant. I must tell you these things before I go.*

One afternoon everyone seemed to drop by at the same time so Marlene decided it was time for the upcoming holiday to be discussed. From her new position on the bed by the window, she said, "This may come as a shock to you but I'll not be cooking Thanksgiving dinner here. So who has a plan?"

Tentatively, Jessie asked, "Are you able to come out to our house?"

"I think so. If not, you can do it without me. You may have noticed that I'm pretty alert and while there won't be any touch football for me, if George and Carolyn can get me to the car and into your house, I believe I can sit on your sofa with style."

The mood in the room changed to one of anticipation and planning. Who would bring what? How about the time?

Kate directed her question to both her mother and Carolyn. "Is there a particular time of day that's usually better than another? I mean, do you get very tired at night or is it hard to get started in the morning?"

Carolyn answered, "A pattern would be unusual. Sometimes we sit here all night long and talk or doze or read. Sometimes she sleeps all day. But you can see it's daylight and she's as alert as any of us. So go figure. You set the time and we'll have her there even if she sleeps all day. But what can we bring as our share of the dinner?"

Eileen spoke up. "You two just get the mama there. We'll do the rest of it. I'd love the opportunity to honor you for all you do and the way you take care of my mom." She rubbed her mother's arm and smiled down at her. Then looking back at Carolyn and George, she said, "Please be our guests and just enjoy the day. You've enabled us to be a family now. And I'm making a crab salad."

Kate used her elbow to punch Carolyn in the ribs as they were standing next to one another. "Wow, that's pretty good, huh? I can't see a bowl of broccoli that would measure up to that. For the little kid in this configuration, she's right on. Come and just enjoy. You've always been family to me. This is appropriate."

So the decisions were made and as the day grew closer, there was a little trepidation about venturing out. Mostly, Marlene wanted to look festive. It was tough.

"No, I don't want to see you wearing those bright colors. You're too yellow to begin with. What if we tried a little lipstick?" Carolyn went to get her own and attempted to put a little on her friend's face. "No, that won't work, you've lost too much weight. Okay, let's try going with the problem.

"You are thin, you are pale and you are jaundiced. Let's see if I can find a simple beige top. While you may look all one color, if the top fits well, then we won't be trying to change what is. Since you'll be sitting down all the time, you won't run the risk of losing them if we put a pair of black slacks on you. Or, I can always buy you a pair in the children's department. I think you'll look classy if stuff doesn't hang on you. So size is most important. Then, if that doesn't work, we'll dye your hair red. At least that will change the point of focus."

So on Thursday morning, they started early. Carolyn washed and combed Marlene's hair into the ponytail she had worn almost all of her adult life. "How do you feel about cutting this? It's getting a little hard to handle in the bed. Maybe we can get you to a hairdresser sometime next week. What do you think?"

It was a shocking thought to Marlene and it took her a while to answer. "Of course, but couldn't you just whack it off yourself?"

"No. We could start braiding it. That would prevent the tangles and still leave you with your beautiful hair. I think I had a dumb idea that time. Good thing it doesn't happen often."

When Marlene had on the new clothes and her hair braided, George attempted an opinion as honest as Carolyn's.

"You really do look put together. Hey, Carolyn let's just get her a whole new wardrobe." Turning back to Marlene he said, "I'm proud to escort you today, ma'am."

The terrifying part of all this is how much I love them and I'll never be able to let them know. So she smiled and raised her arms so they could help her up. "I do feel better all dolled up. Let's hit the town, gang."

What they laughed about later, was that Marlene really did sleep most of the day; she had used all her energy getting ready. But her consciousness came and went often enough that she was able to watch Jason become a part of the family. She saw all the daughters relate to Robert and Jane so they were never left out. She experienced the young ones being near her, unafraid of her and her illness. They were just kind and cautious. At one point, when the adults were setting up a game, she encouraged the children to climb up on the sofa with her and was able to keep her arms around them as they told her what was going on at school and their plans for Christmas.

"Gram, will you be here for Christmas?" Jane was comfortable asking the question, although Robert shot her a glance of annoyance.

"I certainly hope so, even if I sleep the whole day. But maybe your mom and aunts will bring dinner to my house. It was quite a chore getting ready to go out. Will you and Robert come over and decorate a tree for me before Christmas? This time you'll have to do it all alone. I won't be able to help. But I'll keep Carolyn and George out of your hair so you can do it any way you want."

The children wiggled around to look at her with joy in their faces. She'd given them the best of gifts, honesty, hope and helpfulness.

DECEMBER

Where is the time going? Why does it matter? She heard sounds of people around, in the room, in the kitchen, voices speaking quietly, dishes rattling, soft footsteps. They didn't mean anything to her. She kept her own counsel now. The Women were around often, but as yet they didn't acknowledge her. They puttered about or did their hard labor. Sometimes they just sat, but they never spoke to her. In the images, there were always children somewhere around them and, as great ladies, they mothered. But they appeared to have their eyes on a different place. *How did they remain conscious of everything around them, the duties, the demands, the constant needs pressed on them and still retain their position on some universal plateau?* So their consistency in coping gave her the security she needed to go on. She slept, rousing herself to greet visitors, always returning to her own thoughts.

Dr. Lynn visited her early in the month and when they were alone, she asked him, "Why am I so unconcerned now about all the things I attempted to do when I learned I was sick? Shouldn't I feel badly that I don't think much about the family or friends anymore. I'm very content in the quiet, alone."

He looked at her a long time before answering. When he spoke he looked directly at her. "I think that if the patient is comfortable, knows her life was lived with integrity and is fearless, she accepts what's happening to her. Even without pain, you're aware that your body is shutting down, that you're moving on. I think you're right on course."

They exchanged pleasantries about the visit, each pleased to have been with the other. She thanked him for coming; he quietly held her hand for a moment and was on his way.

In her quiet times, she enjoyed remembering the things that were important to her. She thought of the afternoon she had listened to all three daughters while Kate told them about Jason, the new boyfriend and she smiled at the memory.

Jessie had been sitting here, on Marlene's bed and Kate and Eileen were sitting on the sofa which was pushed up against the bed. In the middle of the small talk, Kate had reached up and taken Jessie's hand, for the first time in her adult life, and said, "I have a new boyfriend. You'd better know now because he'll be at our Thanksgiving dinner."

Eileen jumped up and tucked her feet under herself, as she became part of the moment. "Who is he? What's he like? Where did you meet him? Is it serious?"

Jessie had gotten quiet as she reached her other hand out to touch her younger sister's hair. Marlene noted a maternal look on Jessie's face as they listened to Kate recite all the wonderful facts of the man who might be joining this family.

Marlene's thoughts traveled to the Japanese Woman who had haunted her in Carolyn's garden; the lady who was never allowed to leave her home. Remembering her own vivid images of The Woman sitting near the pond, under a tree playing her shamisen, she accepted the message given her by the friend behind the wall. If you leave the stuff outside the wall alone, it takes care of itself. These three women, Jessica, Kathleen and Eileen, can be outside the wall or in because now they were capable of caring for one another. Not one of them will ever be alone.

The holidays approached while she waited inside herself for her own freedom.

Carolyn asked her, "Would you rather they not all come here on Christmas Day?"

"No, let them come, unless I make them uncomfortable. They really don't bother me at all."

Rubbing Marlene's forehead, Carolyn said, "No, Mi'ja, they worry about disturbing you. But everything you wanted for them, they have.

They can let you go, but obviously, want to be around as much as possible while they can. We'll keep the festivities short and the noise subdued. I'm glad you can let them be here."

On Christmas Eve, George sat next to her all night. When she woke, he talked about the first Christmas they had spent together. "I remember how you went through all the hoops with your family Christmas Eve. You told me about spending the night there and being called up at six o'clock in the morning to open presents. You said there was a big breakfast and preparations began for the dinner. I got there sometime after noon and it was high living all the rest of the day. Jane and Robert were great even though they didn't know me very well then. Or maybe I was the adult who didn't have so many responsibilities. At any rate, I think I spent most of the day with them while you involved yourself in daughters, food preparation, gossip, housekeeping, and table setting. I thought at the time that you were a rather noisy bunch of women. Doug joined me with the kids and even found time for us to go out to the garage occasionally for short reprieves.

"But through all of it I knew when we left there, you'd be all mine for the next few days. So I enjoyed myself, the kids, the family feel of all of you being together, never knowing until these last few months how many issues you all had to deal with."

He leaned over the bed. "Still awake? Am I boring you?"

She smiled at him and said, "No. I've thought about remembering Christmases, but it was too much. I like having you remember for me. Go on."

"Well, late in the night we told all of them goodbye and wished them Happy New Year. I thanked them for including me and we got in the car to drive to Monterey. You were asleep before we hit the freeway and slept all the way. We stayed at the beach until New Year's Day. It was our first real getaway and it was when I knew I loved you." He was very quiet.

Marlene spoke just above a whisper. "It was the time I learned how much one needs to be away. I loved you because you let me walk alone, read alone, stare at a rock alone, and yet never feel alone. You've given me that gift all the time I've known you and it's really paid off now—

when you have given me the liberty to die the way I wanted. Love isn't enough to say thank you, but it's all I have to give you now."

Christmas Day came and Marlene felt good about what was happening around her but wanted to keep her distance, so she slept or pretended to sleep most of the day. In the afternoon, she woke to see Jane lying down on the sofa beside the hospital bed. When Marlene saw her granddaughter's eyes were open, she asked, "Would you like to sleep up here with me?"

Jane's response was slowed only by the question, "Are you sure you'll be all right?"

"Yes." So Jane carefully climbed up and laid down next to her Gram. It wasn't long before she was asleep and Marlene was able to watch her special child. It wasn't much more than that, just watching and loving.

JANUARY

There was nothing as dreary as the valley in the winter. Part of what Marlene had liked about it was the exuberance of spring, when out of the gloom and the gray and the fog, the first little signs of life broke through. Now, even though her bed was still by the window, she seldom looked out. Actually, she wasn't awake very often. She wasn't aware that her conversations with The Women were sometimes aloud, if mumbled, and that no one was able to understand her or clarify what she was saying. She didn't know they blamed it on the morphine for if they had stopped to think about it, she was using very little. She simply slept most of the time. Occasionally, in those early weeks of January, she would rally and hold conversations with her living family and friends.

There was a day when she woke to find Carolyn gone and Kate with her. She felt no pain and her head was clear. That was another phenomenon no one could explain—why sometimes she was so clear and at other times so fuzzy.

But on this day she saw Kate before her daughter knew she was awake. Marlene watched for a moment. Kate was leaning against the arm at the opposite end of the sofa, facing her mother, but deeply engrossed in her reading. *What a wonderful young woman. I love it that I can call her my friend.*

"What are you reading, dear? And how is it you're not at school?"

Katie looked up a bit startled, as her mother hadn't been awake at all that day. However, the expression of surprise was quickly replaced by the sweetest smile Marlene could have asked for.

"I really want to be alone with you at least once a week and this week Jessie and Eileen will be here for the weekend. There's no problem with being out of school right now and I love the days I'm here. Anyway, I'm reading that book you read on vacation, the one about women adventurers." She held up the book. "Feels good to remember the outrageousness of our ancestors or foremothers. How many are there today bold enough or passionate enough to willingly take on the power structures?" She moved up onto her knees and leaned over the back of the sofa, laying her hand over her mother's hand.

Marlene smoothed the hair away from Kate's face. "Those women have always been there and they're here now. Maybe it doesn't look like there are many mountains left to climb, but there will always be women who are strong and those who leave legacies for any woman interested in taking up the challenge. Sometimes it's in less visible contests, but it requires every bit of the bravery as before and will be as lasting. Trust me that they're here. I believe you'll be one of them."

They talked for a few more minutes. Then suddenly Marlene was very tired and closed her eyes, knowing Kate stayed a while where she knelt, just watching her mother rest.

On another day, Jessie was there when she woke.

"I brought the kids by yesterday, but I think you didn't know we were here. You were so right, Mom. They're very clear about what's happening. It is something you gave them and I'm so grateful to you for it. It still scares me to think of explaining or comforting them if they were still as innocent as I believed them to be." She paused. "Anything I can get for you?"

"No, thanks, there's nothing I need. Enjoy those children, Jess. You're very lucky." Then she drifted off again into her world of sleep and rest and waiting, secure in the knowledge that her eldest daughter had accepted reality and her own ability to deal with it.

It was near the end of the month when Carolyn told Marlene that George had been by the previous day, but Marlene had been quite unresponsive. Later that day, when she woke and saw him with a look of anticipation, she was stirred with the preciousness of him.

"You look like the canary—you know." She smiled at him with the warmth she was feeling.

"There's something I really want you to see." George leaned over the bed, but kept one hand behind him. "Last fall you talked of putting flowers to bed for the winter. But here," and he reached out to her with a little pot that held a hyacinth in bloom.

She didn't take it in her hands, but turned her head so that her eyes were on an equal level with the flower. Tears filled her eyes.

"It's the most beautiful thing I've ever seen. Look how pure…and the aroma…" She wasn't able to speak anymore as tears fell on her pillow. She didn't reach for the flower, she reached for George's hand. "Thank you."

Setting the flower down, he clasped her fingers with one hand and with the other, he wiped her tears. "That's how I think of you, never letting real beauty pass you by. I'm so glad I found it for you in time. I really wanted you to see spring again."

"I wonder," she said, "had I known the world would turn out so well without my help, would I have been as driven as I was? All my years don't add up to that beautiful purple flower that smells so fine. I can't even take credit for the women my daughters have become. She felt more relaxed, less anxious as if some particular moment had passed. "Please put it on the window sill here, where I can see it and smell it."

They sat together for a while and then Marlene dozed again. It was in the night that she woke and looked again at the flower. Carolyn sat on the sofa and looked up to watch her friend.

"Do you want to hold it?"

"No, seeing and smelling is enough. Does George know what an amazing gift this is?"

"I think so, he's been searching for that first sign of spring. It seemed very important to him that he find it before you were gone. It meant as much to him to give it to you as it does for you to have it."

While quietly looking at the flower, Marlene drifted off to sleep again.

Eileen was there in the morning. They sat quietly and admired the flower together, something they had not been able to do since Eileen was little. They were holding hands when Marlene dozed off, and she was more asleep than awake during the rest of the day. During the night she rallied and asked Carolyn if everyone would be coming around over the weekend.

Carolyn simply said, "Yes." She sat on the bed near Marlene.

"Mostly, it was good, huh?" Marlene's voice was soft, but clear.

"It sure was. You helped make it good for me. Thanks."

"I guess we were just one person that got split up and we're lucky we each found the other half," Marlene said. It was quiet for a time, then. "But now it's time to go."

"You relax and do whatever feels right for you. You pulled it off, you know. The three daughters have become a unit now, an adult, responsible and caring unit. They'll be fine, if a little sore for awhile. George knows you needed him and you let him help. That's all he wanted. Well, that and he found your flower in time. It might take him a little longer because he's alone, but he'll be fine too." Carolyn lay down next to Marlene. She held up both of their hands and entwined their fingers.

"As for me, well, I'm only filled with gratitude that we set out together to find our way and followed the journey—sticking with it all the way. *Si, mi amiga,* it was mostly good and what wasn't good was useful. I like who we are and what we've accomplished. There are no regrets here."

Marlene responded, "I should have known it, seeing you're such a gutsy broad. But I like what we've done too and I love you very much. Thanks."

The next night George sat by her bed, but she spoke only once or twice. She uttered half sentences. "Please look…" "Here…" "Don't go…"

In the morning, the family began to drop by. She was aware they were there. She would speak to them, reach for their hands and then her eyes would dart away as if she were seeing something elsewhere in the room. Compared to the passiveness of the sickness they had grown accustomed to, she seemed distracted, preoccupied, agitated.

She was. As the family drifted back and forth between the hall landing, the kitchen and the living room where she lay, she was aware of the coming of The Women…her friend in the red dress, the lady from the refugee camp who crocheted. They still didn't look at her; they just all stayed busy. Oh, the woman Megan from the medieval days was gathering her herbs and berries.

Marlene said to Eileen, "I'm so glad you're here so I can say how very proud I am of you. I wish I could see the rest of your life, but I know I don't have to worry about it. It will only be my loss and…" she tried to raise her head. *The street woman, the one who used to sit near the corner in San Francisco was setting up her stool and piling her shopping bags right there in the dining room.* "Here…blanket…" Her eyes came back to Eileen and she could only smile, exert a little pressure on the hand she was holding, and close her eyes.

And, so it went, with each family member getting all mixed up with her new friends. Yet, The Women still would not look at her, each one staying busy at her assigned task. Jessie and Kate were standing together at her bed and she wanted to talk to them but the shopkeeper on the Baja Road had put the Cokes on the counter for the two women travelers.

"The war…doing to you?" She asked the woman in fatigues who was fighting for her country in the jungles; fighting so she could go home and mother her children in peace. The severe appearance of the women from the wagon train brought such a sense of determination to The Group that the Chinese mother, whose child was in such pain from her bound feet, could only wring her hands and look around for solace.

Kate was standing next to her bed holding her mother's left hand when the other hand, nearest the window, flew up and reached for something. Then Marlene smiled.

The cat, who had been lying against her legs for several days, leaving for only moments at a time, stretched out his paws and laid them across her feet.

All The Women had moved just outside the window and they were looking right at her. They were holding their arms out to her. She was trying to reach them. As her hand fell back to the bed, she knew she was going with them. She said "thank you" to The Women, but the family thought it was for them. The echoes of the past were silenced now. And she was gone.

EPILOGUE

They were all there on the beach south of Rosarito. It had taken some months for them to come together for this event, but they were ready now. Marlene's final wishes that her ashes be spread in the Pacific Ocean below the California border were about to be fulfilled. The small boat that would take them out to sea was tied right there at the bottom of the rocky slope. Each person had flowers and George carried the urn.

As they made their way down the beach, Kate fell, dropping the flowers she carried. She slid all the way to the bottom of the grade and sat in anger and humiliation with her hands over her face. She knew the seat of her shorts had torn.

"Well, Mom," she said out loud, "you always hated the thought that we would ever think clothes or what we looked like might impede our willingness to move ahead, to risk, to look back. So here I am, coming to say goodbye with my butt exposed and I guess you'll say, 'That's fine.'"

Eileen and Jessie laughed at the imagery and then sat down on the ground with Kate. They held each other and remembered other things Marlene had believed, her sense of adventure, her fearlessness, her knowledge each of them would be okay. Echoes of her voice would carry them, together, the rest of their lives. Tears and laughter put into place all the things they would carry, together, the rest of their lives.

The small craft and captain, waited patiently for them. They walked out through the shallow water and hoisted themselves into the boat, which then moved out the required two miles where the captain shut down the motor.

Each person, in his or her own way, put flowers in the water as George scattered the ashes. Each encountered the quiet and themselves. When they were healed, they knew and shared her peace. It was all she would ever have asked—'that they do it together with the strength and love of real friends.' They each had a copy of a poem Harriet had sent with them.

> She draped herself in a patchwork
> Quilt of pride in those final days.
> Each block a fond memory
> Of her helpers along the way
> She'd simply wrap the women
> around her spent body
> And join them gladly in the
> Never-ending passing on
> Of power and truth.

THE END

Printed in the United States
71464LV00003B/88-93